OUTRAGEOUS FORTUNE

A Frontier Adventure

by

R. E. Mahoney

OUTRAGEOUS FORTUNE

A Frontier Adventure

by

R. E. Mahoney

Write the Future
1800 W. 39th Street
Kansas City, Missouri 64111
www.w84gdo2@gmail.com

Copyright © 2021
R. E. Mahoney

5 7 9 10 8 6 4

ISBN: 978-1-952411-65-6
LCCN: 2021941442

Design & Layout: W.E. Leathem
Editing: Cathy Bogart

This Book is Dedicated to two people
(OK, three if you can figure it out):

To Cathy, my High Priestess of the Written Word. Everything I wrote was perfect - you made it per- fecter.

And to Dad (the Original R.E.) and all those Sunday afternoons we spent with Quirt Evans, Jacob (Big, Jake) McCandles, George Washington McLintock, Sean Thorton , The Ringo Kid, Reuban "Rooster" Cogburn, Tom Doniphon.

Acknowledgements

To all those inter-dimensional, nonlinear, shape-shifting, (technically) extrarrestrials:

YOU KNOW WHO YOU ARE!

You who have NO respect for the space-time continuum. I had a *normal* life before you came along, and I have only one thing to say to you:

Thanks!

Man plans, God laughs
~ Yiddish Proverb

PROLOGUE

The priest's blue eyes glowed in the match's flame as he lit the candle. His black hair formed a widow's peak on his forehead and his smile created an evil looking visage as the candle's flame grew.

"Michael, in 1,844 years the church managed to convert all the pagans, yet we still celebrate this heathen holiday," the priest said, placing the candle in the large pumpkin. He then picked up the square lid by the stem and after a couple of turns it dropped into place. The man and boy stepped back and watched the flames fill the two massive jack-o-lanterns sitting on the porch. The candle's light cast two inverted, elongated faces down the large stone steps.

"You have a lot more heathen traditions to remember now, Uncle Mike."

"Yes Michael, and in the last six months you have been a big help in my studies. But I swear, if I learn one more word in an Indian language I will be saying my next mass in Sioux!"

"Lakota. Calling them Sioux is an insult! It is the name the French gave them which means venomous snake that crawls in the grass. You need to remember that!"

"I wish I had your gift for languages. I know every time I am saying mass, you are out there catching my mistakes."

"Only three last time."

He messed up the boy's black hair. He then put his arm on Michael's shoulders and looked at the house before them. "The Dugan Castle. I couldn't believe it when your father told me he was going to have one built just like it for me in the Town of Kansas. Imagine me, Michael, starting the first Catholic Church in the Town of Kansas."

The massive brick house looked like most houses but larger. On each side were what his father called keeps. The two-story, round structures were topped with ramparts. Many a day Michael and his older sister, Patricia, would pretend to battle a rival clan or sometimes they would be warring clan leaders.

Michael dropped his head and sat down on the stone steps. "Why are you leaving so late? Your wagon train could get stuck in the snow in the mountains. Wait until Summer."

The priest stood before the boy. "So I can help you convince your father to let you pick your college?" He smiled and asked.

"Why can't I pick my own college? I'm almost eighteen!"

"You are just seventeen."

"I'm still thinking about what we talked about on my birthday."

The smile on the priest's face faded. "The Seminary."

The boy looked up with fear in his bright blue eyes. "You didn't tell father, did you?"

"Did I not promise I would not to tell anyone?" He came and sat next to Michael. "Going into the priesthood to spite your father would not go over well at your interview."

Michael looked up at the man. "Why did you become a priest, Uncle Mike?"

Father Mike looked off into the darkness. "I fell hopelessly in love, Michael. With a woman I knew I could never have."

"I am still seriously considering the Seminary."

"You know what your father would say?"

Michael sat up straight and shook his finger at the priest. "Just another one of his adventures," he said in a deep mocking voice.

"How many "adventures" have there been? I've lost count. Chemist, Biologist, Astronomer?"

"Sailor."

"Recently a whaler if I remember correctly."

"That was three years ago. I've been an archeologist and anthropologist since then."

"And now you want to be a priest. You always like doing something, but it never works out. Besides, aren't you engaged or something to Jane?"

"Or something."

"There! Marry Jane, become the head of Dugan Manufacturing, and carry on the family name."

"Patricia has a son and twins on the way." countered Michael.

"You know that is not what I am talking about. The Dugan name. You are his only son, Michael."

"I would rather go with you."

Father Mike laughed. "Me take you to the frontier before you graduate? Your father would kill us both."

A woman pushed open the massive oak doors behind them. "Michael!"

"Yes?" the two harmonized.

"Mother" answered Michael.

"Martha." answered the priest.

She smiled down at the two and shook her head. "Michael, come in, we are getting ready to bob for apples."

The two walked up the stone steps through the towering doors. Michael ran ahead. The woman caught the priest by the arm.

"Please tell me you talked him out of this priest foolishness?"

The man put his hand on the woman's. "I tried, Martha, I really tried."

4

CHAPTER I

After two weeks aboard the Riverboat Chariot, Michael Dugan had concluded that the Missouri River looked the same from the stern as the bow. He stood at the rail of the upper deck. A bright red paddle smashed down into the muddy water as another rose from the water giving a deep groan.

"Good morning, Mr. Dugan and Happy Birthday," a deep voice said behind him.

Michael turned and saw Captain Malcolm Foster approaching. "Good morning, Captain Foster and thank you."

"I missed you at breakfast."

"My apologies. I was too excited to eat. When do we dock at the Town of Kansas?" Michael asked with excitement.

The captain gave a tight smile and looked at this watch. "About two hours."

"Isn't the nineteenth century a marvel, Captain Foster?" said Michael smiling. "From Boston to the frontier in three weeks."

Something caught the captain's eye on the bank of the river. He shielded his eyes from the rising sun. Michael followed the man's gaze. A white tarp was flapping in the early fall breeze. It was the remains of a covered wagon. Its back wheels stuck out of the water. The skeletons of two mules lay nearby still harnessed. Arrows could be seen sticking out of the side of the wagon. Michael Dugan had lost count of the wagons he had seen like this in the past two weeks.

"Someone trying to make the crossing on his own," the captain growled. "Why didn't the fool go with a wagon train or by steamboat?"

Michael looked as the scene came nearer. "Last word we had from my uncle, he was going to cross from St. Louis to the Town of Kansas on his own."

They watched the wagon pass aft. The captain looked at his watch again. "I need to make rounds."

The captain walked forward. The Chariot was a large passenger riverboat. Michael was glad. He has seen stacks of various hides on the pier when he boarded the Chariot at St. Louis. The smell was stifling. Since he had left Boston, his time on the Chariot had turned out to be the most tedious part of his trip. On the trains at least the scenery changed.

Speaking of scenery, Michael looked at his father's watch, then hurried toward mid-ship. Michael stood at the rail. This had become the highlight of his daily routine. After breakfast with Captain Foster, he would go on deck and enjoy the passing shore. The first days of early fall foliage were a wonder. It became like a picto-lamp he had gotten one Christmas. It was a series of drawings of an acrobat inside the shade of the lamp. As the lighted images turned it gave the illusion of the figure performing flips. But it soon became dull, even when he sped up the figure or ran it backwards. The banks of the Missouri became just as boring. But he was not there this morning for the bright leaves. This would be his last chance to see her.

Michael did not know her name. He barely had the nerve to look upon her when he knew she was not looking. She had boarded when he did in St. Louis. Her red hair was always done up. She wore the most beautiful dresses he had ever seen and had the fairest skin.

But it was her eyes. She had brilliant green eyes.

Right on time she came walking by. Normally accompanied, mostly by men, today she was alone and wore the green silk dress that formed to her perfect shape. There were white frills around her neck and cuffs.

She looked at Michael and gave a courtesy smile and bowed her head. Michael smiled, pinching the brim of his hat, and returned the nod. It was after she was out of sight that Michael Dugan realized he was holding his breath.

"Quite a looker, ain't she?" Michael heard from behind him.

He turned. Leaning with his back against the rail was a man. He seemed about ten years older than Michael and little taller. He wore a tailored dark suit. But what Michael noticed most was the two pistols the man wore in holsters across his chest.

In Michael's coat breast pocket was a detailed itinerary. A day-by-day, hour-by-hour, almost to the minute schedule carefully made out by his father's secretary. Also everywhere Michael went someone was following him — perhaps his secret guardian angel. Some introduced themselves. On the Chariot it seemed it was the job of the entire crew to look out for him.   He had seen this man board in St. Louis. Michael was watching him. He assumed he was someone else his hired by his father.

"Mike Seward!" he said offering his hand.

He wore black leather gloves. Michael knew that gentlemen removed their gloves before offering their hand in greeting. But then gentlemen didn't brandish weapons.

Michael shook the offered hand. "Michael Dugan."

"Another Mike!" Seward gave a smile that did not quite reach his hard grey eyes.

"I prefer Michael. What were you saying about the lady?"

"Miss Jessica Kilgore. She is quite known as a Private Entertainer," Seward waited for some sort of reaction from the young man. He saw only annoyance.

"See some of your Private Entertainers sing, dance, or read poetry. All private performances for gentlemen and, I hear, ladies."

"What does Miss Kilgore do?"

"Fortune Teller." Michael looked at the man blankly. "She tells your future."

Michael leaned on the rail. "How do you know so much about Miss Kilgore, Mr. Seward?"

"I make it my business to know who I am traveling with, Mr. Dugan: heir to Dugan Manufacturing. Biggest spare part supplier in New England."

"Biggest on the East Coast," corrected Michael.

"I happen to know Miss Kilgore keeps a cabin on the Chariot and the Riverboat Sultana out of New Orleans."

"I didn't know fortune telling paid so well. She must be very good."

Seward sighed, deciding to change the subject. "I can't help but notice you are always armed, Mr. Dugan. Is that one of those new revolvers you wear on your hip?"

Michael sighed in annoyance. He turned to face the passing bank. "It is a Colt Revolver."

"Mind if I have a look at it?"

"Mr. Seward, If you know so much about me, you would know I promised my parents I would not remove this gun from its holster until I meet my Uncle

Mike." explained Michael, annoyance turning to anger.

"Are you proficient with the weapon?

Michael eyes narrowed as he turned to face the man. "Yes. If you must know, I am proficient with the weapon," he said through clenched teeth. "I am ashamed to say so, and ashamed to even have the thing in my possession. It is obvious, Mr. Seward, you have a fascination with guns. I, however, do not share your fascination. Good day, Sir."

Seward raised his hands and backed away. "Just tryin' to be friendly."

Proficient. Michael Dugan hated the word. He glared down into the dirty water rushing by. He felt the same way about the gun now as the day it came into his life.

Michael rememberd standing outside his father's study. He had been summoned there less than a half dozen times before. The last time was to be told of the death of his beloved grandfather.

He rapped lightly on the doors.

"Come in, Michael," he heard his father say.

He pushed and the doors slid apart with a rumble. Michael saw his father standing behind his carved, antique oak desk. The desk was from the captain's cabin of the Angel, the ship that had brought his grandparents and their two teenage sons from Ireland to Boston. At countless family gatherings, Michael had heard the tale of their harrowing voyage in 1823.

Mounted on the wall to his left was the masthead of the Angel. A beautiful woman proudly holding in front of her the Dugan family crest .

The glow of two whale oil lamps on his desk lit the figure of Patrick Dugan. It seemed to Michael his father always towered over him. Even at forty years of age, his father was in top physical form. His curly red hair and trimmed beard were just now showing streaks of yellow.

"Close the door, Michael."

Michael slid the doors together with a slight boom. When he turned back, his father's attention was on the desk.

Michael stepped forward. On the desk was a gun, a pistol the kind of which Michael had never seen before.

"It's called a revolver. It's a prototype," his father explained. "An invention by Mr. Colt. It can shoot six times without reloading. I have made some modifications."

The handle had polished wood inlays. The body was silver. The long barrel was coal back and reflected no light.

"Father, what use do you have for a gun?"

"It is for you. For your little frontier adventure."

Michael laughed. "I am spending the winter with Uncle Mike, a priest. I will not need a gun."

"The Town of Kansas is on the frontier. You mother and I think it best you have something to---"

Michael's eyes narrowed. "No! I leave in two days. I have met all your terms and requirements. This!" Michael pointed to the gun. "This is too much!"

His father straightened to his full six-foot-three height. In the light of the lamps, anger turned the man's wide eyes into angry pools of blue. "You will become proficient with this weapon or there will be no asinine frontier adventure."

"Outrageous!"

The next morning Michael and his father took the carriage to the outskirts of Boston. They came to an old building. Above the door was a hand lettered sign: Logan's Firearms.

As they pulled up to the porch a man walked out.

"Good morning, Mr. Logan," said Michael's father.

The man walked down the steps to the carriage. "This our student?" He looked at Michael with a forced smile. To Michael, the man's brown eyes were stamped with a deep wariness.

"This is my son, Michael. Michael, Mr. Logan."

"Just Logan," he said offering his hand.

Michael climbed out of the carriage and took the man's hand. "Good to meet you, Mr. Logan."

"Here is the weapon." Patrick Dugan offered the gun to Logan.

Logan looked at the gun. "Take your weapon, Michael."

Michael took the revolver from his father.

"I will be back in an hour," said Patrick Dugan.

"Wait a minute!" protested Logan. "I cannot teach this boy how to shoot in an hour!"

"Michael is a very fast learner. One hour." Michael's father slapped reins on the back of the horse and was gone.

Logan looked after the carriage and then at Michael. He simply shook his head and started toward the side of the building. Michael followed.

They came around behind the building. In a fenced area stood three flat wooden figures in the shape of men. Large holes were cut in their misshapen heads and chests. "If you learn one thing from this, Mr. Dugan, remember this: attempting to use the Colt Revolver without the proper training could result in serious injury or death."

They stood at a table facing the figures.

"You don't like this gun, do you Mr. Logan."

"One man, one shot." stated Logan. "I was thirteen when I helped whip the Brits at the battle of New Orleans with Andrew Jackson. I helped Sam Houston beat the Mexicans down in Texas."

Michael smiled. "Were you at the Alamo?"

Logan suddenly turned his head and glared at Michael. "Boy, don't joke about things you do not know a damn thing about." Logan looked out at the targets. "Single shot pistols and rifles won us the Revolution. Now look what Mr. Colt went and did." Logan lifted the gun and looked at Michael. "Six shots! Where does it end?"

" I have no use for any kind of gun," said Michael.

"Well, it's better to know the proper way to use any weapon and never have to use it, then need to and not know what you are doin'. " Logan handed Michael a belt with a holster on it. "Put this on."

"Does it go across my chest?"

"No, it is a belt. It goes around your waist and the holster goes on your hip." Michael put on the belt and positioned the holster on his right side.

"Put the weapon in the holster." Michael did as instructed and he suddenly felt off balance with two and a half pounds of metal at his side.

"Loosen the belt and lower the holster so when you hang your hand the gun handle is at your fingertips." Michael did as he was told. "Those targets are twenty-five feet away. That is the maximum range for an accurate shot with a Colt Revolver. Closer, you can't miss. Any farther and you should have a rifle. Try pulling, aiming, and firing. Aim for the chest area."

Michael pulled the gun, pointed at the middle figure and pulled the trigger. The barrel shook, but the hammer fell.

"Put it back in the holster."

"It is not as easy as I thought it would be. The gun is heavy."

"Try it again."

This time the Colt seemed steadier. As he pulled it a few more time it became easier.

"When do I get to shoot?

"Let's make sure you can hit something first. Try three shots this time. Shoot the middle one, then the one on your left, and then the one on the right."

"Why that order?" asked Michael.

"Well, the one in the middle is probably the boss. Maybe seeing him get killed will make the other two hesitate. The one on your left is the boss's right hand man. Maybe the third one is a tag along. Hopefully, he will see the two get killed and run. I consider three shots in five seconds proficient."

Michael pulled the Colt and aimed at the middle figure and pulled the trigger.

"Bring the gun up."

"Recoil?"

"Or the gun will try to break your wrist."

Michael raised the gun, then brought it down aiming at the figure on his left and then pulled the trigger. He turned and aimed at the third figure.

"Why am I not shooting the middle figure again?"

"He should be dead. Waste of time and ammunition."

Michael pulled the trigger.

"Keep that up and do it faster."

Michael repeated the task half a dozen times, getting faster and more accurate every time.

"How is our student doing?" Michael heard his father say coming up behind him.

"It has not been an hour," protested Michael as he turned around. It was then he saw his father had brought his mother.

Patrick Dugan ignored Michael. "Mr. Logan, this is my wife, Martha. She came to see her son's shooting skills."

Logan stepped toward the man. "He hasn't learned---"

"I haven't learned the finer points," said Michael looking at Logan. "But Mr. Logan seems to think I have the basics down. Reload the gun, Mr. Logan."

"You haven't even learned to load, Michael?" asked his father.

"Proficient shooting is more important than loading." Logan said handing the loaded gun to Michael Dugan. Michael placed the Colt in his holster and turned to face the targets. "Set the targets, Mr. Logan." Logan walked over and placed pieces of wood over the chest holes. "Set the head targets too, Mr. Logan." Logan shrugged and did as told. He then stood behind Michael Dugan.

"What do you consider proficient, Mr. Logan?" asked Patrick Dugan.

"Three shots in five seconds" answered Michael

"Three accurate shots in five seconds, I assume," said his father standing behind Michael.

Michael's eyes narrowed. "Call it, Mr. Logan."

"Draw your weapon and fire at will!" said Logan loudly.

Michael pulled the Colt, aimed at the center figure and pulled the trigger.

Once a large piece of metal fell two stories slamming flat on the factory floor, mere feet from Michael. That was nothing compared to the gun firing. He barely kept the Colt from flying out of his hand. He brought the gun down and took aim at the second target. He fired.

The gun violently twisted his wrist to the right. He straightened the Colt out as it flew up. He turned and aimed at the figure on the right. It was agony to pull the trigger. His wrist felt like it was about to shatter. He just wanted this over. The gun fired and kicked up. By sheer will he stopped as the Colt was pointed straight up.

"Holster your weapon, Mr. Dugan. " said Logan grimly "Let's see who the crows get to eat."

Michael brought the gun down, pointed it into the holster and let it drop. He let his arm fall to his side, sure he would never be able to use the hand or wrist again.

The smoke cleared. They looked at the targets.

There were ragged holes in the chest of two figures. Michael forced himself not to smile. The third figure had a hole in the center of its head.

"Three accurate shots in five seconds," announced Logan. "I am declaring Mr. Michael Dugan proficient with the Colt Revolver." Logan took the gun out of the holster.

Michael turned to face his father. Their eyes met. "I will be leaving for the Town of Kansas first thing in the morning, as we agreed." Michael walked around his father.

His mother appeared in front of him, terror in her wide blue eyes.

"Michael, could you kill someone?" she asked.

"Trust me, Mother, it will never come to that. Uncle Mike will take this horrid thing away from me as soon as he lays eyes on it."

"Michael, you know you have a temper."

"MOTHER!"

"Promise me you will never use that gun in anger. Promise Mother you will use it only to save your life."

Even though it caused him great pain, Michael Dugan lifted his right hand and placed it on his mother's arm. He leaned over and kissed her cheek. "I promise, Mother." He started off.

"Mr. Dugan." Logan called after him. "You are forgetting your weapon." Logan shoved the Colt in the holster. "I reloaded it for you."

Michael looked forward to the Chariot docking, seeing his uncle, and being rid of the damn gun.

"Be there somethin' interestin' in the water?" asked a female voice in a very familiar brogue. Michael looked up into two beautiful green eyes. "Excuse me bein' forward but we be meetin' before?"

"No, Ma'am." Michael stammered. "I have yet to have the pleasure."

"Miss Jessica Kilgore." She offered a green velvet gloved hand.

Michael took the offered hand and looked into those eyes. "Michael Dugan." Hardness came to Miss Kilgore's eyes as she pulled her hand from his. "I understand you are a fortune teller," Michael said, hoping he had not done or said something to offend the woman.

"Who be tellin' you that?" demanded Miss Kilgore accusingly.

"Mr. Seward."

Her eyes narrowed. "That Mike Seward be a bad 'un, Mr. Dugan. He be a hired gun. Be stayin' away from the likes of him." A smile returned to her face. "But he be tellin' the truth. I do read the tarot in private sessions. You see I am the Celtic Princess of Ireland."

"I read about the Celts and the Pagans when I was studying anthropology."

"Pagan is bein' such a nasty word. I prefer Celt."

She leaned on the rail and eased closer to the young man. "Mr. Dugan, have you ever be havin' your fortune told?" she smiled with a lilt to her voice.

Michael reminded himself he was seriously thinking about becoming a priest. Failing that, he had a girl (whose name he could not recall) at home to whom he was almost engaged. He also knew he should move back. And if Miss Kilgore moved closer Michael Dugan would seriously consider doing just that.

"No, Ma'am, I have yet to have an opportunity to have my fortune told."

She eased closer, her emerald eyes becoming twin kaleidoscopes. "I am bein' in town for the Fall Solstice. Perhaps you can be comin' for one of my private readin's."

"My Uncle, Father Mike Dugan, has a house in town. If he approves, perhaps you can come to his house for dinner. You can tell both our futures."

Sadness came to her pretty eyes. "If I be havin' the time I may be stoppin' by."

"At least come for dinner and meet my Uncle."

"We have already met," she whispered in Gaelic.

"What?"

"INDIANS!" Someone shouted. Michael saw people were pointing forward. Far ahead, up on a low bluff where the river narrowed were a group of Indians on horseback. The Chariot turned hard toward the center of the river. The crew of the Chariot appeared carrying muskets. Captain Foster came running up panicked.

"Miss Kilgore, you must return to your cabin with the rest of the passengers. You too, Mr. Dugan."

Michael had seen Indians from the train and Chariot. They were always in the distance.

Never this close.

The Chariot steadied up in the middle of the river. Michael went to the rail for a closer look. The Indians would be passing only feet away. He ran up to the bow as it passed by the group. "It is not a war party!" Michael called to the crew "If it were we would probably all be dead by now." He walked aft keeping the Indians abreast of him. The men with muskets walked behind him. The Indians watched them. "Lakota!" Michael said to himself. "They are Lakota," he said to the armed men.

"SIOUX!" The muskets went up and took aim.

There were seven of them. Michael knew it had to be a hunting party. He looked at the larger Indian in the middle. His face was horribly scared as if burnt in a fire.

That Indian was dressed differently than the rest. "A Medicine Man! You are a Lakota Medicine Man!" Michael realized the Indian didn't speak English and if he did he already knew who and what he was. He came to the stern of the Chariot. The group had assembled with their muskets in the center of the deck. Michael found himself standing in front of them.

Michael decided he needed to show respect to the Indians. He stood up, straightened, and looked at the Indians. He raised his right hand. The stern moved on, the Indians' expression did not change. They just looked at Michael. He remained in his position until the Lakota were out of sight. He realized the gesture probably made him look stupid — stupid or crazy.

Things returned to normal as the Chariot made her way. An hour later she went around a bend. To the right was a massive sandbar. Wooden pylons and boards protruded from it.

"That used to be the Port of Independence," explained Captain Foster. "There was a bad flood last year. It wiped it all out. Now we have to dock at the western port. Some call it Westport." He turned and smiled at Michael. "Better known as the Town of Kansas. Our next stop!"

A half-hour later the Chariot came to where the Kansas and Missouri rivers met. Captain Foster sent word for Michael to join him in the wheel house. When he got there Captain Foster was at the helm. To his right, Michael saw ships lined up along a long rock ledge along the bank of the river,

"The flood took out the dock, the part of the town closest to the river," explained Captain Foster as he eased the helm to the right. "The only thing left was that rock ledge. But it makes a perfect pier."

Michael saw a space between two moored paddle wheels. It looked not much bigger than the Chariot and Captain Foster was steering right toward that spot. At the last minute the captain swung the wheel left. To Michael they were inches from the boat in front of them. The Chariot eased along side it.

"Back one third."

The man beside the captain was at the helm. He grabbed the handles and pulled them back. Michael had learned that he controlled the speed.

The Chariot eased backwards. Captain Foster swung the wheel left. The stern moved slowly into the space.

"All stop!"

Men on the dock threw over giant bumpers. But the stern looked to Michael as if it would ram the boat behind them, crushing their paddlewheel. The boat stopped on its own. Michael realized the river's current had stopped them. The Captain turned the helm toward the dock.

The ship moved forward toward the paddlewheel in front of them. They were gaining speed as the Chariot neared the dock. Michael was sure the Chariot would hit the rock or ram the boat in front of them. Or both! The bow turned away from the dock but was still heading for the other ship.

Michael was sure collision was eminent!

"Back one third!" shouted the Captain.

Michael held his breath as he waited for the paddlewheel to turn. Finally, it did. The Chariot stopped moving forward and eased next to the dock. Michael felt this was as much excitement as he could handle for a while.

"Welcome to The Town of Kansas, Mr. Dugan." announced Captain Foster.

Michael went to his cabin and grabbed his two bags. They were just securing the gangplank when he arrived. Michael saw Seward following him.

"Can I help you, Mr. Seward?"

"I just want to make sure you find your uncle."

"Deliver me to him, you mean."

"The Town of Kansas can be dangerous. I would hate to see anything happen to you."

"I am not sure what Father Mike will think when I arrive armed and escorted by a hired gun." Michael stepped onto the gangplank.

Captain Foster was at the gangplank saying his farewells to departing passengers.

"We will be heading back to St. Louis day after tomorrow, Mr. Dugan," said the captain not meeting Michael's eyes, "If things don't work out."

Michael walked down the gangplank wondering why Captain Foster would say such a thing. He forgot all about that when he spotted the post office. He walked over to it with Seward right behind.

They entered the office. There were several men standing around. There was a man sorting mail behind a counter.

"Can I help you gentleman?" he asked.

"Good morning, I am Michael Dugan. I would like directions to Father Dugan's house."

One of the men looked at Michael with wide eyes, then he ran out the door nearly running into Seward. Michael and Seward watched the man jump on his horse and ride off.

Michael turned back into the room. Everyone was now looking at him and Seward.

"Dugan did you say?" asked the man behind the counter.

Michael walked up to the counter. "Father Mike Dugan. He has a house here in town. It's right next to where the church is to be built."

"Was Father Dugan expecting you, boy?"

"Father Dugan is my uncle. It is sort of a surprise visit." The men in the room looked at each other. "We have had mail for Father Mike Dugan. I've been instructed forward it."

"Forward?" Michael was perplexed.

"Who instructed you and forwarded where?" asked Seward.

"The Post Master in Westport ordered all mail for Father Mike Dugan is to be forwarded to that post office."

"Westport?" asked Michael confused. "This is Westport."

"This is the western port," explained Seward. "Westport is a town about four miles south."

Michael looked at the clerk. "Are you telling me Father Mike Dugan does not live in The Town of Kansas?"

The clerk looked at the men around the room. "All I know, boy, is that his mail is be forwarded to Westport. You need to check with the post master up there."

Mike felt lost. Where was the house his father built his Uncle? Where was his Uncle Mike?"

Michael turned to Seward. "You said Westport was four miles away. How do we get there? Walk?"

"Actually, I have business in Westport," said Seward. "Let me see if I can get us a ride."

They stepped onto the street. Michael saw a sign with hand lettering spelling out Westport and pointing up a road. "There!" They walked toward the sign as a wagon came from behind.

"Excuse me, sir." said Seward walking beside the driver. "Would you be heading for Westport?"

"I am."

"Mind giving us a lift?"

The driver pulled the reins and brought the two mules to a stop. He looked at Seward and Michael. "OK, but you have to ride in the back." He slapped the reins and mules started moving.

"Much obliged."

Seward ran to the back of the wagon. He jumped up. Michael threw his bags.

The wagon began moving faster. Michael ran and made a leap. Seward grabbed under his arms and pulled the boy in. Michael saw they were not the only passengers. Six negroes sat at the front of the wagon. They were all in chains.

"Sorry you have to ride with the stinkin' niggers," shouted the driver.

"Slaves," said Michael looking at the shackled men as they looked at him.

"Why are you surprised?" asked Seward looking at the slaves. "There were a hundred below decks on the Chariot."

"My father said no man should be owned by another." Michael said almost reciting.

"Do yourself a favor. While you are in these parts, keep that opinion to yourself. Missouri is a slave state."

"I thought we were in Kansas."

"The Town of Kansas is in Missouri. So is Westport."

"My father hires escaped slaves to work in his factories. He said they are his best workers." It wasn't the negroes that bothered Michael. It was the chains.

Michael noticed they were behind several wagons. More wagons behind them. Buildings became smaller and farther apart. Soon they were in open prairie.

"I have never heard of Westport." Michael finally said.

"I have been there a couple of times. It's the jumping off place for people heading west. It's the last place for people to stock up. All the trails go through there. Oregon, Santa Fe, California. It's kind of a wide open town and it can be a little rough. Like I said. I have business there."

"I thought I was your business."

Seward looked at the Michael puzzled. "I am just trying to keep you out of trouble."

"What kind of business do you have in Westport?"

"Hopefully long term employment."

Dugouts and log cabins began to appear. The slat wood houses.

"Could they have decided to move the church to Westport?" Michael wondered aloud.

"Let's find out where the mail is," said Seward. "At least it is not being returned."

"That means Uncle Mike must have made it to the Town of Kansas." Michael said assuring himself, "He is now living in Westport."

More houses and buildings began to appear on the side of the road.

"Hey driver!" called Seward. "Would you know where we can find the post office?"

"The Harris House." shouted the driver. "Mr.

McCoy is the postmaster and he owns the Harris house. I am going by there."

The wagon made a sudden right turn and some of the wagons turned with them.

Others continued on. The road was smoother. Brick buildings were on either side. Yes, Michael thought, this is a better place than the Town of Kansas. The church was moved to here.

The wagon stopped in front of a nice, three story building. "Harris House."

The two jumped off, and Michael grabbed his bags. They walked into an ornate hotel lobby.

"Good morning, gentleman," greeted the desk clerk. "Will you be needing a room?"

Michael hurried up to the counter, "Is the post office here?"

"We handle the mail for Westport."

"They said in the Town of Kansas that my uncle's mail was being forwarded to here."

"Your uncle's name?"

"Father Mike Dugan."

The curt smile on the clerk's face dropped, and he cleared his throat. "And you are?"

"Michael Dugan, I am his nephew."

The clerk looked at Michael then to Seward. "One moment please." The clerk turned and walked away. He disappeared behind a wall. Michael heard hushed whispers on the other side. The clerk returned followed by a taller man in a suit.

"What is the problem?" asked the man curtly.

"As I just told this man. I was told the mail for my uncle Father Mike Dugan was being forwarded here."

"I am Mr. McCoy. I own this hotel, and I am the postmaster. That mail is not here."

"Where is it?" asked Micheal.

"Federal Law dictates all mail will be delivered. It has been."

"Delivered where?" asked the frustrated Seward.

McCoy looked down his nose at them both. "To Father Mike Dugan's house, of course."

Michael sighed with relief. "They did move the church here. Where is Uncle Mike's house?"

"You on foot?" asked McCoy.

"For the moment." Seward put in.

"I can have the hotel carriage take you there." McCoy signaled to a man across the lobby. The man came to the front desk. "Take these gentlemen to where we deliver Father Dugan's mail. Drop them off and come right back."

They followed the man out front to a carriage and climbed aboard.

"I knew it! " Michael said smiling "They moved the church to Westport."

The carriage headed west then made a sudden right turn heading north. They proceeded north and then came to a smaller road and turned west. They topped a hill and in the distance Michael saw a large house at the top of the next hill. But to Michael the house didn't look right. The carriage rolled down the hill and crossed a bridge over a small stream. It came to the top of the hill.

"What is this?" Michael asked in disgust

The carriage turned up the circular driveway and stopped in front of the house.

To Michael, the house was a grotesque version of his family home. The house was built with flat rough rocks that seemed simply stacked on top of each other cemented together.

"This was supposed to be made of brick," said Michael as the two climbed out of the carriage. "They didn't even shape the stones."

Without a word the carriage driver whipped the horse. Seward was barely able to grab Michael's bags.

"Uncle Mike!" Michael shouted as he ran up the stone steps. There was no answer.

"Boy, just what do you think you are doin' here?" asked someone behind him.

Michael turned and saw three men walking up the driveway. The man in the middle was bigger and wore work clothes, as did the other two. All three were armed.

"I am Michael Dugan," he said from the top of the steps. "This is my uncle's house."

"The hell you say," said the taller man.

"Let's all calm down," said Seward seeing there were three guns to his two.

"This house is abandoned," declared the taller man. "October first I aim to legally claim it!"

"Abandoned?" Michael charged down the steps. "My family paid for this land and built this house."

When Michael Dugan got to the bottom of stairs, Seward stepped in front of the angry young man.

"I am sure this is just a misunderstanding," Seward said calmly.

Michael's eyes narrowed at Seward. "There is no misunderstanding!" Michael pushed Seward aside and faced the three men. "This is Dugan property, Sir, and you are trespassing."

The man smiled and looked at the two men on either side of him. They took a few steps back. "Trespassing am I?" They moved farther back.

"Yes! Get off this property, now!" Michael picked up his bags, turned, and headed for the house.

The larger man pulled his pistol, took aim at the middle of Michael Dugan's back, and fired.

CHAPTER II

Many things seemed to happen at once as Michael Dugan placed his foot on the bottom stone step.   He was shoved hard to his left as he heard the gunshot behind him. Something zipped by his right shoulder and dust erupted from the top step in front of him. He felt a sudden pull at his right hip. He realized Seward had taken the Colt.

He turned in time to see Seward aiming the Colt, his finger on the trigger.   Faster than Michael could comprehend Seward pulled the Colt's hammer back with the palm of his hand and let it go. Seward's first shot hit the man on the left in the chest. His next shot struck the second man between the eyes. He turned the gun toward the large man in the middle.

"No!" Michael dropped his bags and threw himself at Seward, bringing the man's arm down as the Colt fired.

Seward shoved Michael to the ground. His gray eyes were filled with rage. He pointed the gun at the young man. "What the hell do you think you were doing?"

Michael jumped to his feet and took the gun

from Seward. "You were about to kill an unarmed man." Michael shoved the Colt back in its holster.

"He just tried to kill you!" said Seward, exasperated.

"Both of you are dead." The large man said laying on the ground. A hole in his upper left thigh was oozing blood. "Do you know who I am?"

"Someone whose going to jail for attempted murder," stated Michael Dugan.

"I am Nick Hopkins."

A horse galloped up. On it was an overweight man with curly brown hair.

"Looks like I am too late," said the man dismounting.

"Winks! Thank God! I want these two arrested. They are armed intruders tryin' to steal my house," said Hopkins. He pointed at Seward. "That man just murdered my two men and tried to do the same to me."

"Let's all calm down." said the man. "I am Sheriff Winkleman."

The double doors of the house opened and an older slave came out. "Mornin' Sheriff. Did I hear some shootin?"

"Obadiah, Mr. Hopkins has been shot. I need you to go down the quarry and get a wagon to take him to Doc Adams."

"Yes suh, Sheriff Winkleman." The slave ran to the road, crossed it, and disappeared down the hill.

"Sheriff, I want this man arrested." demanded Michael. "Attempted murder."

"Well, technically, I am the sheriff of the Town of Kansas. I come up to Westport if there is trouble. Who might you be, son?"

"My name is Michael Dugan. My family had this house built for my uncle."

"Your uncle was Father Michael Dugan?"

"That's right. I came here for a visit. This house was supposed to be built in the Town of Kansas next to where the church was to be built."

The sheriff looked at the ground. "Son, this house has stood empty for almost six months. It is about to be declared abandoned."

"This is my uncle's house and it's certainly not abandoned!"

The wagon came up the hill toward the group. A man drove the wagon, and Obadiah stood in the back. The wagon turned up the driveway and stopped close to Hopkins and the two dead men.

The driver and the slave jumped down and threw the bodies in the wagon. They then eased Nick Hopkins on board. The driver jumped back in the seat and slapped the reins to the horse's back. It rumbled off, all the time Nick Hopkins glared at Michael Dugan.

"It is going to take a while to get Mr. Hopkins fixed up. He has a room at the Harris. We'll take him there. I will have the Harris House send a carriage for you. We'll get this all straightened out."

"Nick Hopkins just tried to shoot me in the back. If it weren't for the actions of Mr. Seward here, I would be dead. What else is there to know?"

The sheriff looked at Seward. "I have seen you before."

"Mike Seward, Sheriff," He offered his hand. "At your service."

Sheriff Winkleman shook his hand. "What brings you back to these parts, Mr. Seward?"

"A job."

"A job working for who?" inquired the sheriff.

"The man I just tried to kill."

The Sheriff looked at Michael. "Three men shot, but Mr. Seward has only two unfired pistols."

"He used this." Michael hefted the gun out of his holster. "The Colt Revolver."

"But when I rode up that gun was in your holster." The sheriff walked over and mounted his horse. "I will see what Mr. Hopkins says." He turned his horse and rode off.

Obadiah smiled at the two. "Are you two gentleman hungry?" asked the slave.

"I didn't have any breakfast." said Michael.

"Well, lunch is ready and somebody has to eat it." Obadiah pulled open the massive double doors and led them in. "You know you both are in big trouble."

"Why?" Michael said looking around the entryway. "The man tried to kill me."

"That man is Nick Hopkins," explained Obadiah. "He owns most of Westport and runs the rest."

"He doesn't own this house yet." Michael looked around. The inside of the house was like his family's home in Boston. But it was a bit smaller.

Obadiah led them into the dining room. Three places were set on the long polished oak table.

"Have a seat," said the slave. "Let me get you some food."

Michael and Seward sat facing each other. Obadiah brought a plate of stacked hot rolls. Michael grabbed one before the plate touched the table. He took a big bite out of it, suddenly realizing how hungry he was. The slave reappeared with a steaming kettle. With a ladle he filled the big empty bowls sitting in front of Michael and Seward.

"Won't you join us, Obadiah?" offered Michael "There's an extra place."

Seward cleared his throat. When Michael looked at him, Seward shook his head.

"I'll get something later, Massa Dugan."

"Do you live in the house, Obadiah?" asked Michael.

"I have a place out in the barn. No one lives in the house until Master Hopkins move in."

Michael took a spoonful of the hot thick soup. "This is very good. Did you make this, Obadiah?"

The slave beamed proudly. "Master Hopkins says the only reason he ain't sold me is my good cookin'. "

Michael emptied his bowl, and the slave filled it again.

"I got some cherry pie coolin'. " Obadiah said after Michael finished his second bowl.

"I haven't had cherry pie in a long time." said Seward.

"I be right back."

"He is not the hired help," said Steward after Obediah had left the room. "They don't eat where we eat, and they do not live where we live."

"Uncle Mike would never tolerate anyone being treated like that."

The door leading to the kitchen opened, and Obadiah entered carrying two plates with large slices of cherry pie. He put the plates in front of them and set forks next to them.

Michael cut into the tip of the oozing pie and popped it into his mouth. "Obadiah, Mr. McCoy said my uncle's mail was delivered here. Do you know where it is?"

"Sure!" The slave went into the living room and

returned with three pieces of mail. Two letter size envelopes and a large, bulging envelope.

Michael opened the large envelope. It was a bound book filled with various papers.

Michael popped a forkful of pie in his mouth. "These are the receipts from building the house." Michael turned the pages as he ate more of the delicious pie. "These are delivery invoices. The house was supposed to be stocked before Uncle Mike got here." He turned to the back of the book. "This is odd." He looked closer at the page.

"What is it?" asked Seward chewing his pie.

"It is the contract for the construction of the house. Where is said Town of Kansas someone crossed it out and wrote Westport."

"Who would do that?" asked Seward.

"The change is initialed MDD"

"Who is that?"

Michael looked off in thought, then snapped back. "Michael Damien Dugan. My uncle."

"There was a flood last year." said Obadiah. "It darn near wiped out the Town of Kansas. Maybe your uncle decided to build the house up here where there be more people."

"Is there a church being built in Westport?" asked Michael.

"What kind of church?"

"A Catholic church of course."

"Nothin' but Protestants in Westport."

Michael looked at the papers. "All these were signed by Nick Hopkins."

"Yes, Massa Dugan, every time something came, Master Hopkins made sure it got signed for and put away." said Obadiah.

Michael pushed the papers away. "Where is Uncle Mike?"

"The last you heard from your uncle he was leaving St. Louis." said Seward.

"His letter said he had wintered in St. Louis, and he was leaving March first to cross Missouri in a covered wagon alone. He said he hoped he would arrive in The Town of Kansas the first of April."

"The man who built the house was out of St. Louis!" said Obadiah.

"You uncle hears about the flood. He decides to have the house built here in Westport and changes the contract while he wintered in St. Louis." suggested Seward. "The man building the house gets here. Your uncle doesn't make it."

"I heared stories of what happens to people travelin' that far by themselves." said the slave.

"I don't feel right giving the house to Mr. Hopkins." said Michael.

"Give?" said Seward "Who said give it to him.

You are your uncle's next of kin. It is up to you to decide what happens to the house."

"The Chariot is leaving in two days." admitted Michael.

"In that time you and Nick Hopkins can come to a fair price for the house." said Seward.

Michael sighed. "It is an ugly house."

"Built from those ugly rocks from Master Hopkins quarry down hill." said Obadiah.

"And it is not built where it is supposed to be."

"It is what it is where it is." said Obadiah.

Michael sighed. "The family will be sad when I tell them what happened to Uncle Mike, but they will be happy to have me back early. And safe. Maybe it is better I go back."

Michael picked one of the letters. "This is from Father."

"So?" said Seward.

"Uncle Mike was not supposed to know I was coming." Michael picked up the other letter. "This one is from Mother."

"Maybe they were writing to make sure you made it." Seward said licking his plate.

Michael smiled. "You don't know my parents." Michael looked at both letters. He dropped one and started to open the one from his father.

"Carriage comin' up the road." said Obadiah

Michael and Seward stepped on to the porch as the carriage stopped in front of them.

"I am here for a Mr. Dugan." Michael recognized the driver who dropped them off that morning.

"You don't mind if I tag along, do you?" asked Seward.

"Mr. Seward, the more you are around, the safer I feel." said Michael, sliding over to give him room on red cushioned seat.

Soon they were turning up a side street beside the Harris House. Michael and Seward got out and walked around to the front. Michael saw a young Indian sitting on the corner. He had a dark brown skin laid out in front of him. On it were various necklaces of finely worked leather and intricate bead designs.

But what caught Michael Dugan's eye wasn't what was on the ground, but what was around the Indian's neck. It was a crucifix that looked very familiar.

Seward looked at Michael then down at the Indian. "Damn Sioux!" He took Michael by the arm and moved him toward the hotel's main entrance.

Mr. McCoy met them at the door. "This way gentlemen."

They followed McCoy into a large ground floor suite. On the bed was Nick Hopkins. The bedding was soaked in blood. Hopkin's left pant leg was cut open up to his crotch. Hopkin's thigh was wrapped with bandages.

"How is our patient, Dr. Adams? asked McCoy.

The old doctor ran his hand through his wiry salt and pepper hair. "I have done all I can do. I got the bleeding stopped. But if I try to dig out that bullet, Mr. Hopkins would probably bleed to death before I was done." The doctor snapped his bag closed and left. Mr. McCoy followed him out and closed the door.

Hopkins glared at Michael. "This is all your fault!"

"My fault?" protested Michael. "You tried to shoot me In the back!"

"I already told the sheriff how you were going for that damn gun!"

"OK!" shouted Sheriff Winkleman. "I am conducting a hearing here to decide who gets charged with what."

"Nick Hopkins! Attempted murder."

"That boy is a murderer." countered Hopkins.

"Actually, " put in Seward calmly, "I did most of the shooting."

"He is the boy's hired gun! They are both to blame."

"Will everyone please be quiet and let me conduct this hearing!" said Sheriff Winkleman.

"Now, as I understand it, this all started in a dispute over the ownership of the house.

"That house is abandoned, and I am claiming it!" stated Hopkins.

"Nick, that house is not legally abandoned until the first of October. That is a week away."

"The Dugan family built that house. I am Michael Dugan, and I am claiming it."

"He is a child! He can't---"

"I turned eighteen today!"

"And how do we even know you are who you say you are? You could be---"

"I saw the manifest of the Steamboat Chariot." Seward put in. "That is Michael Dugan of Boston."

"That can be verified later," the sheriff said. "But for now that's good enough for this hearing."

"Let's get to the part where he murdered my men and tried to kill me!" demanded Hopkins.

"I have heard Mr. Hopkin's version of events. I would like to hear Mr. Dugan's story"

"It is simple. I arrived at my uncle's house when Mr. Hopkins and his two henchman, all armed, walked up. I informed him he was trespassing on Dugan property. I turned to go into the house, and Mr. Hopkins tried to shoot me in the back. Mr. Seward pushed me out of the line of fire, saving my life. He then took my revolver from my holster and dispatched the two men who were drawing down on us. He would have killed Mr. Hopkins had I not intervened."

"Is that how it happened, Mr. Seward?" asked the sheriff.

"Mr. Dugan makes it all sound more dramatic. I saw Mr. Hopkins pull his pistol. I pushed Mr. Dugan out of the line of fire. Realizing I only had two single shot pistols, I drew Mr. Dugan's Colt revolver."

"How familiar are you with the Colt Revolver, Mr. Seward?"

"I have seen the gun used once or twice. Anyway, the two men were drawing on me and Mr. Dugan. I killed them both before they could get a shot off." said Seward with professional pride. "Mr. Hopkins would be dead too if it weren't for Mr. Dugan."

The sheriff turned to Michael.   "Why did you do that?"

"The three men had only single shot pistols," explained Michael. "Mr. Hopkins had fired his gun. As I explained to Mr. Seward, he would be shooting an unarmed man. That would be murder."

The sheriff looked at Nick Hopkins.

"I don't remember that part," mumbled Hopkins. "But I still have two dead men."

The sheriff continued to look at Hopkins. "Mr. Dugan probably saved your life."

"No," stated Seward. "He did save Mr. Hopkin's life. If Mr. Dugan had not have done what he did, Mr. Hopkins would be dead. Guaranteed."

"I am ruling the deaths self defense," announced the sheriff.

"Damn it!" spat Hopkins.

"And as for the house in question. The house is now the legal property of the Dugan family. Mr. Dugan here can do with it what he wants."

"What about this man trying to shoot me in the back?" demanded Michael. "I still want to press charges."

"When the Marshal comes to town you can take that up with him."

"And when will that be?" asked Michael.

Sheriff Winkleman looked down at Hopkins. Hopkins smiled. "Not for a while I suspect."

"Mr. Dugan is planning to leave on the Chariot day after tomorrow," said Seward. "In that time he and Mr. Hopkins can come to a fair price for the house."

"I have to pay for that house? Again?

"What do you mean again?" asked Michael.

"Mr. Hopkins," the sheriff spoke up, "feels, with all the effort he put into the house in the past six months, he has already paid for it. Isn't that right Mr. Hopkins?"

"Yes! That is exactly what I meant. And two days won't make that much difference one way or the other."

Michael looked down at Hopkins. "I will be going back to my house and unpack. Tomorrow I will drop by and we can discuss a fair price for my house."

Hopkins glared up at the boy. "Yeah, Mr. Dugan, me and you do have some unfinished business. Right now, I need to have a word with Mr. Seward here. Boy, you can go."

Before he left, Michael took Seward aside. "When you are done here," he said quietly, "I have something to discuss with you also." Michael walked out the door. The sheriff started to follow.

"Winks, you stay."

The sheriff shut the door.

"Seward," said Hopkins, "hundred in gold if you make sure that boy does not make it back to my house."

"Now, Nick," said the sheriff. "Let's think about this."

"Think about what? The boy dies, I get the house."

"Nick," explained Sheriff Winkleman "That kid's parents are very rich. You kill their only son, they'll want to know who did it. That means the Federal Marshal looking into it. They may bring the army out if they think I can't keep order. You remember what is was like during the election last year? All those officials nosin' around."

"I had to donate a lot of money to those people."

"Exactly! Imagine what it would be like if his parents came here demanding those politicians find out who killed their boy."

"Or had their boy killed." said Seward.

"So what do I do?"

"Nothing." said Seward.

"That is what I was thinkin'.," agreed the sheriff.

"Michael Dugan enjoys his little frontier adventure in Westport." Seward explained. "You give him a fair price for the house. He goes back to Boston and tells the family the tragic tale of his uncle, Father Mike Dugan, being lost on his solo wagon trip from St. Louis to the Town of Kansas."

"OK" said Hopkins reluctantly.

"That matter settled." said Seward. "Why am I here? Your letter said you had a job, you offered me my price, but you didn't say what the job was." Hopkins reached into a box beside his bed and pulled out a leather bag and gave it a toss. The sounds of coins could be heard as the bag landed at the foot of the bed in front of Seward. "You have my attention."

"Mike Seward, I hear you are soulless."

"Well, I have been called a sociopath but I prefer amoral."

"The point is, Mr. Seward, you don't care who or what you kill." said Hopkins.

"You want the boy dead?"

Hopkins smirked. "That will be a bonus if it is done right. My problem is with the boy's uncle. The Good Father Mike Dugan."

"What happened to the good father?" inquired Seward.

Hopkins looked up at the sheriff. "Let us just say he is no longer with us. Your job is to make sure he stays that way."

"So the job is to wait around Westport and kill the priest that is already assumed dead."

"If the need arises."

"You know my daily fee and as usual killing is extra."

"And, if the opportunity presents itself, a generous bonus for the boy," said Hopkins. "I will arrange for you to have a room here at the Harris. I will take care of your other requirements. Food, drink, and other needs."

"There are always my other needs." Seward said with a smile.

"Now get Mr. Dugan home. If someone kills him, make sure you kill them. Make it all nice and legal."

Seward picked up the bag with the coins and smiled. "My thirty pieces of silver."

"What silver? There a twenty gold ten dollar double eagles in there!"

Seward tossed the bag back to Hopkins. "I will pick that up later." Seward left.

"Winks, go find me the Devilbiss brothers."

"The Devil Twins? What do you want with those crazy slave catchers?"

"Like I said, me and Mr. Dugan got some unfinished business."

Michael walked out onto the street in front of

the Harris House.   He was relieved to see the young Indian still sitting on the corner.

"You are the boy with the magic gun," said the Indian smiling up at Michael.

Michael looked down at the Indian. "You are a Lakota."

"Most white men call me a Sioux."

"Sioux is what the French called the Lakota. It means snake in the grass."

"Venomous snake in the grass," corrected the Indian, standing and offering his hand.

"I am Thunder Eagle."

"Michael Dugan." Michael knew that Indians did not shake hands. Michael also learned to always shake an offered hand. "The gun is not magic. It is called a revolver." He turned to show the Indian the Colt.

"I will trade you for it." Thunder Eagle bent down, picked up a necklace, and held it up. "You wear this, no Indian will harm you."

"I cannot trade for the gun. But I am interested in what you are wearing around your neck."

Thunder Eagle looked down. He lifted the cross so Michael could look at it. "A man traded it to me. He said it will keep white man's devil away."

"It's a crucifix. My uncle is a Catholic priest. I gave him one just like for Christmas two years ago."

"This may be it." He took it off and handed it to Michael. "If your family is this Catholic does that mean you have to become a priest?"

"I don't have to. I am thinking about becoming one."

"My father is a Medicine Man. He says I must become one too." Thunder Eagle pointed to the crucifix. "It has writing on the back."

Michael turned the crucifix over. "To Mike, my favorite Uncle, Michael," he read.

"This is my Uncle's. Where did you say you got it?"

The Indian shrugged. "I traded it for a necklace to a man going west last spring. I have never heard of this Catholic. How does it work?"

"Work?"

"I would like to learn about this Catholic. Can you teach me?"

"About being Catholic? I am leaving in two days."

"You teach me a little Catholic Medicine. I teach you a little Lakota Medicine."

Michael shrugged. "My house is across the road from the quarry."

"I will be there in the morning."

Seward came walking up. "What the hell does this damn Sioux want?"

"Do you know him?" asked Michael.

"He is a Sioux! That's all I need to know."

"This is my uncle's." Michael held up the crucifix "Thunder Eagle said someone traded it to him last spring."

"He was probably part of the war party that attacked your uncle's wagon." Seward turned to Thunder Eagle. "What did you do?" said Seward accusingly. "Take that off the dead priest as a trophy? I guess a lot less messy than scalping."

"No!" protested the Indian. "I traded a man for one of my necklaces. I now give to this man as my gift."

"Thunder Eagle said he wants to know about being Catholic."

Seward sneered as he gave the Indian a look up and down. "A Sioux? Religion? They are all murderers and thieves." Seward thought for a moment. "It's the Colt. He plans to kill you and steal the Colt first chance he gets." Seward grabbed Michael by the arm and they headed toward the waiting carriage. They were nearly back to the house when Michael spoke.

"Did you get the job, Mr. Seward?"

"Let's just say the job is being reevaluated by all parties concerned."

"Good, because I want to hire you, Mr. Seward." The carriage pulled up in front of the house.

"Hire me? " asked Seward surprised. "For what?"

"For protection of course." Michael said climbing

out of the carriage. Seward planned on returning to the Harris House after dropping Michael off. Instead he got out. The carriage rolled away.

"You want to hire me to protect you?"

"I was clueless when Mr. Hopkins was about to shoot me. You, Mr. Seward, grasped the situation and took action." Michael undid the gun belt. "It is a two day job. All I can offer you is a room and Obadiah's good cooking." Michael Dugan held the Colt and gun belt out to Seward. "Will you take the job, Mr. Seward?"

Seward looked at the Colt then at the smiling boy. "Looks like you just got yourself a hired gun." He took the gun. They shook hands.

CHAPTER III

"I thought sure someone was gonna come by and tell me you two was dead or in jail," said Obadiah as they pulled open the doors.

"No," announced Michael. "Sheriff Winkleman ruled the killings self-defense and this house is mine to do with what I will. I will be staying here until the Chariot leaves day after tomorrow."

Seward held up the gun belt. "And I am your resident hired gun."

The three walked into the living room. "There are plenty of rooms upstairs," Obadiah said. "I will make one up for Master Seward."

"What time is dinner, Obadiah?" asked Michael.

The slave looked at him blankly. "What time do you want dinner, Master Dugan?"

"At home we always eat dinner at six sharp," said Michael.

"Six it is! What time is it now?"

Michael pulled out his father's watch. "A little after four."

"I need to go back to the Chariot to get my bags," said Seward. "I will be back in time for dinner." Seward pushed open the double doors and was gone.

"I already put your bags on the bed in your room," said Obadiah. "I didn't know if you were going to need them unpacked."

"My room?"

"Yes, Master Dugan. The Master Bedroom."

The slave turned and walked into the dining room, heading for the kitchen. Michael walked up to the thick oak steps. Something occurred to him as he reached the top of the stairs. His room is what would be his parent's room at home. He and his older sister Patricia, had the two smaller rooms down the hall. The large room across the hall was the guest room.

Michael opened the door to his left. His bags lay on the big bed. The windows looked out onto the drive and the road beyond. Part of him wanted to take his bags down the hall to his room. If his uncle were here this would be his room. But, Michael thought, it was only for two days. He could play master of the house for two days. And the master of the house gets to sleep in the master bedroom.

Michael unbuckled the straps on the bags and threw open the first one. This bag held two dress suits, one black, one brown, carefully packed by his mother. He picked up his black suit. He found it was strangely heavy. And it made an odd chinking sound. He reached into one pocket and pulled out a cloth bag. He set the suit down and looked in the bag. It was full of gold coins. Michael smiled and shook his head. His mother wanted to make sure he had plenty of money. His father had limited him on how much he should travel with.

By the time he had gone through both suits he had found money in every pocket.

His sensible father had packed his second bag with his work and casual clothes. He opened it. He opened the drawers of the dresser to put the work and casual shirts in. He picked up the first shirt and found it heavy. He unfolded it to find many coins. When he finished unpacking the bag he found more than his mother had stashed.

Michael hung up the suits and put the shirts and pants in the drawers. He looked at the bed covered in loose coins and in bags of various sizes and denominations. He set one of the bags on the floor and pushed the hoard off his bed and into it. He closed it and pushed it under the bed.

In the other bag he saw two things were left. One was a large Bible. Next to it was another volume almost as big — The Complete Works Of William Shakespeare. Michael could not believe his uncle had left them. He took the books out of the bag, closed it and slid it under the bed.

Michael picked up the books and brought them downstairs. He walked up to the doors of the study. Out of habit he raised his hand to knock. He laughed at himself and pushed the doors apart. He entered. In the middle of the room was an ornate desk. He stood looking at it. He half-expected his father to walk in and demand what he was doing in his study uninvited.

Michael walked behind the desk, placing the two books on it, went out, and quickly closed the doors behind him. He scolded himself. He was acting like a child sneaking into his father's private room without permission.

Michael walked into the dining room. The lunch had long been cleared. He then went into the kitchen. The dishes had been cleaned and put away. Obadiah stood at a large butcher block slicing up a massive piece of meat.

"Hello, Master Dugan," said the slave putting down the knife. ""Can I get you somethin' ?"

"Some water, I guess."

"Sure!" The negro opened a cupboard and got out a glass. He then went to the back room. Michael followed. Obadiah stood at a pump. With two strokes of the handle, water gushed out, quickly overflowing the glass. He handed the dripping glass to Michael.

"This is sure better than haulin' water up that hill from that creek."

"Thank you." When the cold water hit his lips, Michael realized how thirsty he was. He drained the glass and handed it back to the slave.

"Want some more?"

"No, I just want to take a look around the place."

"Barn's out back," said Obadiah returning to the kitchen and going back to cutting the meat. "You can saddle the horse and go for a ride before dinner."

"I don't ride."

The slave gave Michael a confused look. "I thought all young men rode."

"Not my family. We take carriages."

Michael walked out the backdoor and up to the barn. He looked inside. The barn smelled of horse, hay, and manure. A wagon and a carriage were parked inside. He heard a snort and saw two horses, standing in their stalls. One horse was large and the other small and black.

Michael had been able to drive a wagon and carriage since he was twelve. He walked between the wagon and the carriage. He saw the third stall. In it was an old rickety cot. Next to the cot was a small table with a half-burnt candle on it. Michael realized this is where Obadiah stayed. He thought for a moment about allowing the slave to sleep in the servants' quarters next to the kitchen. But it would only be for two nights. What would be the point? As Michael left the barn he wondered what Obadiah would do during the winter.

In the distance he saw various wagons moving on the road that had brought them from the Town of Kansas. There were two lines. One was moving slowly west, the other east. Most were covered wagons.

He walked down the hill, getting closer to the

plodding caravan. Some drivers waved, others looked straight ahead.

The two men on horseback were there before Michael realized it.

"Well, who do we have here?" one of them asked.

The horses were identical as their riders. Both men had blond hair that hung down in oily strands. Their half closed blue eyes void of emotion.

"I am Michael Dugan."

"I am Cane Devilbiss. This here is my brother Jarrod. You are that boy who murdered our friends and shot our boss."

"Your boss tried to shoot me in the back. Those killings were ruled self-defense." Michael said, noticing Jarrod and Cane were armed. He also remembered he had given the Colt to Seward.

"Mr. Hopkins said you were trying to steal his house," said Cane.

"It was ruled that this property belongs to the Dugan Family. The Dugan family paid for this land and built the house on it. I have a right to be here."

"Yeah," said Jarrod. "Mr. Hopkins don't see it that way."

"Mr. Hopkins is not the law."

The brothers looked at each other and grinned. "You ain't been in Westport very long have you, boy?" They both grabbed the handles of their guns. "And ain't gonna be much longer, either." They slowly started to pull their pistols.

Michael heard two pistols cock behind him.

"Well, if it ain't the Devil twins," said Seward coming up behind Michael, a pistol in each hand and aimed at the Devilbiss Brothers.

"You better not be callin' us that, Seward," warned Jarrod Devilbiss.

"Or what? Please! Pull those guns." chided Seward. "Me ridding the world of the likes you two would make my day."

Both men shoved their guns back in their holsters.

"Now, as Mr. Dugan just informed you. He is the legal owner of this property. I am seeing two armed intruders on his property. Property I have been hired to protect."

"Mr. Hopkins know you are workin' for this boy?"

"Why don't you just run along and tell him."

The twins turned their horses and galloped away.

"That is the second time you saved my life today, Mr. Seward."

"Just doin' my job," said Seward putting his pistols back in their holsters. "From now on in Westport, you don't leave the house without me."

They walked up the hill and through the barn.

Seward inspected the horses. He didn't even look at Obadiah's cot.

As they walked toward the house, they saw a carriage come up the road and turn into the driveway. The passenger looked at Michael and gave a wave with her dainty gloved hand, her green eyes sparkled in the setting sun.

Michael took off running. He came to stand at the steps as the carriage came to a stop.

"Good evening, Mr. Dugan."

Michael was out of breath. "Good evening, Miss Kilgore."

"I be seein' you be findin' your uncle's house," she said looking at the house.

"Yes, Ma'am. Such as it is."

She brought her eyes back to Michael. "Be your uncle here?"

"No, Ma'am," Seward said coming up behind Michael. "It is believed Father Dugan was lost on his journey here from St. Louis."

"Miss Kilgore," said Michael, "to what do we owe the pleasure of your visit?"

"Have you be forgettin' then, Mr. Dugan, you be invitin' me to dinner just this morning?"

"Yes, Ma'am, I mean no Ma'am. I thought you were staying in the Town of Kansas."

"The Town of Kansas?" she said indignantly.

"There be nothing there. I be stayin' at the Harris House, as always. Am I still be invited to dinner?"

"Yes, Ma'am, of course." Miss Kilgore opened the carriage door and offered her hand.

As Seward reached for it, Miss Kilgore's eyes turned hard, and she withdrew the hand. Michael Dugan offered his hand. Miss Kilgore placed her dainty, gloved hand in his, and he helped her out of the carriage.

"Should I wait, Miss Kilgore?" asked the driver.

"No, but be havin' the Harris send me a carriage in an hour."

"Yes, Miss." The driver slapped the reins on the back of the horse and was gone.

The woman looked at the house. "It is a beautiful house."

"It was supposed to be in the Town of Kansas and built of brick like my home in Boston."

Miss Kilgore got a slight smile on her face. "It be remindin' me of the ancient castles in Ireland. These two towers. What be they called?" she asked.

"Keeps." Michael answered. "Shall we go in?"

Miss Kilgore glanced at Seward as they walked up the steps. "What business you be havin' here, Mr. Seward?"

"I am staying here." Seward informed the woman with a smile. "Mr. Dugan has hired me to be his protection during his stay in Westport."

She gave a short laugh.

Michael pulled open the doors for her. Miss Kilgore looked around the large living room as she removed her wrap. Michael took the wrap and put it on the coat rack at the entrance.

"Would it bein' too much of a bother, Mr. Dugan, to be given me the nickel tour?"

"Not much to it," said Michael. "The bedrooms are upstairs." He led her to the sliding doors of the study and pushed them apart. "This is my father's---the study." She entered, looking at the room. Miss Kilgore moved to the desk, seeing the books laying there.

"Are you a fan of Shakespeare, Mr. Dugan?"

"He is my uncle's favorite. I like him, but I prefer Edgar Allan Poe myself."

She looked at him as she left the study. "You are a man of varied interests, Mr. Dugan."

"My father calls them my adventures."

She laughed as they entered the living room. Michael liked her laugh. She took a turn looking at the room. "What bein' in there?" She nodded toward two smaller doors across from the study.

"That is the parlor," said Michael.

"A parlor? Really?"

"Yes, Ma'am, my mother insisted. If my father had a study for his business, she would have a parlor to entertain." Michael explained, opening the doors.

The room was as large as the study, but was obviously designed with a woman in mind.

"What a lovely room. It be puttin' my suite at the Harris House to shame. If I be stayin, here," said Miss Kilgore "I could be entertainin' my clients in here."

"You mean telling your fortunes." said Michael.

"I think Mr. Dugan is too young to understand what a private entertainer does," said Seward.

Miss Kilgore whirled to face Seward with fire in her eyes. "And I be supposin' I should be a hired killer, such as yourself, Mr. Seward."

"At least I don't pretend to----"

Michael stepped between the two. "Why don't we go see how close Obadiah is to serving dinner?"

They walked out of parlor, through the living room and into the dining room.

Obadiah came out with two large plates.

"Obadiah," said Michael, "This is Miss Kilgore, she will be joining us for dinner."

"Obadiah! It has been too long!"

"Miss Kilgore! " The slave smiled. "I am makin' steak!"

"I am blessed!"

The slave placed the two plates and soon came out with a third.

"Obadiah, set that at the head of the table, please," said Michael as he moved a chair to the end of the table. "Miss Kilgore," he said moving the chair out. "Would you mind sitting at the head of the table?"

"I be honored." Michael held the chair for her as she sat. He watched as the woman removed her gloves. For the first time he could see her elegant, dainty hands.

Michael quickly took a seat on her right. Seward sat across from Michael.

Obadiah set napkins and silverware for them. He also placed wine glasses in front of each setting. He poured wine for Seward and Miss Kilgore. When it came to him, Michael covered his glass with his hand.

"Milk for me, Obadiah."

Seward looked up. "You don't drink?"

"My father does not allow drinking in the house."

"I thought you Irish were big drinkers."

"Drinking and the Irish Brogue were both discouraged in our house."

Obadiah reappeared with a pitcher of milk and filled Michael's glass. "There you go, Ma'sa Dugan." The slave disappeared into the kitchen.

"I wish he would stop calling me that." Michael said quietly.

"Be callin' you what?" asked Miss Kilgore taking a sip of wine.

"Master. Why can't he call me Mr. Dugan?"

Obadiah returned with a basket of rolls in one

hand and a plate of steaming baked potatoes in the other. He placed both on the table.

The three helped themselves to the potatoes, cut them open and buttered them.

Obadiah came in and placed a serving platter in front of Michael. It was stacked high the biggest steaks Michael had ever seen.

Michael drove his fork into the top steak and brought to his plate. The ends of the piece of meat hung over Michael's plate. He cut off a piece and popped it his mouth.

"Obadiah!" said Miss Kilgore in rapture. "You be out doin' yourself! This meat be meltin' in my mouth. As always your seasonin' be perfect."

They quietly dined for a while.

Finally Miss Kilgore spoke. "Mr. Dugan," she said buttering a roll. "Would it be too bold of me to be askin' you a question?"

Michael put a piece of meat from his third steak in his mouth. "Not at all, Miss Kilgore."

"What be your family business?"

"Dugan Manufacturing." said Seward cutting into a steak. "Biggest spare parts supplier in New England."

"Biggest on the East Coast," corrected Michael.

"How be you family be gettin' into that business?"

Michael sighed, remembering the company's

boring brochure Dugan salesmen would carry with them.

"When my family came to Boston from Ireland my grandfather got a job selling small white toy windup dogs on the street. They were cheaply made and would break. People would throw them away. My Grandfather would collect the broken ones from the trash. He would bring them home for my father and Uncle Mike to play with. One night my father and my grandfather took one of the dogs apart. Between them they figured out a small part was breaking in all of them. They made a replacement part and fixed all the broken dogs. They painted them black and sold the black dogs saying if they broke they would replace them. They started taking other things apart and seeing what part would break, and would make a dozen of them. Our slogan is "It's a Dugan!" Our trade mark started out as a cute black dog. Now its looks like a angry black wolf.

"I have been taking things apart and putting them back together since I can remember," explained Michael. "My sister would get furious when I would dismantle her Christmas toys."

They laughed.

"I am hopin' you be puttin' them back together." said Miss Kilgore.

"Most of the time." The room erupted in laughter.

"Forgive me for bein' personal," continued Miss Kilgore. "A guaranteed life of wealth and privilege.

Why then would you be wantin' to be comin' a priest?"

"Oh, a priest will be the last of my pursuits. I tried so many things."

"You be mentionin' anthropologist on the boat this morning.'"

"Nothing ever seemed to work out. Everyone would say I was just not cut out for it."

"Why priest?" asked the woman.

Michael looked at his plate and sawed his meat. "Uncle Mike always seemed so happy."

"But you can't---" mentioned Seward. "Ya' know, have intimate relations with a woman."

"Did you have The Calling the preachers talk about?" asked Obadiah.

Michael popped a piece of meat into his mouth and chewed it. He did not look up. "I have not had The Calling yet. But something did happen."

"Would it bein' a sign of some sort?" asked Miss Kilgore.

"Yes Ma'am, I had a sign, I guess you can call it that." Michael said with mild annoyance.

"What was it?" Seward inquired with a grin. "Angels coming down from above?"

Michael's eyes narrowed as he looked across the table at Seward. "It is a rather personal matter."

"You be havin' your uncle's eyes." Miss Kilgore said absently.

Michael looked up at her. "You met Uncle Mike?"

Miss Kilgore's eyes widened. "Why yes, I thought I be tellin' you that." She gave a nervous laugh.

"It was in St. Louis." Obadiah quickly said.

"Yes! We be meetin' on the Riverboat Sultana. I keep a cabin on the Sultana."

"What was Uncle Mike doing on the Sultana?" asked Michael.

She hesitated. "He be on a tour, if I be rememberin' correctly. It was so long ago.

Yes, the family he be stayin' with for the winter in St. Louis be takin' a tour of the Sultana. He came aboard just before we be sailin' for New Orleans. I be rememberin' now."

Michael leaned back in his chair. "You remember him from that long ago?"

Seward cleared his throat and smiled.

Miss Kilgore's green eyes fixed Seward with a warning look. "It is hard to forget an attractive man with striking blue eyes dressed as a priest. He always seemed so happy. We be talkin' for a while."

"You . . . and a priest," smirked Seward.

Miss Kilgore's eyes narrowed and a loud thump was heard under the table. Seward winced in pain.

"He be talkin' mostly about his family. How he be goin' to the frontier. You thinkin' you might be wantin' to be a priest?"

"Why would he tell you about that?" demanded Michael angrily. "It was supposed to be our secret!"

"Calm yourself, Mr. Dugan. Who would I be tellin'?" Her demure smile returned to her red lips.

"I have some cherry pie," announced Obadiah. "Who wants desert?" They all raised their hands.

"I be twice blessed!" said Miss Kilgore excitedly. "First Obadiah's steak, and now I be havin' his famous cherry pie!"

"How do you know Obadiah?" asked Seward as the slave returned with three plates of cherry pie.

"And who said I be knowin' him?"

"You said it had been a long time since you have seen him," said Michael.

"And you said you have had his steak before," said Seward looking at the woman with a smirk. "And it seems you are familiar with his famous cherry pie."

Obadiah set a plate in front of Miss Kilgore, putting his back to Michael. "I used to be a cook on the Chariot," said Obadiah looking down at Miss Kilgore, then looking at Seward.

"Yes! "Miss Kilgore said. "Of course. I be enjoyin' your wonderful meals."

There was a knock at the door. Obadiah went to answer it. "Miss Kilgore, your carriage is here," said the slave when he returned.

To Michael the woman seemed to give a sigh of relief. "Where be the time goin'?"

Michael jumped to his feet and stood behind Miss Kilgore's chair and pulled it out for her. She stood and smiled at him. "Mr. Dugan, I be thankin' you for a very interesting evening." She said as they walked to the front doors. Michael took down her wrap and handed it to her. Her smile grew as she put the wrap on. Michael pushed the doors open and the cool late September breeze greeted them.

"I plan to sell the house, so we will both be sailing on the Chariot when it leaves day after tomorrow," said Michael opening the carriage door and helping her in.

"I be lookin' forward to you sittin' for one of my Tarot readins.'"

"I, too, will be looking forward to that."

Just before the carriage pulled away, Miss Kilgore leaned down and gave Michael a peck on the cheek.

After the carriage was gone he turned to see Obadiah and Seward grinning at him.

"Mr. Dugan," said Seward, "I do believe you are blushing."

The three walked into the house. Obadiah shut the doors behind them. The slave turned in time to see Michael give a big yawn.

"Ma'sa Dugan, you have had a long day. You need to get to bed," said Obadiah.

"Master Seward, I put your things in the room across from Ma'sa Dugan's room. It's the room facin' the front so you can see trouble comin.' Let me get you some candles."

Obadiah went to a shelf and picked up two candle holders, each containing a long white candle. He handed one to each of them. The slave struck a match and lit both the candles.

"Thank you, Obadiah," said Michael.

"I will clear the table and get everything washed and put away. What time do you want to get up tomorrow, Ma'sa Dugan?" asked the slave.

Michael shrugged. "Sunup I guess."

"I will get breakfast ready then wake you up."

"Good night, Obadiah." The two men walked up the stairs by flickering candle light.

"Good night, Mr. Seward."

"Good night, Mr. Dugan."

Michael opened the door and closed it behind him. He placed the candle on the night stand and got undressed. He lay his clothes on a nearby chair, not sure if he would be wearing fresh clothes tomorrow. He pulled on his night shirt, drew the covers back, climbed into the large bed, and pulled the covers up.

Michael Dugan was SURE he would never be able to sleep. He leaned over and blew out the candle. Off in the distance he heard the clinking of wagons. He also heard the faint sound of music, loud talk, and laughing coming from the nearby saloons. Stars shined through the windows.

Michael thought about it. In one day he had seen a real Lakota Medicine Man, MET a Lakota Indian.

Did he remember right? Did Thunder Eagle say he was the son of the Medicine Man? Could his father be the same Medicine man he saw from the Chariot?"

He has also met and had dinner with the lovely Miss Jessica Kilgore. And yes, day after tomorrow he would be taking the Chariot back with her. Dare he hope that he would be one of those gentlemen escorting Miss Jessica Kilgore on her daily strolls on the ship? He imagined looking into those smiling green eyes every day for two weeks.

No, he would never sleep tonight. He would be wide awake when Obadiah called him for breakfast. No, he would never sleep tonight. That was his last thought before he fell asleep.

The next thing Michael Dugan knew there was a loud knocking on his door. "Ma'sa Dugan you got to get up!" There was terror in the slave's voice.

Michael raised his head and forced his eyes open. The sun barely lit the room as he looked at the door. "What is it, Obadiah?"

"There's Indians out in front."

Michael half thought he was dreaming as he got up and went to the windows. He expected a war party coming up the drive. Instead he saw a tipi and two horses standing next to it.

"Should I wake Mr. Seward? We are gonna' need both your and his guns!"

Michael saw no movement in the structure. "No, I will see about it."

Michael quickly dressed and opened his door. Obadiah waited there wide-eyed.

"You need to get your gun," said the slave with a quiver in his voice.

The door across the hall opened. Seward appeared dressed and wearing the Colt.

"What the hell is going on?"

"Indians, Master Seward!" said he slave. "They's camped out front!"

Seward pulled the Colt. "We will see about that." He started downstairs.

"Put that gun away," ordered Michael. "It is one tipi. If it were a war party we would all be dead by now."

Seward looked at Michael. "You have a point." He holstered the Colt. "What the hell are they doing here?"

The three walked down the stairs. Obadiah behind Seward, Michael leading.

"Obadiah," said Michael "You get breakfast ready. Mr. Seward and I will see about the Indians."

Obadiah turned and nearly ran toward the kitchen. Michael and Seward pushed open the doors. Seward kept a grip on the Colt and looked on the porch.

"Clear." They walked to the top of the steps. There was still no movement from the tipi.

Seward started down the steps. "Stay here." he whispered.

"Why are you whispering?" asked Michael. "Do you know any plains Indian languages?"

He drew the Colt. "Trust me, this is the only thing redskins understand."

Michael looked at the tipi and sighed. "You stay here."

Michael walked down the steps. He decided he did not want to look like he was sneaking up on the tipi. He walked right up to the entrance.

The top of the opening came up to his chest. He heard a man and a boy arguing in hushed voices in an indian language. Michael had helped his uncle learn some of each major plains Indians languages. All of it, however, was from books. They had to guess at the pronunciations. Michael heard the older man say father. But what language? He listened more. He heard the younger Indian say son in Lakota he thought (hoped). The exchange was getting angrier and louder.

"Excuse me!" Michael said in a loud clear voice. The angry exchange continued without even a pause.

"Stop attacking! I come in peace!" shouted Michael in what he believed was Lakota.

There was silence in the tipi. Michael stepped back as a figure emerged. A very big, very tall Indian was suddenly standing before him. Michael immediately recognized the scared face glaring down at him.

"You are the Lakota Medicine Man!" Michael offered his hand. "I am Michael Dugan."

The Indian turned his glare to the house.

Michael followed his gaze. He saw Seward aiming the Colt at them.

"Put that away," ordered Michael.

"Not a chance. He kills you, I kill him. Simple as that." said Seward easing down the steps.

Did Michael hear that right? The man he hired for protection would kill the Indian after the Indian killed him?

The Medicine Man bent down and talked to the other person in the tipi, pointing in the direction of the house and Seward. Another figure emerged.

"Thunder Eagle!" Michael said smiling. "What are you doing here?"

"I told you I would be here this morning. Did you forget? You said you would teach me Catholic Medicine."

The Medicine Man started talking and pointing to Seward now at the bottom of the steps still aiming the Colt at them.

Thunder Eagle looked at Seward then to Michael. "You know, if we wanted you dead, we could have killed you in your sleep."

"I told him that. That is Mr. Seward. I hired him to protect me. Michael turned to Seward. "Put that gun away before I take it away from you."

Seward put the Colt back in its holster, but kept his grip on the handle.

"Is this your father?" asked Michael.

"Yes! This is Fire Oak."

"Michael Dugan," he offered his hand. "We saw each other yesterday."

"We don't shake hands," explained Thunder Eagle. "Even looking him in the eye very disrespectful."

Michael dropped his hand and his eyes went to the ground.

Fire Oak pointed to Michael and said some words in Lakota. Out of the words said Michael understood two words: stupid and boy. Fire Oak continued to speak pointing to the tipi, then at Thunder Eagle, to himself, and then Fire Oak forcefully pointed west.

"My father does not want me to stay with you and learn your Catholic medicine."

"Tell Fire Oak I am leaving tomorrow. In that time, if he gives you his permission to stay, I will teach you nothing of my Catholic Medicine. But I would be honored to learn more about the Lakota from you."

Thunder Eagle translated. After which Fire Oak looked down his nose at Michael and snorted. He gave a dismissive wave to both the boys. Fire Oak began to talk as he walked over to the horses and mounted one. He continued speaking as he turned his horse and looked down at the two boys. The Medicine Man spoke as he pointed to the boys, the house behind them and gave a sweeping gesture that seemed to take in all of Westport. The boy's eyes remained on the ground. Fire Oak finally gave a slashing motion toward the boys and turned his horse around and galloped off.

"What did he say?" asked Michael.

"He said I can stay," said Thunder Eagle. "And he hopes you enjoy your visit."

"I have never been in a tipi before," said Michael. "May I?"

"Welcome!"

Michael dove into the structure. Thunder Eagle followed.

Long poles stuck in the ground gave the structure its cone shape.

"Is this buffalo?" Michael asked as he ran his fingers over the sloping walls.

"Yes, the skin of two buffalo. I killed them myself." said the Thunder Eagle with pride.

"You hunt buffalo?"

"Since I was a child."

"On horseback? With a bow and arrow?"

"How else?"

Michael saw the tipi was empty. "Where are your things?"

"My father would not let me bring them. He wasn't sure if he or you would allow me to stay."

"It is only until tomorrow. May I sleep in here tonight?" asked Michael.

Thunder Eagle smiled. "I would be honored."

Seward stuck his head in the tipi. "Obadiah said breakfast is ready."

"Thunder Eagle, this is Mike Seward. Mr. Seward meet Thunder Eagle. Why didn't Obadiah come get me?" asked Michael.

"He is scared to death of Indians," explained Seward. "He won't even come out of the house with him here."

They climbed out of the tipi. "Thunder Eagle you are welcome to breakfast."

"I need to get my things." The Indian jumped on his horse and galloped off.

Michael smiled at Seward. "I am sleeping in a Lakota tipi my last night on the frontier!"

"Who do we have here?" Michael saw a buggy turn off the road onto the driveway. It was being driven by a man in a long black coat and matching wide brimmed hat. Beside him rode a stern looking woman in a buttoned down black dress.

The buggy pulled up to them.

"Good morning," said the man curtly after bringing the buggy to a stop.

"Good morning." said Michael.

"Are you Father Mike Dugan?" the man inquired.

"Father Dugan is my uncle. I am Michael Dugan."

The man stepped out of the buggy. "I am Reverend Elijah Clark of the First Baptist Church of Westport. This is Abagail, my wife." The woman nodded, a stern look in her sallow face.

"Pleased to meet you both," said Michael offering his hand. "This is Mike Seward."

"Is Father Dugan here?" asked the reverend after finishing the greetings.

"It is assumed that my uncle was lost in his solo passage from St. Louis to the Town of Kansas." explained Michael.

"Sorry for your loss, I am sure." Reverend Clark's words were perfunctory and void of sympathy. "So there will be no Catholic Services?" the man asked with a satisfactory smile on his face.

"I came here to learn from my uncle about becoming a priest. Unlike Protestants, we Catholics don't just allow anyone to lead our services." Michael informed the reverend curtly. "Hearing of my uncle's tragic death, I will be leaving tomorrow and going back to Boston."

"There are many people, including myself, that will rejoice to hear that," said Reverend Clark in a self-righteous tone. "Westport is a fine Christian community. We don't want or need the sort of people your kind seem to attract, Mr. Dugan."

Michael folded his arms in front of him. "And what sort would that be, Reverend?"

The man of the cloth nodded toward the tipi. "Savages for one."

"Thunder Eagle is the son of a Medicine Man. Thunder Eagle is as interested in my beliefs as I am in his."

Reverend Clark looked at Seward. "Hired guns."

"Mr. Seward saved my life twice yesterday."

"He also gunned down two upstanding members of my flock just yesterday."

"Outrageous! If it weren't for Mr. Seward your upstanding members of your flock would have shot me in the back!"

The Reverend Clark smiled at the young man. "And keeping company with the likes of one Miss Jessica Kilgore."

Michael Dugan dropped is hands to his side. "What about Miss Kilgore?"

Seward put his hand on Michael's shoulder. "Steady."

"She was seen leaving this house last night," said the Reverend suggestively.

"Reverend Clark you seem to know an awful lot about the comings and goings of this house," said Seward.

"As if it is any of your business, Reverend Clark. I invited Miss Kilgore to dinner."

The minister gave the young man a self-righteous smile. "Of course you did, Mr. Dugan, and I am sure you and Mr. Seward enjoyed her after dinner entertainment."

"Miss Kilgore joined us for dinner," stated Seward. "That was all."

"It is between you and God if you two choose to keep the company of someone known as The Witch-Whore." Seward grabbed the side of the buggy, putting his arm between the reverend and an outraged Michael Dugan. Reverend Clark sneered as he climbed back into his buggy.

"As you said, Mr. Dugan, you are leaving for Boston tomorrow. Mr. Hopkins will be taking possession of the house. Mr. Hopkins is another fine Christian. He is in church every Sunday.

"Jesus was really big on back shootin, runnin' whore houses, and slave tradin' was he, Reverend Elijah Clark?" asked Seward.

The reverend snatched up the buggy whip and glared at Seward. Seward put his hand on the Colt. "Good-bye, Mr. Dugan. Have a pleasant trip back to Boston." The man whipped the horse and roared off.

"Mr. Hopkins do all that you said?" asked Michael watching the buggy go.

Seward turned toward the house. "If it can make

money, legally or otherwise, my boss probably takes a part of it."

"Your boss?"

"My future boss." said Seward quickly.

Obadiah pushed open the doors to them as they came to the top of the steps. "I seen you talkin' to Reverend Clark."

"Do you attend his church, Obadiah?"

Obadiah laughed. "You say the funniest things, Master Dugan."

They came into the dining room. Breakfast was laid out.

"Obadiah, do we have any coffee?" asked Seward.

"Just made a pot."

"I will have some too, Obadiah," said Michael, taking a chair. "And where is the book of receipts I was looking at?"

"I put it right over here with the mail." The negro brought the book and set it beside Michael. Obadiah went into the kitchen as Michael placed eggs onto his plate. As Michael looked at the receipts Obadiah brought in two big coffee cups and a pot of coffee. He set the cups in front of the two and filled them. Michael put cream and sugar in his coffee while looking at the paper work.

"Does Mr. Hopkins own the quarry down the hill?" asked Michael.

"Mr. Hopkins didn't buy it," said Obadiah. "No

one owned it. He just took it over. Mr. Hopkins hires out slaves to dig the rocks out. He charges by the wagon load."

"This house was built from the rocks from that quarry," stated Michael.

"That's right."

Michael bit into a piece of bacon as he turned the pages of the book. "So these receipts for labor and materials is Mr. Hopkins paying himself."

"I know one thing," said Obadiah. "Mr. Hopkins kept those men working didn't matter what the weather. Mr. Hopkins wanted this house done by the first of April."

Michael popped a piece of warm, syrup-soaked pancake in his mouth. "What is a fair price for this house?"

Seward popped some bacon in his mouth. "Just add up the receipts in that book and double it."

Michael nodded and took a sip of coffee, going through the receipts. He came to the last page as he drained his cup.

"Five thousand, two hundred and thirty-two dollars."

Seward nearly choked on his coffee. He sat his coffee cup down. "You just totaled all those receipts in your head."

"Math was one of my favorite subjects. So ten thousand sounds like a nice round figure," said

Michael standing up. "Obadiah, would you mind hitching up the carriage? We'll be seeing Mr. Hopkins and make him an offer."

"No sir, we are walking," said Seward.

"Why not take the carriage?" asked Michael.

"Because we have business to take care of after we see Mr. Hopkins."

Seward led Michael to the door and pushed them open. "What kind of business?"

"You got any money?"

"Some." Michael remembering the treasure his mother and father had supplied.

"How much am I going to need?" asked Michael suspiciously.

"Ten dollars should cover it."

Michael ran upstairs and got ten silver dollars and put them in his pocket. He then ran back downstairs to find Seward waiting.

They walked to the road where the wagons moved in their east and west procession.

"Why are these wagons coming from the west?" asked Michael as they waited for a gap in the wagons. "I can see going west."

Seward grabbed the young man's arm and pulled him through a gap. "Some are traders doing business with the Indians. Others just give up and turn back."

They jumped onto the board sidewalk, barely being missed by a wagon.

"Lots of saloons and whorehouses," admitted Seward as they walked along.

"If that is the business you were talking about, you can do that on your own."

"No, Mr. Dugan. There are other businesses here in Westport. They are out of the way. Blacksmiths, general stores, even a dentist I hear. Westport was here long before the Town of Kansas."

They came to another road that crossed north and south. They stopped and waited again for a break.

"Why are they going south?"

"That leads to the Santa Fe and California Trails."

They made it across just missing being trampled by a team of oxen. They walked up the hill to the Harris House. Mr. McCoy met them at the front door and led them to Hopkin's room.

"Good morning!" Hopkins lay in a robe on the bed. He made no effort to hide the fact he was naked under his robe. "Mr. Seward, I heard you were now working for the boy."

Seward and Michael took two seats in overstuffed chairs facing the bed. "It seems Mr. Dugan was concerned about his safety."

Hopkins laughed. "I can't imagine why."

"Mr. Hopkins, I came up with a fair price," stated Michael

Hopkins pushed himself up into a sitting

position. He reached over and picked up a full glass and emptied it in one swig. He sat the glass down and picked up a lit cigar.

"And what price would that be?"

"Fifteen thousand dollars." Michael had decided to start high.

"I am going to give you five thousand dollars." He took a drag from his cigar.

Michael laughed. "That isn't even what it cost my family to build the house, let alone the land."

Hopkins blew smoke toward the ceiling. "I happen to know, Mr. Dugan, you are leaving tomorrow," he finally said. "Once you are gone I aim to claim the house as abandoned. You will never find another buyer before you leave."

Michael knew Hopkins was right. "Very well."

"The Chariot leaves at noon tomorrow. Come by on your way out of town and I will give you the four thousand."

Michael jumped to his feet. "Outrageous! You just said five."

Hopkins took a drag on his cigar and blew the smoke at Michael. "Yeah, I forgot you callin' it your house yesterday. You need to show more respect to your elders, boy. The price is four thousand, and you are lucky you are getting that."

Michael moved toward the man. Seward jumped up and put his hand on Michael's shoulder.

"We will see you tomorrow, Mr. Hopkins," said Seward pulling Michael toward the door.

Seward quickly opened the door and pushed the angry young man out.

"Four thousand!" growled Michael turning back toward the room.

"Mr. Dugan?" said a female voice behind him.

Michael turned and saw Miss Jessica Kilgore walking up to him. "Good morning, Miss Kilgore."

"What pleasant surprise. What be bringin' you to the Harris?"

"I am having my house stolen." Michael said angrily looking at the door he had left out of.

"Beg pardon?"

"Mr. Dugan and Nick Hopkins just came to a price on the house," explained Seward. "Mr. Dugan is NOT happy with the terms of the deal."

She smiled at Michael. "Perhaps I can be improvin' your mood. I be havin' such a wonderful dinner with you last night. I be wonderin' if you allow me to return the favor by joinin' me for dinner in my room this evenin' ?" She eased up closer to Michael. "I be thinkin' it would be a nice way for the both of us to spend our last night on the frontier."

"Ma'am, I am sorry but I have been invited to sleep in a genuine Lakota tipi tonight."

Seward grabbed Michael Dugan's arm and pulled him aside. "Are you crazy, stupid, or both? You would rather spend the night sleeping on the ground in a tent with a Sioux than spend a night with THE Miss Jessica Kilgore?"

Michael tore his arm from Seward's hold. "Miss Kilgore and I will have two weeks together on the Chariot on the way back to St. Louis. I will have plenty of chances to have dinner with her. I will never have another chance to sleep in a real Lakota tipi. How I spend my last night on the frontier is my business, Mr. Seward, not yours!"

Michael Dugan turned back to Miss Kilgore who had a quizzical look on her pretty face.

"Miss Kilgore, It will be my pleasure to dine with you on any night you choose on our trip back to St. Louis."

"I will look forward to it." She gave a slight smile, turned, and walked away.

"We have some real frontier business to attend to," said Seward.

They walked out of the Harris House and across the street onto a wooden sidewalk.

They then turned down a side street. Seward led Michael down an alley. They came to a large lot with three corrals. Two were filled with horses, in the third stood a single multi-colored horse.

On the top rails of the pens were a dozen saddles.

"Good morning," said a man coming out of a nearby shed. "Can I help you?"

"We are looking for some horses and saddles," said Seward.

The man gestured to the two corrals. "Take your pick. People comin' back after tryin' their luck out west. They sell me their horses and saddles for a ticket home."

Michael looked beyond the corrals to a covered stall where a dozen negroes were squatting.

They started to come to their feet when they saw Michael looking at them.

"Interested in a slave?"

"NO! We are not." said Michael looking at the horses in the pen. His eyes were drawn to the lone horse in the third pen. "Someone own that one?"

"No, that is an Indian Pony." Michael waited for a further explanation. "He just wandered in here one day. I probably will have to sell it to the army for meat."

Michael walked over to get a closer look at the animal. "He's beautiful." Michael said

"What is wrong with him?"

"Once an Indian Pony gets a master, it don't like any one else. Indians say it is a spirit thing."

Michael stood at the fence. The horse turned his multi-colored head and looked in Michael's direction. It then turned and plodded over to him.

"Ain't never seen that before," said the man. "He would not let another horse or man near it."

Michael raised his hand. The horse lifted its head over the rail. Michael felt the horse's hot breath on his fingers as the horse smelled his hand. "He seems tame to me." Michael looked at the man. "Will he take a bridle?"

"It is not like a dog, Mr. Dugan." Seward called.

Michael scratched the middle of the horse's monstrous head and smiled. "I never had a pet." Michael shouted back.

"I got a bridle if he wants to try," the man told Seward. Seward shrugged. "You gonna be responsible if anything happens?"

"Sure. The kid gets killed, I kill the horse. I will pay for the horse."

The man took a bridle off a hook and handed it to Seward.

Seward took the bridle from the man, and they walked to where Michael Dugan stood. "You know what you are doin'?" asked Seward handing the bridle to Michael.

Michael's eyes were bright with excitement as he climbed up the rail and dropped into to the corral next to the horse. He walked into the middle of the pen. The horse followed.

Michael held up the bridle expecting the horse to bolt. It raised its head. Michael raised the bit to its mouth. It slid right in. As he put the bridle on Michael felt his heart racing.

Michael stood beside the horse. He got a handful of rein and mane. He took a deep breath.

"Mr. Dugan, wait!"

He jumped as hard and high as he could. He found himself balancing his torso and legs on the horse's back. He swung his leg over. He was suddenly sitting on a horse. The horse did not move.

Not sure what to do next, he slowly tightened the reins. Michael braced himself, not knowing what to expect. The horse brought its head up. Michael gently kicked the ribs of the horse. The horse moved forward. Michael smiled at the stunned men leaning against the rails outside the corral. He kicked the ribs again and pulled the reins to the right. The horse walked in the direction indicated. The horse walked in a circle. He pulled the reins in the opposite direction, and the horse made a circle in that direction. Michael pointed the horse's head in the direction of the gate and with a light kick to the ribs the horse walked toward the gate. Seward opened the gate, letting the smiling young man and horse out.

"How much do you want for him?" asked Michael.

"I would get a dollar for the meat from the Army. A dollar and I will throw in the bridle."

"Deal!" Michael reached into his pocket and tossed the man a silver dollar.

Seward picked out a chestnut and after a bit of haggling. He had a nice saddle and horse.

Seward stared at Michael as they rode towards the house. "You never had a horse before?" asked Seward.

"Never had an animal of any kind. Father said pets were a waste of time and money."

"If I didn't know any better, I would say that horse knew you." Seward looked ahead.

"There's your bunkmate."

Michael saw Thunder Eagle on his horse. Behind him his horse dragged two poles strapped a few feet apart. On the poles was a large bundle.

"Where did you get that horse?" demanded Thunder Eagle.

"Why do you ask?" Michael smiled proudly as he brought the horse next to Thunder Eagle.

"That is an Indian Pony. You should not be able to ride him."

"Bareback at that," said Seward.

After dinner Michael stood at the entrance of the tipi with his pillow and blanket.

Thunder Eagle poked his head out. "Welcome."

Michael excitedly ducked in. The inside of the tipi had changed since that morning. There was a fire in the center. Along the side were various tools and weapons.

"You sleep over there." The Indian pointed to a clear place.

Michael put his pillow down. He saw Thunder Eagle give the pillow a look of disapproval. "I have never slept on the ground before," said Michael laying down.

The Indian stretched out on a skin. "What do you want to know about the Lakota?"

Michael propped his head on his hand. "How did you get your name?"

"My first buffalo hunt. I was riding my horse in the middle of a large buffalo herd as I shot arrows. My father said I looked like the eagle flying over a thunder cloud." He gestured with his hand. "My full name is Eagle That Flies Over The Thunder Clouds".

Michael smiled, "Wow."

"Would you like to know how my father got his name?" asked Thunder Eagle.

"Yes, please!"

Thunder Eagle brought his face close to Michael's. The fire put tiny orange dots on the Indian's dark eyes. "He was on a vision quest in the Black Hills. He sat under a great oak for eight days with no food or water."

"Eight days?" Michael questioned. "No one can live without water for more than three days."

"You tell him that. On the eighth night a great ball of fire came out of the sky and hit the great oak. It exploded in a fire before my father."

"That's why his face looks like that."

"Face? He let the Great Spirit mark all of him! Face. Chest. Arms. Hands. Everything!"

"That is amazing," whispered Michael in awe.

"Do you want to know what my father calls you?"

Michael looked at the ground. "I heard this morning. Stupid Boy."

"No. Well, yes, but that is not all. He calls you Stupid Boy Who Stands Out.

"Still, he thinks I am stupid."

"No, well maybe, in Lakota we have the same word mean crazy and stupid. That word is not bad or good in Lakota. It means touched by The Creator."

"So your father thinks I am touched by the Creator?"

"No, my father thinks you are like all the white people. Stupid or Crazy."

The two talked for a while. Finally they slept. Michael dreamt of thundering buffalo herds and a mighty oak tree exploding and a tall, large naked man, arms raised, being bathed in its fire!

Michael Dugan was being shaken awake by Thunder Eagle. "The dark man is calling you."

"His name is Obadiah." Michael said in annoyance. He looked around forcing his eyes to focus. His body was stiff from sleeping on the ground. He did a big stretch realizing he was very hungry.

"Obadiah will not leave the house."

Michael sighed as he crawled over and poked his head out of the tipi. "Good morning Obadiah," he called.

"Good morning, Ma'sa Dugan," answered the negro. "I see the Sioux didn't cut your throat in your sleep like Master Seward said he probably would."

"No, he did not."

"Breakfast is ready."

Michael ducked back inside. "You must have breakfast with me!"

"The man with the guns won't shoot me?"

"Mr. Seward only shoots people I pay him to shoot."

They climbed out of the tipi and walked toward the steps. "Obadiah is afraid of me."

"Don't take it personally. I think he is afraid of Indians in general." Michael noticed Thunder Eagle had a large knife in a sheath at his side. He had a firm hold on the knife's handle. Frankly, Michael did not blame him.

Michael expected Seward to meet them at the door, fully armed. Michael pulled open the doors and entered. There was no one in sight.

"Obadiah?" Michael called.

"Yes, Ma'sa Dugan," called the negro from the kitchen.

"Where is Mr. Seward.?"

"He said last night, since you are were spendin' the night the way you wanted, he'd spend the night the way he wanted. He didn't get in 'til real late."

Michael sighed in frustration. "Obadiah, we will be having a guest for breakfast."

"I'll set a extra place." Obadiah still sounded like he was calling from the kitchen.

"Obadiah, I would like you to come out here and meet my friend Thunder Eagle."

There was silence. "Now, Obadiah."

The door between the dining room and the living room opened a bit. Obadiah peeked out. "Nice to meet you, Ma'sa Sioux." The slave shut the door.

"Dammit." Michael hissed. "Obadiah, you are embarrassing me in front of my guest. You come out here at once."

The slave came out and stood next to Michael, keeping his wide eyes down, not looking at Thunder Eagle.

"Obadiah, this is Thunder Eagle. He will be joining us for breakfast."

Neither man said or did anything.

"Breakfast is set out." Obadiah finally said.

Michael and Thunder Eagle followed the slave into the dining room. The Indian took the chair with his back to the wall. Michael sat across from him. Obadiah's eyes widened as the Indian rolled up a pancake and started eating it.

"Can I get some coffee, Obadiah?" The negro almost ran into the kitchen.

"Do you own Obadiah?" asked Thunder Eagle grabbing a fist full of bacon.

"Yes and no. He comes with the house."

The Indian munched the bacon. "He is like your horse. You can sell or trade him."

"No, I like Obadiah. I would never sell him."

"So he is like a dog. Like a pet."

"Obadiah is not a pet."

"He calls you master."

Michael was thinking of a proper response when Obadiah came out with a pot of coffee and filled his cup. Michael decided that he would be happy after he left on the Chariot with Miss Kilgore. He will leave Nick Hopkins to deal the people in this house. He would be leaving Westport behind him and going home.

Michael saw the two unopened letters laying on the table in front of him.

"I put those there for you, Ma'sa Dugan," said Obadiah. "I can throw them old letters away if you want."

Michael looked at the letters. He was not surprised his father secretly let Uncle Mike know he was coming. The letter from his mother was another matter. He opened the letter from his mother. As he suspected it laid out the whole scheme. It ended with: "I know you will make sure our son returns home safely ."

Obadiah and Thunder Eagle saw Michael blink back tears as he gently set the letter aside.

He wiped his tears away and opened his father's letter.

It was basically the same as his mother's.

Until the end.

Michael had picked up his just filled coffee cup as he read. The cup was almost to his mouth. Michael Dugan's eyes widened and the cup stopped. He jumped to his feet, knocking the chair over. He glared at the letter.

"Outrageous!" He dropped the letter to the table, looking at it is if it were something unholy. "You bastard!" he said loudly. "You son of a bitch!" Michael screamed.

In a rage, the young man flung his coffee cup against the wall behind Thunder Eagle. It exploded into tiny pieces. Michael gave no notice to the Indian jumping to his feet and drawing his knife.

Michael Dugan's breath came faster and deeper. He glared down at the settings on the table. "Damn you! You bastard!" Crying in rage, with the back of his arm, he swept everything, including the two letters, off the table, sending it all crashing to the floor. Tears overflowed Michael's blue eyes. He glared down at the table. Michael began to take deep breaths. Both the slave and the Indian felt Michael Dugan would turn over the table. Tears ran down the boy's reddened face. A quiver came to his deep breaths. "That son of a BITCH!" Michael whispered harshly through pursed lips. "Dammit!" Michael said in annoyance as he tried to wipe the tears from his face. His breath lessened. His eyes narrowed as walked over and looked at the two letters on the floor. A calm came over Michael Dugan. "Obadiah. " he said evenly still looking down at the letters.

"Yes, Master Dugan," said the slave quietly.

He turned to the negro, his reddened eyes still narrowed. "I will be needing a paid servant and a cook for the winter. Will be a paying position. Would you be interested in that?

"Yes, Master Dugan. I surely would."

Michael took a breath and calmed himself.

"I wish you to do two things right away. First: I cannot and will not have the hired help living in a barn with animals," he said curtly. "You will move your things into the servants' quarters as soon as possible."

"Yes, Master Dugan. What is the other thing?"

Michael paused, looking into the negro's eyes. Michael's eyes were still narrowed.

"Secondly: the hired help do not call their employer "Master." For the remainder of your employment with me, you will address me as Mister Dugan."

"Yes Mas—Mr. Dugan."

Michael looked at the Thunder Eagle, his knife still at the ready. "Thunder Eagle, I apologize for my outburst. I will be staying in Westport a little longer than I planned," said Michael curtly. "You may stay here, and I will teach you all I know about the Catholic Medicine. Now, if you excuse me, I need to have a word with Mr. Seward." Michael started out. He stopped and looked at the mess on the floor as if it had just appeared. "Obadiah, before you do anything, clean up this mess."

Michael came up the stairs wiping the last of his tears from his face. He came to Seward's door, stood up straight and knocked. Michael heard female voices, and Seward shushing them.

"Who the hell is it?"

"It is Michael Dugan. I need to speak with you. It is rather urgent."

After quite a bit of whispering the door finally opened. A shirtless Seward opened the door. Two naked women waved at Michael from the bed. One smiled, pointed at Michael, then crooked her finger invitingly.

"Good morning, Mr. Seward."

"It was a good morning, Mr. Dugan. As you can see I am in the middle of something here," frustration dripping from Seward's every word. "What can I do for you?"

"I have decided to stay in Westport."

"What?" Seward's brow furrowed. "How much longer?"

"My father's----my itinerary says I will be leaving April first. Would you be willing to extend our arrangement for six more months? Obadiah has agreed to stay on as paid help."

"Yeah, I guess so," said Seward.

"Very well. I will be writing a letter to Father and posting it on the Chariot."

"What about Nick Hopkins?"

Michael's eyes narrowed as he gave a tight smile. "Yes, we will be dropping in unannounced to Mr. Hopkins. Be ready in a half hour."

Michael came down stairs and went right into the study, slamming the doors together.

Seward came down. Obadiah was sweeping up the mess. Thunder Eagle still stood with his knife out. He looked at Seward. Seward raised his hands.

"OK, what just happened?" inquired Seward.

Obadiah straightened up holding a letter. "Ma-Mr. Dugan was readin' this letter."

Obadiah held out the pages to Seward. "It's from his father."

Seward snatched the letter from the slave.

"What does it say?" asked Thunder Eagle. "It made Michael Dugan mad enough to kill."

Seward walked over to the table as he read the letter. "It's from his father. Telling his brother about his son's surprise visit. Saying he wants his uncle to make things as difficult for Mr. Dugan as possible so he will want to come home." Seward set the first page on the table.

He read the second page silently. Anger came to his gray eyes as his lips tightened. "Damn!" Seward continued to read. "What a bastard. I don't blame Mr. Dugan. I would want to shoot the son of a bitch myself."

"What does it say?" asked Obadiah.

"Fortunately," Seward read in a deep mocking voice. "I will not have to pay you to do this favor for his mother and I, as I had to pay the others to make sure Michael's past asinine adventures turned out to be failures."

"What do asinine mean, Master Seward," asked Obadiah.

"It means stupid, Obadiah." No one noticed Michael Dugan standing at the dining room door. Michael walked up and snatched the letter from Seward. "Obadiah, bring Mr. Seward's and my horses around. We will be leaving shortly." Michael turned and went back into the study. He slammed the doors together, shaking the house.

Seward ran upstairs. Soon angry female voices were heard and then two half-dressed women came running down the steps.

A little later Michael came out of the study. He scanned the living room, then opened the doors and looked outside only to see Obadiah bringing up the horses. Michael rolled his eyes and went back inside.

"Mr. Seward!" he called upstairs.

"Coming, Mr. Dugan." Seward came running down the steps.

"Where is my Colt?" Inquired Michael.

Seward ran back into his room and reappeared buckling on the gun belt. Outside the two mounted and rode off.

"Our first stop is the Chariot." Michael said, kicking his horse in the ribs.

Seward urged his horse to catch up.

They came down to the pier and stopped at the gangplank.

"Stay with the horses, I won't be long," instructed Michael.

Captain Foster greeted him with a salute. "An early boarder, Mr. Dugan. Shall I send a boy for your bags?"

"That won't be necessary." Michael reached into his coat pocket. "I have decided to winter in Westport." He handed the captain an envelope. "Please post this in St. Louis. It's a letter telling my family everything they need to know. Has Miss Kilgore boarded yet?"

"She is in her cabin. Main deck 23. Michael hurried away. He came to cabin 23 and knocked.

"Who is it?" she called.

"It is Michael Dugan, Miss Kilgore."

The door opened. "Mr. Dugan, you be boardin' early."

Michael dug into his pants pockets and pulled out a pair of green velvet gloves.

"You left these when you came to dinner. I was going to bring them when I boarded. You see, Miss Kilgore, my plans have changed."

"Oh?"

"Yes Ma'am, I regret I will not be joining you on your trip to St. Louis. I have decided to winter in Westport. So this is good-bye."

She raised her hand to his lips. "Until we meet again, Mr. Dugan."

"I so look forward to that pleasure, Miss Kilgore." He took her elegant, dainty hand, blushing. He lightly kissed it.

Michael turned and quickly walked away, heading toward the gangplank. Captain Foster motioned him aside as he started to step on to the gangplank.

"Mr. Dugan," he said quietly. "Very few paddlewheels come to the Town of Kansas during the winter," warned Captain Foster. "You may want to reconsider."

"I am staying Captain Foster. I will see you April first. I will give your regards to Obadiah."

"Obadiah?" The captain smiled and nodded to a boarding passenger. "Nick Hopkin's old slave?"

"Yes, I understand he was formerly your cook on the Chariot."

"Mr. Dugan, you are mistaken. I have had the same cook for years. And to my knowledge, Obadiah has never set foot on the Chariot."

Perplexed, Michael walked down the gangplank.

"Something wrong?" asked Seward as Michael mounted.

"Probably nothing," said Michael looking at The Chariot. He turned to Seward with a smile. "One more stop."

Michael and Seward walked into the Harris House and headed for Nick Hopkin's rooms.

Mr. McCoy ran across the lobby and put himself in front of the suite's door.

"Can I help you gentlemen?" he asked.

"We---I have business with Mr. Hopkins."

"Is he expecting you?"

"Yes and no." Michael pushed Mr. McCoy aside, opened the door, and the two walked in.

Hopkins lay on the bed with a woman. Both were naked.

"Good morning, Mr. Dugan."

"Good morning, Mr. Hopkins." Michael dropped down in one of the chairs facing the bed. Seward stood behind.

"You are early. I haven't had a chance to get your three thousand dollars together."

Michael's eyes narrowed as he got a tight smile on his face. "I thought we agreed on five thousand."

Hopkins looked at the young man. "It was four thousand. I decided three thousand will do."

Michael came to his feet and stood at the foot of the bed, looking down at the naked Hopkins.

"Mr. Hopkins, I too have come to a decision. I have decided to turn down your offer."

"Good! You leave, I get the house."

Michael's tight smile faded at he looked at the naked man through narrowed eyes.

"I have decided to winter in Westport. I will have a nice house to stay in and will have plenty of time to find another buyer."

"Good luck with that, Boy." Hopkins gave a laugh. "Everyone knows that is really mine. You are there because I LET you stay there."

Michael Dugan calmly looked down at the naked man. An odd smile slowly came to Michael Dugan's face. Michael leaned down, planting his hands at the foot of the bed. "Let me tell you something, Mr. Hopkins. I will burn that damn house to the ground before I take a penny less than ten thousand dollars for it." He straightened up. "Good day, Sir."

Michael Dugan turned and stormed toward the door, Seward opening it for him.

As they crossed the ornate lobby of the Harris House, Michael Dugan could hear Nick Hopkins bellowing behind him. "We had a deal Dugan! I don't care who your father is! You are a dead man. A dead man!"

CHAPTER 4

"I'm going to need a raise!" said Seward as they dismounted at the entrance to the barn. "I AM suprised the Devil brothers didn't come after us."

Michael smiled as he led his horse into the far stall. It was empty. Obadiah had put his old cot carefully against the wall near the stall. Michael first wondered why the slave didn't throw the thing out. There were two beds in the servants' quarters. Then he remembered. in the spring, whoever bought the house would move the slave back into the barn.

"How did Master Hopkins take the news?" asked Obadiah, meeting them at the back door.

"He said I was a dead man," said Michael.

"With Master Seward here, you gonna' be hard to kill."

They went inside and into the dining room. Michael looked around. "I guess I am here for the winter," he said sitting at the table.

Seward sat across from him. "What makes you think your father will even let you stay here without your uncle?" asked Seward. "What's to stop him from sending someone to drag you back home?

"I gave my family certain facts. I cannot help if they come to certain conclusions from those facts."

Seward leaned back ih his chair. "What did you tell them?"

"I said I arrived safely. That Uncle Mike took the Colt away from me and is keeping it safe. Right now Uncle Mike is taking good care of me." Michael grinned across the table at Seward. "Isn't that all true, Uncle Mike?"

"You know what, Mr. Dugan, I think I am having a bad influence on you."

"Obadiah, have a seat," Michael pulled out a chair beside him. "I am here for the winter. What is the first order of business?"

Obadiah thought as he took the chair, "Food, will be the main thing, I guess."

"We're not stranded in the Mountains," stated Seward. "We can buy food in town."

"We could get snowed in," said the slave. "Best to have enough food for a month or so, just in case."

"What is our food situation now?" asked Michael.

"For two grown men and me?"

"Four. I invited Thunder Eagle to stay."

"Let that redskin get his own food!" said Seward.

"Four men, Obadiah."

"We got about a week's worth of food, eatin' like you do," said the negro.

"Like WE eat," corrected Michael.

"We still have the Nick Hopkins problem," Seward said. "He may put the word out. We may not be able to buy anythihg."

"You think he would try to starve us out?" asked Michael?

"Right now, I don't think there is anything Hopkins won't do to get this house," said Seward.

"We have plenty of firewood," said Obadiah. "We may starve, but we won't freeze."

There was a knock on the door. They all looked at each other. "We expecting someone?" asked Seward.

"No."

"Well, I am sure the Devil Brothers would not bother to knock," said Seward.

They got up and walked into the living room. Seward drew the Colt, "Open the door, Obadiah."

As the slave walked toward the door, the knocking was heard again. This time harder and faster. Obadiah cracked the door and peeped out.

A smile came to his face, "Look who it is!"

Obadiah opened the door. In walked Miss Jessica Kilgore.

She smiled at Michael. "Hello again, Mr. Dugan."

"Miss Kilgore," Michaerl stammered.

Miss Kilgore looked around the room, "Yes, this will be doin' nicely," she said.

"Do, Miss Kilgore?" asked Michael. "Do for what?"

She turned to him. "I would like to be your boarder. I also be decidin' to stay in Westport for the Winter and Spring Solstice. I be needin' a place."

"Here?" Michael stammered, trying to grasp the idea. "YOU want to live ... HERE?"

"I will be willin' to pay a dollar a day as I did at the Harris." She waked over and looked upstairs, "You said there be extra rooms upstairs?"

"No, Ma'am, I mean yes Ma'am. I mean Mr. Seward has already taken the larger guestroom."

She turned to Michael, "And the master bedroom?"

"That is my room."

She looked at Michael coyly.

"There ARE two small rooms abailable," Michael said.

"One of those will have to do. I will pay a dollar extra a day for sleeping quarters."

"Three MEN are already living in the house," stated Michael. "Obadiah, Mr. Seward and myself will be living here also."

"And my friend, Thunder Eagle — I be seein' a tipi in front. So four, counting yourself, Mr. Dugan," she said. "I think, if we all be actin' like proper ladies and gentlemen, this arrangement will be suitable for everyone."

Before Michael could think of another argument, Miss Kilgore walked over and opened the doors to the parlor, "Better than I be rememberin' it."

Michael followed her into the parlor, "Miss Kilgore--"

"Mr. Dugan, if you be feelin' my being your boarder will be an inconvenience or too ... awkward, I am sure I can find another place in Westport."

"Miss Kilgore, it would be my -- OUR pleasure to have you stay here for as long as you wish. When would you like to move in?"

Miss Kilgore walked to the front doors and pushed them open. Parked in front of the house was a wagon stacked with furniture and trunks. On top of it all was tied an ornate brass tub. Three men stood waiting at the wagon.

"These men were kind enough to be offerin' to help." She walked back to Michael who was looking at the tub. "I will be needin' a private entrance. I'll not be wantin' my clients' comin' and goin' to disturb the house."

"I am sure I can arrange to have a door put in," he stammered.

The words were barely out of Michael's mouth when a second wagon turned into the driveway with three large men aboard. The wagon was filled with picks, sledge hammers, lumber and varoiouss other carpentry tools.

Michael looked at Miss Kilgore.

"I be takin' the liberty to be hirin' these gentlemen."

Michael, Seward and Obadiah stood back and watched the spectacle.

Miss Kilgore directed the unloading. All they noticed was the brass tub being carried upstairs. In the commotion, no one noticed Sheriff Winkleman ride up. He walked up to Seward.

"We have a problem," said the Sheriff.

"What would that be?" inquired Seward.

"That," he pointed to the tipi.

"That is Thunder Eagle's tipi," explained Michael. "What's the problem?"

"Town ordinance. No red skins or niggers allowed in town after dark."

"Where is he supposed to go?" asked Michael.

"Home! The Sioux have a camp a couple miles west of here."

"Sheriff Winkleman," said Michael in annoyance. "Thunder Eagle is my guest and has permission to camp on my property."

"Well, he can't ..."

"What if I take responsibility for the Redskin?" offered Seward.

The Sheriff looked at Seward. "You?"

"If the Sioux starts any trouble..." Seward grabbed the handle of the Colt. "I'll deal with it."

"Ya know, I have been thinking about gettin' me a deputy for Westport."

"How much does it pay?"

"Two silver dollars a month."

"Seward shrugged, "I'll take the job.""

"Raise your right hand," Seward did as instructed. "You swear to uphold the law here in Westport the best you can?"

"I do," said Seward fighting to keep from laughing.

"You are now Deputy of Westport. The Sioux is in your custody. You'll need to come by my office to pick up your badge."

The sound of the work caught Winkleman's attention. He walked over to the east side of the house. The workmen had just broken through the wall.

"Making some improvements to the house, Mr. Dugan?"

"Miss Kilgore has decided to winter in Westport. I have offered her lodgings," explained Michael. "She will be entertaining clients in my parlor and needed a private entrance."

The sheriff laughed as he walked over to his horse. "Mr. Dugan," he said, hauling his large form onto the horse, "You DO attract some interesting characters." He rode off.

"Deputy Seward?" said Michael incredulously.

"That's three jobs I have to keep track of."

"Three? Protecting me and Deputy of Westport. What is the third?"

"That's right. Unlike you, I was never good with numbers."

By dinner there was an ornate door in the west wall of the parlor. Over dinner, the practical side of running the house came up.

"We don't have enough food for even a month for five people," stated Obadiah.

"And we'll be needin' another slave," put in Miss Kilgore.

"Servant" corrected Michael. "Why?"

"Poor Obadiah can't be expected to be takin' care of four people," stated Miss Kilgore. "And I will need a female servant."

"I can always use the help," said Obadiah.

Miss Kilgore sipped her water. "As I be recallin', the McCoys be havin' trouble with their new female slave. Ebony, I believe her name is," she said looking up at Obadiah.

Obadiah looked back at Miss Kilgore. "Young slaves take a bit to be settlin' in," said the negro. "She'll be all right."

"She be a runnin' away twice. Mr. McCoy won't be puttin' up with that sort o thing much longer. He'll probably be happy to be rid o her."

"We'll see." said Obadiah reluctantly.

The next morning, MIchael looked at the suitcase he had put the money in. He had counted it before he went to bed. There was four thousand dollars in coins. He had separated them by value. He, Seward and Obadiah were going into town to buy supplies IF anyone would sell to them.

The other errand, Michael did not look forward to: going to the McCoys to see about buying their female slave.

Michael put fifty dollars in one leather bag to pay for supplies. He had no idea what a slave would cost. He put ten twenty-dollar gold pieces in another leather bag and tied both bags to his belt.

"Quite a bit of money you got there, Mr. Dugan," observed Seward, sitting on his horse.

Michael climbed up onto the wagon's seat next to Obadiah, "Never thought I would be a part of buying another human being."

He took the reins from Obadiah and slapped the back of the horse. Seward trotted alongside them.

The merchants seemed happy to do business with them. Of course, Seward and the Colt may have helped persuade them. Michael let Obadiah place the order and came outside with Seward as the supplies were being loaded.

"People seem perfectly willing to sell to us," observed Michael.

"We won't starve, anyway," Seward nodded

toward the other side of the street. "Our friends are keeping an eye on us."

Michael saw Jarrod and Cane Devilbiss leaning against the wall, grinning at them.

"Don't worry, they kill you, I will kill them. I promise," assured Seward.

"How about you kill them BEFORE they kill me."

"Why, Mr. Dugan, that would be murder."

Michael looked at the Devil Twins across the street, "You really think people would care if or how those two die?"

"I'm a sworn deputy," Seward pulled the Colt and offered the handle to Michael. "I can look the other way."

Michael looked at the gun, then Jarrod and Cane. He dropped his eyes.

Seward put the Colt back in its holster. "They are probably under orders to keep their distance."

"All loaded," said Obadiah. "Twenty dollars."

"TWENTY?" growled Seward. "A load like that shouldn't even cost ten."

Seward started at the store.

"Twenty is fine," said Michael untying one of the bags on his belt. He opened it and counted out the coins. Obadiah went in to pay the bill.

"I don't know if they think we are rich or are tryin' to run us out of money," said Seward. "Let's go see if we can get a better deal on McCoy's problem slave."

Soon they were coming up to a large, three story house. Four great white pillars held the front veranda. Michael and Seward walked up to the front door. Michael used the shiny black door knocker shaped like an attacking lion.

A man in a butler's uniform opened the door, "May I help you gentlemen?"

"We are here to see Mr. McCoy," Michael informed the man.

"Is he expecting you?" inquired the man.

"We understand Mr. McCoy may have a problem slave he may be interested in getting rid of," said Seward.

"One moment." The man closed the door.

"I bet they make us come back," said Michael.

"Can I help you?" An older man in work clothes came walking up from behind the house.

"I'm Michael Dugan. We are here to see about buying your problem slave."

The man extended his hand, "Name's Charlie Crawford. I'm the McCoy's slave tender. Pull your wagon around back. If I can find her, I'l fetch her out. She done ran off twice. I had to put the irons on her, but sometimes that don't stop 'em."

Michael got back in the driver's seat and pulled

the wagon onto the road leading to the back of the house. "I would think Mr. McCoy would be doing this."

"Sell a slave?" laughed Seward. "It's like buying or selling any other work animal. Who better to sell them than the person who tends them?"

Michael felt a tightening in the pit of his stomach. He just wanted to get this over with.

Michael stopped the wagon in the back of the house. There was a stable on the left with horses in the stalls. Charlie Crawford came walking out holding a thick chain. He led a female negro out of the stable. She was naked. On her wrists and ankles were rusty iron shackles. A chain was cinched around her neck, held tight by a large lock.

Michael looked at Obadiah, "She is just a CHILD!"

Obadiah patted Michael on the knee. "Hush Mr. Dugan," the slave said looking straight ahead.

Seward dismounted and walked over to the girl, "I see she can still walk good."

The girl looked straight ahead with anger in her eyes. She was forced to hold her head up because of the tight chain around her throat.

"Yeah, Mr. McCoy doesn't like the idea of doin' things permanent to a nigger. He said to sell her and get an older male. Interested in tradin' her for that one?" Crawford said, pointing to Obadiah.

"No! We are not!" stated Michael.

Seward came to stand in front of the girl. He reached up and lifted her girl lips with his thumbs, "How old is she?"

"Old enough to breed," Crawford looked at Michael and raised his eybrow suggestively. "She is fifteen I reckon."

Obadiah gave a low growl.

Seward walked around her, "She ain't marked up or branded. How much?"

"I am thinkin' about three hundred."

Seward laughed, "I can get a full grown man with skills for four hundred." He wrinkled his nose, "Young, untrained AND a runner. Hundred is the best we can do."

Michael could barely contain himself. Seward was haggling over this child like he had done for his horse just yesterday.

"This ain't no field nigger," countered Charlie Crawford. "She is a house nigger. She does house keepin'. She is a fine cook. I have tasted her cookin' myself. Two hundred or she goes back to the barn."

"This is OUTRAGEOUS! Michael came to his feet. "DEAL! SOLD!" He tore at the strings tying the bag to his belt. "DAMMIT!" Finally it came lose. Michael threw the leather bag at Charlie Crawford. It landed at his feet. "That is two hundred dollars. Get someting to cover her up. NOW!"

The man opened the bag and slowly counted the coins. He winked at Michael and walked into the stable. He came out with a filthy, tattered horse blanket and threw it over the girl's shoulders. "I am throwin' in the irons. I reckon you will need them."

He tossed the keys to Seward.

Seward took the chain and led the slave to the back of the wagon. "We don't need to damage the supplies," said Seward to no one in particular. He hitched the chain to the back of the wagon. "She can walk."

Michael's jaw dropped as he came to his feet, "To hell with the--"

Obadiah reached up, took Michael by the shoulder and sat the young man down. "Drive slow, Mr. Dugan. She be alright."

Michael drove the wagon as slowly as possible. The shackles around her ankles caused her to fall twice. The first time, Seward, cussing, got off his horse and stood her up. The second time, he jumped off his horse, dragged the girl to her feet and drew back his hand.

Michael jumped up, "MR. SEWARD!"

Seward looked over his shoulder.

Michael Dugan's eyes narrowed as he slowly shook his head.

Seward hesitated, then brought his hand down. He forcefully stood the girl up. Seward glared at Michael as he got back on his horse.

As soon as he stopped the wagon at the front steps, Michael jumped off and ran up to Seward, "Give me the keys!"

"Mr. Dugan, we may want to wait until we are inside. As soon as you take those things off, she may run."

"GIVE ME THE DAMNED KEYS! NOW!"

"It's your two hundred dollars. I ain't goin' after her." He tossed Michael the keys, "You ain't payin' me to chase slaves."

"Leading a child behind a wagon like a horse — what is wrong with you? He walked over and knelt down in front of the girl and started trying the keys to the lock on her shackles. "She is a human being, for God's sake!"

The lock popped open. Michael pulled the shackles off, stood up and threw the shackles down the hill. He started to work on the ones at her wrists. Tears of rage blurred his vision.

Obadiah climbed off the wagon and walked over to the young man. The slave took the keys from him and soon the shackles came off. Michael took the shackles and threw them as far as he could.

Obadiah was working on the lock holding the chain around the girl's throat.

Michael saw the pain in the girl's dark eyes, "Obadiah! You are huring her!"

"I know, Mr. Dugan," said the slave in frustration.

Michael watched as Obadiah had to tighten the chain in order to get the propper angle for the key to go in the lock. Finally, it popped open and the chain dropped.

Michael came to stand before the girl. She looked at him blankly.

"Your name is Ebony?"

The girl gave a slight nod.

"Ebony, I am Mr. Dugan," he did not know what else to say. He turned to Obadiah, standing behind him. "Obadiah, this is Ebony. I want you to take care of her."

"I surely will, Mr. Dugan."

Miss Kilgore came running down the steps, "Oh! The poor thing!"

"Miss Kilgore, get her into some clothes. Take some of mine if you need them."

He turned to Obadiah, "Obadiah, I am putting you in charge of Ebony." Looking at Seward still on his horse, "No one else. Get her food, whatever she needs."

"Yes, Mr. Dugan, I will take real good care of her."

Michael realized Obadiah was crying, "Obadiah, what is wrong?"

The old slave looked at Michael with tears in his eyes, "Ebony is my daughter."

CHAPTER V

Over the next few days an odd routine set in. Obadiah got his daughter settled in. The two cooked and did the housework. Thunder Eagle mostly stayed out in his tipi, still going to town to sell his trinkets. Michael would see smoke coming out of his tipi, and would go out every once in a while. Thunder Eagle would teach him the Lakota language. Michael said he wanted to know enough Lakota to keep hims from getting killed.

Michael observed that Miss Kilgore had a steady stream of clients. Sometimes a carriage would be sent for her. Michael came to realize everyone had something to keep them occupied. Everyone but him.

By Sunday Michael was beginning to wonder if he had made a mistake staying on in Westport. How was he to spend his time for the next six months?

"People here to see you." Obadiah informed him as he took the breakfast plates away.

"People? What people?" asked Michael.

"They told me they are here to learn about bein' Catholic."

Michael had forgotten all about his offer to teach Thunder Eagle about being Catholic. He pushed open the front doors expecting to see Thunder Eagle. Instead he found a dozen people waiting. The majority were Indians. But there were some negroes.

"Who are these people?" Michael asked Thunder Eagle.

"Some come to learn about Catholic Medicine," explained the Indian. "Others just want to know about the magic gun."

'The gun has nothing to do with being Catholic," said Michael.

A young Indian in the group spoke in Lakota.

Michael looked at Thunder Eagle. "He wants to know about the man that was tortured and killed by his enemies and came back to life and killed all his enemies."

"That was Jesus. He did not come back to kill his enemies. He is supposed to do that in the future."

"What about the man who walked across the big lake?"

"That was Jesus too. Or Moses." Michael sighed in frustration. "Why don't you come inside and I will try to answer your questions as best I can."

Michael led them into the living room. With the lack of seating they sat on the floor in a circle.

For an hour Michael tried to answer every question. At the end the group mostly looked at him blankly and politely nodded.

"Thank you all for coming." Michael said getting to his feet. He hoped he had discouraged them from coming back while hoping he had not done too much damage when a real priest came to Westport.

An Indian came up to him and talked to Michael in Lakota. He talked fast and Michael only got a few words.

"He said, he liked to hear more about Catholic Medicine. He is coming back and bringing more people." The group nodded, agreeing. "You will make a good holy man."

Michael herded them out and pulled the doors closed. He saw Miss Kilgore, Seward, and Obadiah smiling at him.

"I am not qualified to do this." Michael said flatly.

"I think you be doin' fine," said Miss Kilgore. "For it bein' your first time."

"I don't have anything but my uncle's Bible," said Michael.

"You can read them stories," said Obadiah. "and tell them what they mean."

"Sooner or later a priest will show up," said Seward. "You will have a congregation all ready for him. He can fix whatever you get wrong."

Later that morning Michael realized he now had something to occupy a little of his time anyway, deciding what Bible stories to read. He looked at his father's watch. It had stopped. Michael had forgotten to wind it. "Keep it safe and wound!" were his father's instructions.

He looked at the ornate clock on the mantle. It too had stopped. Michael had not noticed. With nothing to do, he had no reason to keep track of time.

"Obadiah," he called to the kitchen.

The slave came out of the kitchen. "Yes, Mr. Dugan."

"This clock has not been wound," he said.

Obadiah reached behind the clock and found the key. He turned the clock around, put the key in the back and wound it as Michael would his watch.

Obadiah turned the clock back around and opened the face. "What time is it, Mr. Dugan?"

"I don't know. I noticed that clock had run down when I saw I failed to wind my watch."

Michael saw the doors to the parlor were open, and Miss Kilgore sitting on the couch inside.

Michael walked to the doorway. "Excuse me, Miss Kilgore."

Miss Kilgore came to her feet. "Good morning, Mr. Dugan."

"Good morning," said Michael walking into the room, looking at his father's watch. "Miss Kilgore, do you have the time?"

"Time for what, Mr. Dugan? I be expectin' a client."

Michael looked up. "No. I---"

"I can be tellin' him to—"

"That won't be necessary. I simply failed to remember to wind my father's watch. I would like to know if you have the correct time."

Miss Kilgore pulled on the small chain on her blouse and a small watch came out of her pocket. It was beautiful. She pressed he stem and its lid popped open, revealing a jeweled face.

"It be noon straight up." she announced.

"Noon straight up, Obadiah." Michael called into the other room as he set his father's watch.

"Noon straight up." repeated Obadiah.

"You have a beautiful watch." Miss Kilgore observed.

"My father lent it to me for my trip," explained Michael. "He wanted to make sure I kept to his Itinerary he had made out for me. The watch was my grandfather's who died a few years ago."

"You bein' without an itinerary now. There be no need to be checkin' the time. Must bein' nice to be a man of leisure."

"No, Ma'am, on the contrary, I came here expecting to help build a church. Now I have nothing to fill my time."

"Sure you be at leisure in Boston," she sat on the couch.

"Oh no, Ma'am," he joined her on the couch. "If I was not at school I was working for my father. She turned toward him. "You be sayin' you be good at fixin' things?"

"Yes Ma'am."

"I be talkin' to Mr. Ewing at the second hand store in Westport. His repair man up and went west. Mr. Ewing was sayin' how he be havin' clocks, music boxes, and the like that he can't be sellin' because they be needin' repair."

Michael's eyes lit up. "Really? I will look into that tomorrow."

There was a knock at her door. Miss Kilgore stood. "That be my client."

Michael came to his feet. "Of course, I will go."

Michael remembered walking by the shop when he and Seward went to buy their horses. First thing the next morning he and Seward were tying up their horses outside the old single story building.

"Good morning!" a short, round, balding man greeted them from behind the counter. "What can I show you gentleman today?"

"My name is Michael Dugan."

"Yes! You are staying at the Hopkin's place. You're the man who shot Nick Hopkins and lived to tell about it!"

Michael did not see any reason to explain whose house it was or who shot who. "I understand you are looking for a repairman."

The portly man came around the counter. He was about a foot shorter than Michael "I am George Ewing." he said offering his hand. "Yes! Old Tinker Bob up and went west. Been looking for a replacement for a month." Mr. Ewing looked at Michael up and down. "You are kind of young, Mr. Dugan. Do you have any experience? I don't have the time to train someone."

"This is Michael Dugan of Dugan Manufacturing," announced Seward.

"Out of Boston?"

"The same."

The man smiled. "Let me show you the workplace." They followed the man behind the counter and through a door. "It's a bit small. Part workshop, part storage."

Michael's eye lit up seeing all the tools and the workbench.

"See that clock?" Mr. Ewing pointed to a large antique clock sitting on the work bench. "I bought it for two dollars from a family heading west. I had two offers of ten dollars if I can get the thing running," he said in frustration. I have been trying to figure out what is wrong with it."

Michael turned the clock around. The back was already removed. He peered into the workings of the clock. Michael looked at Mr. Ewing, smiled, then looked at the bench, then to the shelf above. He pulled down a small pair of pliers. He eased the tool into the innards of the clock.

Michael bit his lip. "There!" He pulled the pliers out. "It looks like a grass seed got stuck in one of the sprockets. It should run fine now. A little oil won't hurt but it should be taken apart and cleaned."

A big smile came to Mr. Ewing's round face. "Son! I pay a dollar a day and ten percent of what you fix that I sell."

Michael smiled, "When can I start?"

"Hold on!" said Seward. "I am not going to babysit you here everyday."

"I can set up a workshop in my father's---the study at the house."

"I can have a wagon bring out the work and bring back the fixed things," said Mr. Ewing.

"Looks like you got yourself a job, Mr. Dugan," said Seward.

Michael had just finished clearing off the desk when a wagon pulled up with a workbench, shelves, and three wooden boxes of tools. Before long Michael had everything how he wanted it. Mr. Ewing had even sent a half dozen things to get him started. Michael put on a work apron Mr. Ewing had sent and set to work. He had finished two repairs when there was a knock at the door.

"Come in." Michael was looking at the workings of a music box.

Obadiah looked around at the former study. "Time for lunch, Mr. Dugan."

Michael pulled out his father's watch. "Noon? Already?" Michael stood up and untied his apron.

"You look like you have plenty of work," said Obadiah.

"I am out of practice." Micheal said as he took off his apron. "What is for lunch?"

"Beef stew. Ya' know we are runnin' low on meat. I can have of the farmers slaughter a steer for us," said Obadiah as they walked into the dining room.

"How soon before we run out?"

"Probably little over a week."

Michael took a seat at the table.

"Mr. Dugan, you be lookin' deep in thought."

Michael looked up to see Miss Kilgore at her place at the head of the table. "Good afternoon, Miss Kilgore. You will have to excuse me, I was lost in thought."

Obadiah filled their bowls with steaming stew as Seward came in.

"Good! I am hungry!" he said sitting down.

"So you are no longer bein' the man of leisure, Mr. Dugan?" asked Miss Kilgore cutting into a roll.

"No, Ma'am, Mr. Ewing made me a very generous offer."

"Things are pretty quiet in Westport," said Seward as Ebony filled his bowl. "Almost too quiet." Seward looked at Miss Kilgore. "How is Miss Kilgore today?"

"I be well. Yourself Mr. Seward?" she said taking a drink of milk.

"I am fine." Seward tore open a roll and smeared butter on it. "I notice your business is been steady."

"Yes, Mr. Seward, business is good."

"I am surprised to see women coming to see you," commented Seward chewing a piece of meat.

"Why would it surprise you a woman would want her fortune told?" asked Michael.

"The secret to success in business is to find a need and satisfy it," said Miss Kilgore taking a bite of her roll.

Seward looked across the table at Michael Dugan. "Has Miss Kilgore satisfied your needs yet, Mr. Dugan," asked Seward slyly. "If it were my house I would be getting my needs satisfied on a regular basis."

"Why would you need your fortune told so often, Mr. Seward?" asked Michael.

Seward suddenly started coughing. He finally regained himself. "I am sure your uncle would not approve of you partaking in Miss Kilgore's services."

Michael bit into a buttered roll. "Mr. Seward, how would you know what a priest would and would not approve of?"

"Oh, I am pretty sure he would not want---"

"Mr. Seward." Miss Kilgore said through clenched teeth. "An amoral person, such as yourself, is hardly bein' in the position to be teachin' this young man right from wrong."

Seward came to his feet. "I will not be lectured about morality by a---" he looked at Michael "woman." Seward walked off.

Michael discussed it with Miss Kilgore. They agreed they would need a proper cross to be hung in the living room during their ... Michael was not sure what to call the gathering on Sunday. Miss Kilgore said she would see to getting a cross.

Sunday morning the cross was hanging when Michael came down for breakfast. Michael stopped and looked at the cross. It was beautiful oak. But all four arms were equal. And there were four arcs connecting the arms, making a circle in the middle of the cross, creating a very familiar symbol.

Michael walked over to the Parlor where Miss Kilgore sat. "Miss Kilgore."

Miss Kilgore came to her feet. "Yes, Mr. Dugan."

"Can I have a word with you regarding the cross?"

"Certainly." They walked over to the cross and looked at it. "Well?"

"The standard Christian cross bottom board generally goes to the floor. This is a—"

"It be a Celtic Cross," she said.

"Yes, it is."

"I am Celtic." Miss Kilgore returned to her parlor.

Michael went upstairs and got the Bible. He had decided on the Moses story. He was concerned about the part about escaping slaves.

Michael heard pounding when he came down the steps. Thunder Eagle was standing on one of the dining room chairs nailing something into the cross. Four bunches of feathers now hung from the cross.

Michael watched as the Indian stepped off the chair, stood back, and admired his work.

Michael too, looked at the cross. "Thunder Eagle... what—"

"It is a Lakota Spirit Wheel. I am honored you had it made."

"Spirit Wheel?"

"It just needed to be dressed." Michael looked at a Celtic Cross with feathers hanging from it. "The Lakota Medicine is bad for Catholic Medicine?"

Michael sighed. "If it makes you and your people feel welcome ... fine."

A few more people came this time. Negros, Indians, and a few whites. They stared at the cross, but no one said anything. Michael wondered what his uncle would say if he walked in at that moment.

Michael didn't have to worry about the slave uprising being an issue. It was the staffs turning into snakes that fascinated the group.

"Do you have a staff like that?" asked one of the slaves.

"No, I don't"

"Do Catholic Holy Men have such a staff?"

"That power came from God," explained Michael. "It was meant to show the power of good over evil."

"Like your gun that shoots many times, while the others only shoot one?"

"It is like your knives, arrow, or spears," said Michael. "It is only as evil or good as the person using it."

The meeting ended with whites and slaves singing a hymn. Thunder Eagle sang a song in Lakota. The others liked it.

Michael was barely able to push the doors open because of the wind. The sky had darkened. To the west was a black cloud. Spits of rain hit Michael's face. The group scattered looking up at the threatening sky. Michael saw a familiar figure in a buggy waiting at the bottom of the steps.

"Good morning, Reverend Clark," said Michael.

"Good Morning, Mr. Dugan. So it is true?"

"What is true?" Michael grabbed hold of the buggy against the wind.

"You decided to stay and force your ... religion on the godless savages and ignorant slaves."

Another gust of wind buffeted the buggy. "I

offered to teach Thunder Eagle. He brought the rest." explained Michael.

"You are allowing the witch-whore to live and do her evil work under your roof. You let your slaves live in your house! You are going against the laws of God and nature, Mr. Dugan! "

Michael looked at the approaching black cloud in the west. The reverend followed his gaze. Both saw a dark grey cone shaped cloud dipping out of the darker cloud. Reverend Clark pointed to funnel cloud. "You have brought the Wrath of God to Westport, Mr. Dugan!" The Reverend whipped the horse and headed east.

Michael grew up near the ocean. He had seen waterspouts. But this! Reverend Clark was right. This swirling dark grey monster was about to touch down. It looked like the Wrath of God!

The mammoth tail touched down to the west. Michael ran up the stairs. He watched as the twister picked something up. Michael saw a tiny white square fly up. Then another.

Michael realized the tornado had touched on the trail and was tossing wagons like he had seen waterspouts do boats on the ocean.

Seward and Obadiah pushed open the door. "That's headed this way! INSIDE! NOW!"

If Michael didn't know any better he would swear a great train was roaring toward the house from the west.

Everyone came to the living room. "Cellar, NOW!" ordered Seward.

Seward made sure everyone was in before he shut the cellar door. He and Obadiah held on to the handle. In the dark Michael heard the roar that seemed right above them. He waited to hear the sound of the house disintegrating. Then a vacuum would tear the door out and suck all of them out. Or tons of rocks would fall on the door, filling the cellar and crushing them. The roar grew lower. Then stopped. In the dark was nothing but breathing.

Seward pushed up the door. He poked his head out. "The house is still here."

They climbed out into the light. Seward went to look out the back. "We still have a barn."

Michael wondered if Westport was still there.

Obadiah pushed open the doors. They stepped out onto the porch. Westport was still there. "Thunder Eagle, you tipi is gone." Seward looked to the west. "It must of only touched down for a bit. I have heard twisters stayin' on the ground for miles. Some towns were just gone."

Michael squinted, looking to the west. "It looks like the wagons on the trail were hit."

"Yeah, poor bastards. I would hate to be them," said Seward.

"People could be hurt or dying," said Michael.

"So?"

Michael turned to Obadiah. "Obadiah, get the wagon hitched up and bring it around front. Miss Kilgore, Ebony, bring whatever can be used as bandages."

"Is this part of Catholic Medicine?" asked Thunder Eagle.

"Yes, Thunder Eagle. This is what Catholic Medicine is all about."

By the time Obadiah brought the wagon around, Miss Kilgore and Ebony had two bundles waiting on the steps. Seward rode next to the wagon, the Colt on his hip.

Michael, Obadiah, and Ebony jumped in the back of the wagon. Miss Kilgore handed them the bundles. She reached her hand up.

"Miss Kilgore," said Michael. "Perhaps you should stay here."

Her green eyes narrowed. "You be orderin' me not to go, Mr. Dugan?"

"No, Ma'am, but---"

"Then be givin' me a hand up and let's be goin' to help those poor people."

About a mile west the debris lay on the ground as they rode. First small things. Clothes. Linens. Then Michael saw a smashed clock. It was the one he had pulled a grass seed out of.

The farther west they went the bigger the pieces of debris. Finally, they came to the wagons. For a mile it looked like the twister followed the trail, casting aside any wagon that had the misfortune to be in its path.

Horses and oxen lay dead in their harnesses. Michael heard a child cry to his right. He turned toward a wagon on its side. People lay around it. Michael got his wagon as close to it as he could. Michael jumped from the wagon and the others followed. As Michael approached a man using a long shot gun as a crutch came out from behind the upturned wagon.

"What do you people want?" he asked.

"We are here to help."

He brought the gun up and pointed it at Michael. "I will not have no redskins or niggers touchin' my family."

Michael looked at the others behind him. "He can't mean that. He is in shock."

Michael turned and took a step toward the man. He aimed the gun at Michael's face and cocked both barrels. Another wagon pulled up, and people jumped off. Michael backed away, and they got back on the wagon.

Not long after they got back on the road Michael heard someone cry out. "Help me somebody!" Michael stopped the wagon. They could only see wagons and belongings. No movement.

"Where are you?" called Michael.

"Over here! Under my damn wagon!" Michael

turned the wagon off the road toward where he thought the voice was coming from.

"Which wagon are you under?" asked Michael.

"The one on top of me, DAMMIT!"

Seward rode ahead. "Here he is!"

Michael brought them toward Seward who was near an overturned wagon. He saw a man. Only his head, right shoulder, arm, and hand could be seen.

Michael jumped out of the wagon and ran over. The man had the biggest beard Michael had ever seen. "Are you hurt?"

"That damn twister tossed me around a bit. I am pretty sure my right leg is broke. The name's Nathan Braker. He offered his free hand. Michael shook his hand. He saw that the only thing that kept the man from being crushed was the corner of the wagon had landed on the very edge of an old trunk near the man's head.

"Michael Dugan, this is Mike Seward," he said pointing to Seward who was still on his horse.

"Dugan? You the man who shot Nick Hopkins?" asked Braker?

"I shot Nick Hopkins." Seward said in frustration.

Obadiah and Ebony came around the wagon. Michael did not notice the pistol that lay next to Braker until he had snatched it up and aimed. Seward drew and cocked the Colt just as fast.

"Easy, Mr. Braker, we are tryin' to help you," said Seward.

"There is a Sioux right behind you, Mr. Dugan."

Michael saw Thunder Eagle with his knife out ready to throw.

Miss Kilgore stepped out from behind the upturned wagon and into the Braker's line of fire. "Why Nathan Braker!"

"Miss Kilgore?"

"Mr. Braker you are being very rude to my friends," scolded Miss Kilgore. "You be droppin' that gun this instant before I be havin' this hired gun be shootin' where you be layin'. " The man let the gun fall. Michael angrily kicked it away.

Seward dismounted. "Let's see about gettin' you out of there."

"Obadiah, find something to use for leverage," said Michael picking up a trunk and placing it by Braker's head. Obadiah brought a harness spar from a wagon. Michael put one end under the wagon and laid the spar across the trunk, leaving the other end high.

All stood on either side of the end.

"Thunder Eagle. When we lift, pull him out."

"No!" roared Baker. "I will not have a Sioux layin' a hand on me!"

"Thunder Eagle, take my place." Thunder stood

at the spar. Michael bent down and grabbed under Baker's arms.

"LIFT!"

They pressed down, and Michael pulled. The man screamed in pain as the wagon lifted. The spar was wet from the rain and started to slide. Michael dragged the man back, but his feet lost traction in the wet grass. The wagon slammed back down missing Braker's feet by inches.

Miss Kilgore quickly moved over to examine the man's right leg. "His thigh and his shin both be broken."

"We'll have to set it soon," said Seward.

"We can't be doin' it out here," said Miss Kilgore.

"Let's get him on the wagon and back to the house," said Michael.

"I cain't leave my supplies and gear!" protested Baker. "I need them to get through the winter!"

"Braker!" said Seward. "Its either your supplies or your leg!"

They carried the man trying to keep his leg as straight as possible. The man screamed in pain and anger all the way to the wagon.

They arrived at the house and carried Braker into the living room.

"Put him on the floor," said Seward.

Obadiah turned to his daughter. "Go out to the

wood pile and fetch four strong sticks as long as this man's leg. She ran off, Obadiah following her into the kitchen. Miss Kilgore brought in one of the bundles from the wagon. He pulled out a sheet and started tearing them into strips.

Obadiah returned carrying two big bottles.

He pulled the cork out of one bottle and handed it to Braker. "Whiskey for the pain." Baker snatched he bottle and started guzzling.

"Mind you I set my own leg two winters ago," stated Baker.

Ebony returned with the sticks. Miss Kilgore laid the strip of linen under the man's leg as Obadiah placed the sticks. Michael ripped the man's pant leg open to his crotch.

"It is broke in two places," said Seward. He looked at Braker. "You better drink up, Mr. Braker, this is going to hurt like hell." Braker emptied the first bottle and threw it away. He pulled the cork out of the second one with his teeth and started gulping it.

"Mr. Dugan, have you ever set a leg?" asked Seward.

"Once at one of our factories," said Michael looking as Braker's shin bone pushed up against the skin. "A man broke his leg. I helped set it."

"You can help now," said Seward. "Get a hold of his foot. Obadiah, grab under his arm. Pull hard when I say. Don't stop 'till I say so. Miss Kilgore if you can set the shin, I'll see about the thigh." Seward looked at Braker who was holding a three-fourths empty bottle in his arm. He smiled and nodded.

"GO!"

Michael pulled, and Braker screamed and cussed. Miss Kilgore worked on his shin. Seward squeezed the thigh.   Michael felt a click as the shin set and then a deeper one as Seward set the thigh. Obadiah and Ebony set the splints and were tying them when Braker started to buck. Thunder Eagle sat on Braker's chest. Braker went limp. Ebony tied the last splint.

Thunder Eagle got up.

"He's still breathin." said Seward. "He just passed out."

CHAPTER VI

Michael Dugan again wondered why someone traveling west in a covered wagon would bring something as useless as a music box. With the dust and rain, how long do they expect it to work? He snapped the black lacquered back on the box. He turned it to face him and opened the lid. A ballerina popped up and twirled to a tinkling Mozart.

There was a knock at the door. Michael looked at his father's watch and hoped it was Obadiah with his mid-morning snack.

"Come in," said Michael.

The doors slid apart and the form of Nathan Braker filled the doorway. He leaned against the door jam, favoring is right leg. The leg was still being held stiff by the crude splint they had put on the day before.

Michael jumped up and ran over to the man.

"Mr. Braker, you should not be up."

Michael got under the man's arm. "Dr. Adams said he would come out this morning and set that leg properly." Michael was barely able to support the man's weight as he eased him down on the couch.

Braker laughed. "Ain't the first time I had a busted leg. Those other times I set it myself!" He dragged an ornate footstool over with his left foot and lifted the stiff leg onto it.

Michael returned to his work. "Where were you headed when you got caught in the storm, Mr. Braker?" asked Michael bringing a large antique clock in front of him. "California? Oregon?"

"Boy! Why the hell would I want to go to those places?" he growled. "Too many people out there."

"Where then? Kansas Territory to trade with the Indians?" asked Michael as he tried to find a tool to fit the clock's tiny screws.

Braker glared at the young man. "Trade? With the damn Redskins? I was headed for God's Country. The Mountains. I got me huntin' and trappin' to do!"

Michael looked up from his work. "Are you a Mountain Man, Mr. Braker?"

"People call us that. I have a cabin up there. I come down in the spring and fall to sell my furs. I get supplied, get drunk, get into fights, and get me a woman or two. Then I head back. I was headin' back when that damn twister caught me."

"Living alone in the mountains. I have heard that can be very dangerous." Michael finally got the last screw off the back of the clock.

"Dangerous?" Braker got up and hobbled over and sat in the chair across from Michael.

"Boy! You are the one living dangerously."

Michael smiled. "What do you mean?"

"You shot Nick Hopkins for one. And you let a damn cutthroat Sioux on your property and let him camp here."

Michael sighed in frustration as he removed the workings of the clock. "Why does everyone hate the Lakota? Thunder Eagle has been nothing but friendly to me."

Braker leaned over the desk so close that Michael could smell the whiskey on his breath.

"You took a riverboat from St. Louie?"

"Yes, the Chariot."

"You saw wagons driven into the river?"

Michael looked up from his work. "More than I could count."

Braker shook his large scarred finger at Michael. "That is the work of your friendly Sioux. I still have a Sioux arrow in my lower back that gives me hell when it's going to rain or snow."

"My uncle is presumed lost on his solo trip from St. Louis to here." Michael mentioned.

"I will bet your friendly Thunder Eagle has a hand in that or knows who did."

Michael remembered Thunder Eagle wore his uncle's crucifix. Had he traded for it as he said, or was he wearing it as a trophy?

A knock at the door tore Michael from his thoughts. Miss Kilgore stood at the door.

"Be I interuptin' man talk?" she asked.

Michael stood. "Not at all! Miss Kilgore you have met Nathan Braker."

"Miss Jessica Kilgore!" The man tried to rise.

"Don't be gettin' up for me," she said.

"Too late." the man smirked.

She chose to ignore Braker's crudeness. "How be the leg this mornin, Mr. Braker?"

"Just seeing you, Miss Kilgore, makes me forget the pain."

Miss Kilgore looked at Michael. "I be goin' out to the kitchen. Might you be wantin' somethin'?"

Michael sat. "Yes, ask Obadiah if he could bring in my mid-morning snack."

"And if that old nigger has it handy," said Braker. "Could he bring me in some more of that fine whisky."

"I be seein' what I can do." She walked out and slid the doors closed.

Braker sighed looking after the woman and then turned back to Michael who was oiling the clock's innards.

"You are a tinker, Mr. Dugan?" said Braker.

"I repair things for Mr. Ewing."

"And a preacher."

Michael laughed sliding the workings back

into the clock. "We have meetings on Sunday. I was thinking about becoming a priest before I came here. My uncle is priest. I was supposed to spend the winter with him." Michael pursed his lips trying to get a tiny screw to catch on the inside the clock. "I am afraid my stay in Westport is the last of what my father called my asinine adventures. My plan is to return to Boston in the spring, as my father wishes, to go to business college."

Braker leaned toward Michael. "Have you been with a woman yet, Mr. Dugan?"

Michael looked at the man in annoyance. "Have I what?"

A wry smile came to Braker's bearded face. "Known a woman in the biblical sense."

"I am Catholic, Mr. Braker. We don't believe in sex before marriage."

Braker smiled. "You have intimate relations with a real woman, and you will forget all about bein' a priest." Braker looked at the door Miss Kilgore had just left out of. "A good lookin' man like yourself, I thought you and Miss Kilgore would have some special arrangement. I know if I were you---"

There was a knock at the door. "Come in." Michael said tersely.

Obadiah pushed the doors apart. He carried a tray of small stacked sandwiches. On top was a big whiskey bottle. Braker got the bottle before the Obadiah could set the tray on the desk.

"Thank you, Obadiah." Michael said picking up a sandwich. Obadiah left, closing the doors behind him.

"There is someone else you need to keep an eye on," said Braker grabbing a sandwich and stuffing it in his mouth.

"Who?"

Braker swallowed the sandwich and washed it down with a couple of swallows of whiskey.

"You are lettin' niggers live in your house."

"Obadiah and Ebony?" Michael bit into his sandwich and scanned the shelf above him.

"Slaves have been known to kill their owners and then make a run for freedom, Mr. Dugan."

Michael looked at the tag of a large music box. "Obadiah and his daughter are not slaves. They are live-in paid servants."

"Were they both here when you came?"

"No, we had to buy Ebony," said Michael bringing down the music box.

"What would you do to keep your daughter from being sold again? The Kansas Territory is free and the state line is less than a mile away. They have the run of this house. They know where you keep your money."

"I hired Mr. Seward to protect me."

Braker laughed. "You trust that hired gun? If someone offers a man like that the right money, he would kill you and everyone in this house without a second thought. How much are you payin' him for his services?"

"Room and board. He is also a sworn deputy."

Braker howled. "How much does that pay?"

"Two dollars a month."

Braker almost fell off his chair. "You have any money?"

"I have some."

"Trust me, both your hired gun and those niggers know how much you have and where you keep it." Braker thought for a moment. "This is what I would do if I was Seward. I would tell the niggers if they killed you I would split the money with them. They kill you, he kills them sayin' they killed you and he kills them as they tried to run for the free territory. Seward gets all the money."

"Mr. Braker," said Michael with annoyance close to anger. "It has been an interesting conversation but I have do have work to do. I will get Obadiah to help you back up to your room."

"Oh, I almost forgot why I came in. I have to get back to my cabin."

It was Michael's turn to laugh. "Mr. Braker, your leg is broken in two places. Dr. Adams assured me you won't be able to travel until spring if then."

"What this?" he slapped his splinted leg. "I have had both legs broken at the same time.   Set them myself and still got all my trappin' and huntin' done! All I need from you is to help me get my wagon righted. I gotta' see how much of my supplies those thievin' Redskins stole.

"After Dr. Adams resets that leg and gives something for the pain I will have Obadiah hitch up the wagon, and we will go see about your wagon."

Obadiah drove the wagon. Seward and Michael rode along side. In the wagon, with his reset leg, was Braker. He coddled a bottle of laudanum. Dr. Adams said laudanum was a mix of alcohol and opium. If it tasted as bad as it smelled, Michael felt sorry for Braker. Bringing up the rear was Thunder Eagle, sternly scanning the horizon.

They moved along the road, debris stretching out on both sides.

Michael was shocked that there were still bodies laying were they fell. Only he could not really see the corpses. They were covered with masses of screaming buzzards and ravens.

"No one to claim them," said Seward as Michael watched a vulture and a raven fight over a young girl.

"Why doesn't someone from one of the churches come out and give them a proper burial?" asked Michael.

"Only people who live in Westport get proper burials," said Obadiah.

"What about the others?"

"Well," he smiled. "Master Hopkins owns some

graves plots in all three of cemeteries in Westport. He is a partner with the undertaker. The people who die on the trail they want them to get a Christian burial here in Westport. They pay ten dollars for a nice casket and service led my Reverend Clark. They bury them. The day after the people leave, Master Hopkins has his slaves dig them up. They clean off the casket and bury the body in the part of Master Hopkins' quarry they don't use anymore.

Michael wrinkled his nose. "What people like … these?"

"Master Hopkins will send his slaves out before the bodies get to smellin'. He'll bury them the same place he buries the others. He charges The Town of Kansas a dollar a grave."

Michael felt sad that his uncle would not get a proper burial. Michael pictured his uncle Mike being devoured by vultures and ravens. Then his ghost was doomed to wander the prairie.

"There it is!" shouted Braker. "There's my wagon."

Obadiah turned the wagon off the road, in the direction Braker pointed. The birds with blood splattered beaks gave challenging screams as they maneuvered to the upturned wagon.

Finally the wagon came to a stop. Braker's wagon laid as it was left, a wheel sticking in the air.

Braker climbed off the wagon. "My wagon looks in pretty good shape. He looked at the clutter around the wagon. "Looks like the Redskins got everything that got thrown out." He pointed to Obadiah, "Get the rope. Let's get it righted."

Obadiah unhooked the horse from their wagon and tied one end of the rope to the harness. Michael rigged the other end to the wagon. Obadiah stood at the back of the horse. Michael stood in front of the horse and held his bridle ready to pull the horse forward.

Obadiah hit the horse with the reins, and Michael pulled. The horse gave a snort and moved forward a few steps, and the rope went taut. Obadiah urged the horse on. The rope gave a long creak.

"Stop" ordered Michael. "If that rope breaks it could kill Obadiah. There is a chain in our wagon. We can use it."

"Mr. Dugan, that rope is strong enough," explained Braker as if speaking to a child. "It ain't gonna' break. If it does, I will buy you another nice nigger."

Michael's blue eyes narrowed as he walked up to Braker. "I am deeply troubled by your lack of concern for this man's welfare."

"Man? Mr. Dugan, you don't think niggers are human, do ya?"

Michael turned and walked away from Braker toward Obadiah.

"Obadiah."

"Yes, Mr. Dugan."

Michael Dugan looked at Obadiah then to Braker. "Come with me."

The two came to the head of the horse and both grabbed the bridle. Seward threw a clod of dirt at the flank of the horse as Michael and Obadiah pulled. The tightening rope creaked, and the wagon began to rise. Just as the wagon was teetering on the verge of righting, the rope gave a groan. Then what sounded like a gun shot and the rope parted and the wagon slammed back to the ground.

Michael and Obadiah held on to the bridle as the panicked horse took off, dragging them through the debris. Between their combined weight and screaming orders the horse came to a stop.

Michael let go of the bridle and it fall to the ground, Obadiah beside him. The horse stood looking down at them.

"You probably just saved my life, Mr. Dugan," said Obadiah.

Seward came running up. "You still in one piece?"

"I think so," said Michael getting to his feet. Michael offered his hand to the slave.

"Obadiah, you alright?"

Obadiah grabbed the offered hand and came to his feet. "You saved my life," he said with tears in his eyes.

Nathan Braker came hobbling up. "Everyone no worse for wear?"

Michael whirled, using his full body weight, sent his fist into the jaw of Nathan Braker, knocking him to the ground.

Michael turned to Obadiah. "Get the chain from the wagon and rig it to Mr. Braker's wagon."

"Yes, Mr. Dugan."

Michael walked back toward the wagon narrowly missing stepping on Braker.

After Michael was gone, Seward offered his hand to Braker. "You offended his Boston sensibilities."

Braker took the offered hand. Seward strained to get man on his feet.

"Those Boston sensibilities will probably get that boy killed."

"Yeah," said Seward as they walked toward the wagon. "I know."

Soon Michael and Obadiah got the chain rigged on the wagon and returned to the front. This time Braker stood by the chain and held the reins. The wagon slowly came up and landed on its wheels.

Braker quickly hobbled over and heaved himself in the wagon. Michael could see that trunks, crates, and stuffed bags had been tied down.

"Old Ruby is still here." He pulled out something from a sheath of brown leather with intricate Indian design sewn in to it." Braker withdrew it from the sheath to reveal a gun. A rifle. To Michael it looked like a small cannon. It had a very long barrel and with a muzzle that was at least an inch wide.

"What kind of gun is that?" asked Michael in awe.

"This is Ruby." Braker held up the gun. "She's a buffalo gun. Also good at killin' grizzlies."

"You hunt buffalo?" asked Michael running his finger up the barrel of the gun.

"Boy, I hunt everything from rats to grizzlies. I killed things you never heard of and would not believe if I told you. But yeah, I have killed me my share of buffalo. Best meat I ever ate. Their hides make good warm blankets and coats.

"Can I ... we go on a buffalo hunt?" asked Michael in wide eyed excitement.

Braker looked at the boy. "Boy, I don't kill for sport. I kill to eat or protect myself."

"Obadiah, you said we were short on meat," said Michael.

"Yes, Mr. Dugan, but there be farmers who will sell us all the meat we need."

"Let's ask an expert." Michael looked around. Thunder Eagle was keeping his distance from the group. Michael could not understand why the Indian even came along.

"Thunder Eagle!" Michael motioned the Indian to join them. Thunder Eagle hesitated, looked around and slowly moved his horse toward them. "We are thinking of going on a buffalo hunt."

Thunder Eagle looked down at the group, and then asked Michael. "Why?"

"For meat." said Michael.

The Indian shook his head. "There are farms. You can buy meat from them," he said dismissively.

"See Mr. Dugan," said Obadiah. "We can buy meat all winter, butchered and delivered. Any kind of meat you want."

Michael looked at Thunder Eagle. "Did you find your tipi?"

"No."

"You told me it took two buffalo to make your tipi."

Thunder Eagle stared at Michael and thought for a moment. "Yes, two."

"So we go on a short buffalo hunt." Michael said. "You kill two buffalo. We get the meat for the house. You get the skins for your tipi."

Thunder Eagle looked down at Michael from his horse. "I can hunt on my own. Hunting buffalo is very dangerous."

Michael's eyes narrowed at Thunder Eagle. "It's not up to you," stated Michael Dugan. " I want to be able say when I go home, that I went on a buffalo hunt. We are going. With or without you."

Thunder Eagle and Michael locked eyes for a moment. Then Thunder Eagle shrugged.

"Looks like we are going on a buffalo hunt," said Seward.

CHAPTER VII

"A hunt! How exciting! "said Miss Kilgore over dinner. 'When do we be leavin'?"

"Miss Kilgore," said Michael cutting open his roll. "You won't be going."

Miss Kilgore slammed down her knife. "I would like to be knowin' why not, Mr. Dugan?"

"Too dangerous for a woman." Braker said popping a piece of meat in his mouth.

"The main herd is a full day away," put in Thunder Eagle. "We will have to camp before the hunt." Thunder Eagle had taken the last room upstairs since he lost his tipi to the twister.

"The Sioux women not be goin' on the buffalo hunts?" inquired Miss Kilgore.

"No, they stay at camp, cook and take care of the children. They do butcher the buffalo when we return from the hunt," said Thunder Eagle eating without utensils. Michael felt sure the Indian did so just to annoy he group.

"I agree." Nathan Braker said taking a drink of

wine. "No place for a child either. The men should be the only ones going."

"I am eighteen," stated Michael.

"You are still a child," reiterated Braker. "I will not be takin' a spoiled brat on a buffalo hunt."

"Spoiled brat?"

"The whole point of the hunt is so Mr. Dugan can brag to everyone back home he went on a buffalo hunt." Seward reminded everyone. "If Mr. Dugan doesn't go the hunt is off."

"I won't be missin' my chance to be takin' part in a real frontier buffalo hunt, stated Miss Kilgore.

"Buffalo hunt is not like a fox hunt, Miss Kilgore." Braker said sternly, cutting into his steak. "Someone could get hurt or killed."

"I be goin'." said Miss Kilgore. "Even if I be followin' in the carriage. But I be goin'"

Braker sighed in exasperation. "How many are coming?"

"All of us. Five and you," said Michael.

"Food and supplies for six people for two days. We will have to buy some supplies. Make preparations." Braker thought a moment. "We can leave first thing day after tomorrow."

After dinner Thunder Eagle took Michael aside. "My people are following the main herd. They also will be hunting."

"You think your people are going to have a problem with that?" Michael asked, wondering what he had gotten himself and the others into.

"If they see I am with you, probably not. But you … We WILL be hunting on our … their territory without asking permission."

"Thunder Eagle, if you say so right now, I will call this hunt off."

"You know what the white man says about my people?"

"No, what?"

Thunder Eagle smiled. "If you can see a Sioux, you are already dead."

Michael failed to see the humor in that.

It was a brisk sunny day in late October when the odd caravan formed up. Two wagons and Miss Kilgore driving her carriage.

Nathan Braker lay in the lead wagon. Michael and Seward rode in the driver's seat.

Their horses were tied to the back. Obadiah drove the second wagon with the supplies. Ebony sat beside her father. The men agreed Miss Kilgore's carriage would go second between the two wagons.

Dr. Adams did give Braker an ample supply of laudanum. Braker also brought a good supply of his personal painkiller: whiskey.

They pulled in with the rest of the wagons going west.

"In about a hour you will see a trail going off to your left," said Braker in a drunken slur. "Take it."

"We are heading south?" asked Seward.

"We head south until noon. Then we go west."

"Why?"

"Stayin' way clear of the Sioux."

For that hour Braker regaled Seward and Michael Dugan with his life and times.

"My squaw and two kids in that little cabin," said Braker just after they turned south.

"'Bout drove me crazy. One day I had to get out of there."

"I heard you Mountain Men took Indian wives," said Seward.

"Had a nice squaw, pretty too." The wagon hit a bump. Braker was thrown on his face.

For a moment he just lay there. Finally he pushed himself up. "Where was I?"

"Your pretty squaw," reminded Michael.

"We were together for many a winter. She was always there when ever I came back.

Had boy and a gir by her. Pretty as their mother. Lost them all two winters ago."

"Was it illness?" asked Michael.

"They are gone, Boy, that's all that matters."

Just before they turned west they stopped for lunch. Obadiah had brought two kettles of beef stew. He built a fire and warmed some up.

Michael got a bowl and sat next to Thunder Eagle. "We are being followed." Michael said to Thunder Eagle in almost a whisper.

"They are watching us and letting us know," said the Indian quietly.

"Why? They can see we are no threat."

Thunder Eagle shook his head and shrugged.

They packed up and turned west. Michael was realizing his decision to go on this buffalo hunt was like his choice to winter in Westport. He had no idea what was really involved. He started seriously considering turning back. Buy meat as Obadiah had suggested. Thunder Eagle was quite capable on his own or with his people. Going home. That would be the smartest thing to do for all involved.

Thunder Eagle rode up next to Michael. "There they are."

Michael looked in the direction the Indian was pointing expecting to see Lakota scouts. Instead he saw a wave of thundering brown breaking over a hill less than a mile away. Buffalo. Michael stood, even in the wagon he could feel the ground shake. The herd was moving west. An Indian on horseback came over the hill in the midst of the herd. He aimed his arrow and shot. A large buffalo fell beside him. Before he topped the next hill another animal dropped. Then he was gone. Michael smiled, his blue eyes wide with excitement. He forgot all about going home. He was going on a buffalo hunt.

The caravan rolled west alone until the sun touched the western horizon. Thunder Eagle chose a spot at the top of large plateau. The only way up was a small path just wide enough for the wagons to get up. At the top there was enough room for them to form a tight circle and still have room for the horses to graze.

Thunder Eagle reported they were behind the herd. Michael wondered if the herd stopped at night and if they have to travel to catch them?

Just at twilight, Michael took the five horses to drink at a small stream at the bottom of the plateau. He led them into some bushes, and they bent to drink.

Michael heard a snort of a horse and a hoof hit a rock to his left. He looked, expecting to see a Lakota war party or the Devilbiss brothers. He realized he was alone, unarmed, and well out of shouting distance of the camp.

He saw a single horse standing in the creek. Even in the fading light there was no mistaking the rider. Looking down at Michael he saw the scarred face of Fire Oak.

Michael dropped his eyes, remembering Thunder Eagle had told him looking the Medicine Man in the eyes showed disrespect. Michael gave serious thought to dropping the reins and making a run for it. He knew he would not get far. He was probably surrounded. Were they here to steal the horses? Were they attacking the camp right now?"

"Stupid Boy Who Stands Out," said Fire Oak.

Michael wondered if he should be honored that the Medicine Man had learned to say his name in English. Or insulted Fire Oak called him stupid.

"Great Medicine Man, Fire Oak." Michael said in Lakota, keeping his eyes down.

For a moment Michael could only hear the horses drinking and a breeze through the golden leaves. No war cries, screams of terror, or gunshots came from the camp above. Unless the Lakota had snuck in and cut everyone's throats. They may have killed everyone with arrows out of the dark.

"Thunder Eagle." Fire Oak finally said in English.

"Your son," said Michael in Lakota.

"Your friend?" Fire Oak asked in Lakota.

God, let me get this right. "Yes, The Eagle That Flies Over the Thunder Cloud IS my friend."

Just like the first time Fire Oak had seen him, Michael was trying to show respect, but probably was only sounding stupid.

"You. Keep safe." He heard the Medicine Man say in English. He heard Fire Oak turn his horse around and splash away.

Michael suddenly realized he was holding his breath. What did Fire Oak mean?

Thunder Eagle would keep him safe, or he has to keep Thunder Eagle safe? He led the horses up the path. He staked them out and came into camp. Everyone was there. No one was laying around the fire with throats cut or Sioux arrows sticking out of them.

Logs were dragged up and laid side by side. Michael did not know it, but wooden sides of wagons could be removed to create flat bed. The removable side also made a passable dinner table. The wagon's side was laid across the logs.

Dinner was stew and hard rolls. The only drink was water. Except Braker's whiskey.

All talked about the plans for the hunt the next day. Then there was a howl out of the darkness.

"Coyote," said Seward.

"Too deep. That was a wolf," countered Braker.

Everyone looked at Thunder Eagle who continued to eat.

"Sioux!" said Braker.

"He is a Lakota," Michael corrected. "His name is Thunder—"

"Was it a wolf, coyote, or one of your people?" demanded Braker.

"Why does it matter?" said the Indian still eating. "It is the things that are not seen or heard. Those are the things you need to worry about."

Braker grunted in agreement.

"Things like what?" Michael inquired draining his bowl.

"Things, boy," said Braker. "Things out here I have seen and heard tell of."

Thunder Eagle looked at the Mountain Man and nodded.

Michael leaned back and laughed. "The worst Lewis and Clark expedition reported were wolves, mountain lion, and bears."

Braker laughed. "That is what they said in their report. You should hear what they really saw. What really happened."

"Why would they lie?" asked Michael.

Braker looked at Thunder Eagle. "If people knew the truth no one would have crossed the Mississippi."

"And how do you know this?" demanded Seward.

"I personally talked to the men who were with Lewis and Clark. They had some tales to tell."

"The Lewis and Clark expedition was 1804 to 1806." recited Michael. "That was forty years ago."

"I talked to them over the past thirty years. Besides, I know what I have seen out here. Ask the Sioux. His people know."

Thunder Eagle looked at Michael's eyes widen and nodded.

Miss Kilgore stood and stretched. "If you be goin'

to be tellin' the scary stories, let's be beddin' down for it."

Soon they lay in the semi-circle around the fire. Braker sipped a cup with a bottle near by. He looked into the fire. "Once when I trappin' I was paddlin' down this river. I looked up and out of the tall trees on shore came a head. It was huge! It looked like a snake, but it had big teeth. And in that monster's teeth were two full grown live grizzly bears."

"What? No! A dinosaur?" exclaimed Michael.

"You call it what you want, Boy. I watched that thing swallow those two grizzlies whole. I heard those grizzlies scream all the way down. That thing took one look at me, and I started paddlin' and didn't stop paddlin' for a full day and night."

"There are the Thunder Birds," said Thunder Eagle. Braker looked at Michael and pointed at the Indian and gave a nod. "When my father was a child he was a hunting buffalo. One of the hunters was out in the lead of the great herd chasing a very large buffalo. What he didn't see was a large black thunder cloud ahead of him. As he started to throw his spear, a great bird came out of the cloud. It had no feathers but scales like a snake and two sets of claws. With its front claws it took a large buffalo. With the back claws it grabbed the hunter and his horse. It flew up, back up into the thunder cloud. For a long time my father could hear the hunter, his horse and the buffalo all screaming."

"That sounded like a dragon!" exclaimed Michael.

"Tell the boy about the hairy elephants." said Seward.

Both Thunder Eagle and Braker nodded.

"Mammoths? Out here?" Michael asked in amazement.

"I have never seen them," said Braker. "But I have seen their handiwork."

"Mammoths," asked Michael with excitement in his wide blue eyes. "Really?"

"From what I hear tell, they come chargin' at you out of the west," recollected Braker. "They stomp everything and everyone flat that gets in front of them."

"You say you saw this yourself?" asked Seward.

"I was a wagon master for a wagon train. It looked like six wagons. They were smashed right into the dirt."

"That could have been a buffalo stampede," said Seward dismissively.

Braker filled his cup. "You don't think I know what a wagon train looks like after a buffalo stampede? This was different. Wagon trains circle the wagons for protection. Not these. These six wagons were side by side like they were runnin' from somethin,' and they were heading east. Something came at them from the west. It looked like a giant smashed everything with big flat round rocks. Wagons, belongings, and people smashed flat."

"Surely," said Michael, "They had guns." Braker drained his cup.

"Found plenty of guns, boy. All smashed. One still in a man's hands. We didn't find a single unspent round or ball. Whatever it was they used all their ammunition against it."

"Tell him about the ghost trains," said Seward.

"No!" protested Miss Kilgore. "You be givin' him nightmares."

"What about the ghost trains?" asked Michael laying his head on his pillow.

"This was my first wagon train. I was just a boy," said Braker. "We were about at the half-way point. One afternoon we saw a dozen wagons lined up movin' steady off in the distance. But they weren't on any trail. They weren't headin' east or west. We turned toward them and tried to hail them. Nothing. Nobody was walkin' beside the wagons. So the wagon master sent a couple of riders to check on them."

"What did they find?" asked Michael.

"They found nothing but skeletons."

"Everyone was dead? How can that be?" demanded Michael.

"There be fevers," said Miss Kilgore. "Fevers that be killin' someone in a day or just hours."

"That's what the wagon master figured," said Braker. "Fever swept through the wagon train. I guess the man in the lead wagon was trying to get to a town when he died.

The animals just kept goin, stoppin' to eat and drinkin' ."

"No one did anything?" asked Michael. "You just left them?"

"Even redskins are smart enough to leave the ghost trains alone."

Seward got to his feet. "Some of us are going to have to stand watches."

"'Watches?" asked Michael.

"Yes, Mr. Dugan," Seward laughed. "This is not a family camp out. There are things out there we don't want in camp. If we keep the fire going we shouldn't have any problems," he said looking at Thunder Eagle.

"Two to a watch," said Braker "Keep the other company."

"And awake," said Seward. "Mr. Dugan, you won't have to stand watch."

"I will stand a watch like the rest you," stated Michael.

"I will stand a watch with him." said Thunder Eagle.

"Mr. Braker, you and I will stand the first three hours. Mr. Dugan, I will wake you in three hours. We will rotate until dawn."

"I cans stand a watch," said Obadiah.

"We women be quite capable of keepin' an eye out." Miss Kilgore stated.

"Obadiah, you and the women will take the third watch. By then it should be sun up."

"Me and Ebony can start breakfast."

"What are we looking out for?" asked Michael.

Seward looked out into the dark. "Main thing is to keep the fire going. And listen to the horses. Any trouble comes around, they will let you know."

"You will need this," Michael offered the man his father's watch.

"I am sure our Mountain Man can tell time by the stars." He put the watch in his front pocket. "Mr. Dugan, you need to get some sleep. Three hours is not very long."

Michael got under his covers and laid his head on his pillow. Not far away Thunder Eagle lay. The Indian seemed to already be asleep. Michael pulled his covers up and looked at the fire.

First Michael heard the clop of a hoof on the ground. Then the clinking of wagon tackle.

Then the creak of a wagon wheel. He raised up from his pillow to see a wagon coming toward the fire. The glow of the fire barely showed the outline of the horse pulling a wagon coming towards him. The driver's head was down as if he were sleeping. Michael could only see his broad brimmed hat. He jumped to his feet with excitement. Michael knew who it was. It was Uncle Mike! He had finally made it and followed them out here. Michael jumped a spar and waited for the wagon to get closer. It grew clearer in the dim fire light. He could see the driver's long coat. And Yes! There was the white collar. He ran up to the wagon. "Uncle Mike!" The figure kept his head down, lightly rocking with the movement of the wagon.

Michael jumped onto the wagon and grabbed the figure's knee and shook it. "UNCLE MIKE!" Michael called, shaking the knee again. The knee felt odd. Skinny. The face turned toward him. Michael saw the face was a skull with dried tight skin.

Someone grabbed his shoulder and shook it. Michael sat up. Seward was kneeling next to him, smiling. "Was Miss Kilgore right? The spooky stories give you nightmares?"

"What do you want, Mr. Seward?" asked Michael tersely.

"It is your watch."

Michael blinked and looked around. "Is Thunder Eagle awake?"

"He woke up on his own." Seward nodded toward the fire. Michael saw the Indian dropping a log on the fire. "I think he knows more about what is going on out here than we do."

Michael got up and walked over to the Indian. "How are you doing?"

Thunder Eagle looked into the dark. "I am fine."

Seward walked up to Michael. "Need to discuss a few things with you." He walked away from Thunder Eagle. Michael followed.

"What?" asked Michael hoping Thunder Eagle didn't think he was being rude.

"First you can have this back." He handed Michael his fathers' watch. "I wound it."

Braker thinks there is something out there. He says it's big and circling outside the wagons. He was drunk, and I didn't see anything."

"You said the horses would sense something first."

"Yeah, they have been quiet. Of course Braker says the Sioux are sneaking around out there too. There's something else."

"More monsters?" asked Michael.

Seward looked at Thunder Eagle still standing by the fire. "Depends on what you call a monster."

"What is it?"

"You remember Braker said he lost his squaw and the kids a couple of years ago?"

"I asked him if it was an illness."

Seward lowered his voice. "It was a really bad winter. They were snowed in. They had run out of food. So he goes out hunting. The hunting is bad because of the deep snow. When he comes back..."

Seward looked at Thunder Eagle.

"The Sioux killed his family?"

"Or."

Michael jaw dropped. "You think Mr. Braker killed his family and blames the Sioux."

"That's not the worst of it. Braker said the hunting was bad. He didn't bring anything back to eat. But he made it through the winter."

"You think he----"

"Makes up the story about the Souix killing his family until he even believes it. Just make sure Braker is out to kill buffalo tomorrow and nothing else."

"Thank you, Mr. Seward, I think."

"I would give you one of my pistols if I thought it would do any good. Probably better for me to have it."

"Better? For what?" asked Michael

"Thunder Eagle has his bow and arrow. Braker has his buffalo gun and a couple of pistols. I have the Colt and my pistols. At least we'll put up some sort of fight IF we can get enough warning."

"Warning? For what?"

"Braker believes the Sioux are going to attack tonight. He says they will kill us then take the horses and supplies."

"Thunder Eagle said if he was with us---"

"I am thinking the Sioux consider your friend a traitor. To them he is just one of us now."

"You believe the Lakota will attack us, Mr. Seward?"

"If it happens it will be probably tonight, or they'll wait until tomorrow during the hunt."

"We could all just disappear without a trace like my Uncle?"

"Both Braker and Thunder Eagle told you this was dangerous."

"A buffalo hunt. What was I thinking? I could get us all killed." Terror filled the boy's eyes.

"Hey, we are not dead yet. Keep the fire going. We may get lucky, and they may just steal the horses."

"Why would they just take the horses and not the wagons?" He looked at Seward. "If the Lakota attack they will not leave anyone alive. We have to go back."

"Back?"

Michael turned away from Seward. "Dammit! What have I done?" Tears filled his eyes. "My father was right. This is just another one of my asinine adventures. But this time Little Mikey 's little frontier adventure doesn't work out. Little Mikey Dugan gets himself killed along with his friends." He gave a sob. Michael cried, his voice becoming louder. "No one will know where we are. We will all be eaten by scavengers, and my family will never know what happened to me! My God! What the hell am I doing here? What the hell are we doing here?"

Seward turned the sobbing boy around to face him.

Seward slapped Michael. Then slapped him again harder.

Seward grabbed the front of Michael's coat and pulled his face close to his.

"Your daddy paid those people to make sure you failed those other times." Seward said in a loud angry voice he hoped the whole group could hear. "I don't know who the hell Mikey Dugan is. Mr. Michael Dugan brought us out here. Mikey Dugan decides to turn and run. Fine! At first light, if we are still alive, we can all pack up and go back to Westport. And as far as I and the rest of us are concerned Mikey Dugan can catch the first riverboat back to Boston. What he should have done in the first place!" Seward picked Michael up and threw him. Michael Dugan landed hard on his backside. His eyes narrowed as he jumped to his feet. Everyone was now watching.

Michael Dugan didn't care.

"Mr. Seward," said Michael Dugan through clenched teeth.

"What, Mikey?"

Had it been daylight Seward may have seen it coming. Mr. Michael Dugan put his full weight behind the rage driven uppercut that came up out of the dark. It hit Seward solidly under the chin, lifting him off his feet and knocking him flat on his back.

Michael stood over Seward with his fists clenched hoping — no wishing, the man would get up.

Seward rubbed his jaw to make sure it was in its socket and in one piece.

"Mr. Seward, If we are not dead tomorrow, we will be continuing this buffalo hunt."

"Yes, Mr. Dugan … sir."

Michael walked over to Thunder Eagle. "Why did he hit you?"

"I needed it."

"Why did you hit him?"

"I needed that, too."

They walked away from the fire and toward the perimeter. "Mr. Braker thinks It was my people who killed his family," said the Indian as they walked both looking out in the darkness.

"He also said your people probably killed my uncle."

The Indian shrugged. "Lakota don't attack without good reason. They would not attack a holy man traveling alone."

Michael hesitated then asked. "Will they attack us?"

Thunder Eagle laughed. "Is that what you and Seward were arguing about? That is why you became so frightened?"

"I just don't want to end up like those people from the wagons hit by that tornado," said Michael as they walked round the circle. "Lost or ending up in some unmarked grave."

They sat on one of the spars. "If you do die out here, it will be by my people."

Thunder Eagle looked into the darkness. "They are out there now. Nothing will get through."

"Your people are looking out for us?" Michael could not hide his disbelief.

"My people are looking out for me."

Michael looked out into the silent blackness. "How do you know they are out there?"

Without warning, Thunder Eagle gave a howl. One short and one long.

First there was silence. Then there were various animal noises all around. Some far away, others very close. Then quiet.

Michael thought a moment and smiled. "Yeah, let me go assure everyone, we are all perfectly safe. And when they ask why. Because we are surrounded by Sioux. The man and the Indian laughed.

They walked around the inside of the circle, every once in a while they would throw a log on the fire. Michael thought to himself. A few minutes ago he was convinced he and the others would not live to see the morning. Now? Now he felt safe. Why? Because the same people he thought would kill them were protecting them.

About an hour passed when Michael saw them again. The first time he thought it was a trick of the fire light. This time he stopped and looked into the blackness.

Thunder Eagle took an arrow out of the quiver on his back. "You see something?"

Michael started to walk again. "I thought I saw eyes."

Thunder Eagle's eyes squinted as he looked into the dark. "Man's eyes?"

"I don't know. But they were blue."

The Indian stopped. "Blue? Like yours?"

"Yes. But not as high as a man."

Thunder Eagle put his arrow on the string of his bow as they continued to walk.

"Low like a wolf?"

Before Michael could answer they came to a space between the wagons. Two bright orbs appeared in the dark in front of Michael. "There?" and they were gone.

Thunder Eagle ran ahead bringing up his arrow.

"Wait!" He grabbed the arrow, pulling it down. "What are you doing?"

"I saw it. This was a black timber wolf. It has followed the buffalo from the north. Timber wolves are very big and very bad."

"A wolf this close," asked Michael. "Why aren't the horses going crazy?"

"They should smell the wolf." Thunder Eagle looked into the direction of the horses. They were quiet.

Michael looked into the darkness and saw two bright blue dots in the darkness looking at him. His eyes adjusted. The wolf was standing as if waiting. Waiting for him. Michael eased over the spar of the wagon. Thunder Eagle brought up his arrow. Michael stepped sideways, putting himself between the Indian and the wolf. He slowly moved toward the animal. It sat.

He was half-way to the wolf when he heard Seward.

"What the HELL are you doin'?" Seward whispered loudly.

Michael turned and put his finger to his lips. "SHHHHHH!"

He turned back to see the wolf still sitting where it had been. It shifted on its paws and gave a whine of excitement. Michael brought his hands down and turned his open palms toward the wolf still slowly stepping toward it. Michael could see its massive tail flying back and forth.

Michael could not believe the size of the animal. It was bigger than any dog he had ever seen. Its head came up his chest. If the wolf attacked he wondered, between Thunder Eagle's arrows and Seward's Colt, could they kill the wolf before it tore out his throat? The thought terrified as well as excited him.

He came up to the wolf and offered his open palm. The wolf put his cold nose to it and smelled it with quick sniffs. Bending down, Michael ran his other hand over the wolf's black head and neck. He felt its massive nose sniffing, exploring, and wetly tasting his face. Then the wolf stood. Michael straightened up and looked at the wolf. Did he smell and taste good to the wolf? Is this where a monster wolf tries to kill and eat him? Should he turn and run? The wolf's mouth opened showing his teeth. It seemed to be smiling at Michael. It barked at him as if trying to say something and waited as if expecting Michael to say or do something. It barked again then turned and ran off. Michael watched the blackness swallow the wolf fighting the urge to run after it.

For a moment longer Michael looked into the darkness. He then turned and walked back to the wagons. He saw Seward and Thunder Eagle lower their weapons.

"What the hell were you thinking?" demanded Seward. "That was a Timber Wolf."

Michael turned again to look into the darkness. "It was like he was looking for me," said Michael absently. "Like he couldn't believe it was me." He smiled and looked at Seward then to Thunder Eagle. "It was like he was happy to see me."

CHAPTER VIII

Michael Dugan was not killed during the night. But he did wake to chanting and an angel. Miss Kilgore was bent over him holding a steaming tin cup of coffee. She was wearing a robe the rising sun shined through.

"Good morning, Mr. Dugan."

Michael sat up and took the cup from her. "Good morning, Miss Kilgore. You are dressed differently this morning."

She straightened, the robe forming to her shape. "I be bathin' before dawn."

"Bathing? Where?" asked Michael incredulously.

"In the stream at the bottom of the hill. There be a pool servin' me purpose."

"Miss Kilgore! There be Indians about!"

She looked down at him quizzically. "The Indians never be seein' a woman bathe before?" She turned and walked off.

In the distance Michael heard chanting. He put on his boots and followed the sound. Thunder Eagle faced the half-risen sun with his arms lifted as he chanted in Lakota.

Michael could only make out a few words. Honor. Great Spirit. Michael wondered if he was showing disrespect by listening.

Thunder Eagle stopped and looked at him.

"Good morning," said Michael.

Thunder Eagle smiled. "It is a good morning."

"Were you welcoming the sun?" asked Michael

"No, I was asking the Great Spirit to honor us with good hunting."

"I wish you would have woke me up. I would like to have chanted with you."

Thunder Eagle shook his head. "We are not allowed to teach others our songs."

"Others. White men?"

"Only those born to the Medicine Family learn sacred things. There is a long song my father sings. It ends when the sun is fully risen. My father will not teach me that song."

"Why not?"

"My father refuses to teach me anything as long as I follow the white man ways."

"You don't cause trouble. So you want to make money with your trinkets. So what?"

The Indian looked at him. "Is that piece of metal I gave you — is that a trinket?"

"The crucifix? No, that is sacred."

"To my father everything he makes is sacred. To him selling the things I make to the white man is a sacrilege."

Thunder Eagle sat down and gestured Michael to join him. "What happened last night to you was a very sacred thing," he said as Michael sat and handed the Indian the cup of coffee.

"Last night? You mean the wolf?"

Thunder Eagle took a sip of the coffee. "That was not a real wolf, Michael Dugan."

"Fur, ears, cold nose, and very big wet tongue. It was real."

Thunder Eagle shook his head. "Sometimes there is a love so strong that it is stronger than death. My father would say that your uncle's love for you was so strong it kept him here in spirit. Somehow his spirit and that wolf joined. Last night your uncle came to you to say good-bye."

"What?" The Indian offered the cup to Michael. He refused it.

"The coloring of the wolf and your uncle were the same."

Michael stood. "How do you know what my Uncle looked like? And how do you know he is dead?"

"Your uncle does not look the same as you?"

Michael realized that, to the Indian, white men, like Indians to him, all look alike. Thunder Eagle was simply assuming all Dugans had black hair and blue eyes.

"My uncle was a Catholic Priest. When Catholics die we go to Heaven, Hell, or Purgatory. All priests I am sure go directly to heaven and do not get inside a wolf just to come say good-bye to their nephews."

Thunder Eagle came to his feet and stood before Michael. "If it were a real wolf my people would have seen it. The horses would have gone crazy. And a real wolf would have killed you, or we would have killed it." He handed Michael his cup.

"You are not the only one the Great Spirit sent a messenger to last night," said Thunder Eagle walking toward the wagons. "The white buffalo came to visit me in my dream. It told me something about you"

Michael smiled. "What?"

"We must hunt today like brothers."

"No! You and Mr. Braker are the hunters. I am just here to watch."

Thunder Eagle laughed as he led Michael to the supply wagon. "We must honor the Great Spirit. We will hunt together."

"Thunder Eagle, I haven't shot a bow and arrow since I was ten. I am not going to try it today from horseback."

Thunder Eagle reached into the wagon. "Too crazy for the Crazy Boy Who Stands Out?"

"No, too stupid for the Stupid Boy Who Stands Out."

The Indian pulled something out of the wagon. It was a spear.

It was a foot taller than Michael. The shaft was wrapped with various skins and furs. It was the spear's head that caught Michael's eye. To the untrained eye it looked like it was made from a shard of black glass. But it was obsidian — a volcanic rock that ancient hunters and warriors coveted all over the world. The six-inch head had been skillfully chipped away and honed to a lethal point. Thunder Eagle offered Michael the wondrous spear.

"It is beautiful." Michael said taking it. He centered his grip on the shaft and held it over his head smiling as he looked up at it. He brought it down and offered it back to Thunder Eagle.

The Indian held up his hand. "That is yours for our hunt. You will throw from your horse."

Michael brought the spear up as if to throw it. It seemed very light. He aimed it at the ground and threw it. The dark sharp head went into the ground up to where the head met the shaft.

"You honor me to allow me to use such a spear. I ask the Great Spirit guide my hand whenever I use it."

Thunder Eagle looked at Michael surprised. "You said that in Lakota."

"I know."

Thunder Eagle and Braker agreed the camp would have to be moved off the plateau and closer to the herd. For two hours Thunder Eagle scouted ahead. Soon they turned north-west.

Thunder Eagle informed the group a small group of buffalo had separated from the main herd. The fewer the buffalo the safer they would be if there was a stampede.

By noon they came to a rise. Below them, just beyond some hills they could see the main herd. The caravan moved down the rise to the floor below. Hills rolled up around them. They started to circle up, but Braker had other ideas. "I am going to take my wagon closer to the main herd."

They kept the horses hitched and facing in opposite directions. Seward figured if there was a stampede, one of them would be facing in the right direction.

They ate lunch before the hunt.

"Miss Kilgore and I will be staying at camp with the slaves-----servants," said Seward looking at Michael. Thunder Eagle mounted and was ready to go.

"I am surprised you are not hunting," said Michael.

"No, shooting buffalo with a pistol is like shooting a grizzly, it will only make them mad.

Seward looked at Michael. "I don't suppose I can talk you out of it."

Michael looked at the spear he held. "I will try

it. If I can't do it, I will leave it to the expert," he said pointing the spear at Thunder Eagle.

They rode away from camp, heading for a hilly area to the north. They rode over two or three hills. Then they stopped at the top of one. Michael looked down on a flat valley between two steep hills that narrowed at the far end. A half dozen buffalo grazed below. A larger one grazed in the middle of the group.

"The bigger one is the older bull," said Thunder Eagle looking down at the group. "Watch out for him. It is simple," explained Thunder Eagle. "You chase from one side, I will chase them from this side. Chase them to where the valley narrows. Throw your spear at the group, hope you hit one."

"And leave the big one alone, go after the little ones." Michael said.

He turned his horse away from Thunder Eagle and moved to the other side.

All the buffalo were grazing. Except for the bull. It seemed to be watching Michael.

He took a deep breath and looked at the group below. Him, a spear, his horse, and a half dozen panicked buffalo. Was he stupid or crazy? He looked over to Thunder Eagle.

The Indian looked at him with a very serious look on his face. Michael suddenly knew this was not a game to Thunder Eagle. This was very real. The Indian nodded.

Michael kicked his horse in the ribs, and they were off galloping down the hill.

The buffalo started running, and the horse ran faster. The bull bolted to the left, crossing in front of Michael. His horse turned and gave chase. Michael was closing on the buffalo Thunder Eagle said to leave alone. The horse brought the large buffalo closer. It came along side.

The horse gave a high grunt as if to say: "What are you waiting for?"

Michael brought up the spear and threw it at the bull as hard as he could.

It hit its shoulder with a crunching thump. The animal didn't break its stride. It ran getting ahead of them. Michael saw the spear flopping around on the back of the large buffalo as he ran over the hill ahead. It seemed to Michael the spear did not stick in and was now just tangled in the buffalo's fur. Michael urged the horse to follow over the hill assuming the spear would fall off. The least he could do was retrieve Thunder Eagle's spear.

As Michael topped the hill he saw the buffalo standing at the top of the next rise. The spear hung from its side. Michael saw blood streaming down the big bull's front leg. The buffalo looked at Michael as if to say. "Look what you did." The animal turned and disappeared behind the hill. Michael dismounted. The spear looked as if it was ready to fall. He walked down the hill and up to the top of the next. Ahead was still another hill and no sign of the spear.

He looked at his horse. It stood grazing at the top of the hill behind him. He thought about going back, getting on the horse and following the bull on horseback until the spear came loose. He then looked at the hill before him. He walked down the hill and trudged up the next.

The grass was knee high and tiring to walk through.

He topped the hill. There, just at the top of the next hill was the spear. Michael ran down and then up and picked up the spear. It was wet. He dropped the spear and looked at his hand. It was covered in thick warm blood. He picked the spear back up and started down the hill, knowing he had two hills to get over before he got to the hill where he had left his horse.

Michael stopped at the bottom of the hill. He wondered if a horse was like a dog. If he called it, would it come? Michael remembered he had not named the horse. The horse would not know he was calling him.

He started toward the hill in front of him when he heard a snort from above. Michael hoped it was Thunder Eagle on his horse. He turned. At the top of the hill stood the bull buffalo with its bloody shoulder. It glared down at Michael.

"Hey!" said Michael to the wounded animal. "I got my spear, and you get to live. Let's say we are even."

The buffalo charged.

Michael ran up the hill in front of him. The buffalo had the momentum, but Michael used the spear as a staff and made the top of the hill as the bull started up. Half-way down the hill he looked at the hill ahead of him. He knew he would not reach his horse before the buffalo caught up with him. As Michael turned he saw the buffalo top the hill. Michael shoved the end of the spear in the ground. The bull buffalo bellowed as it launched itself. Michael raised the spear, aiming at where he thought/hoped the beast's heart was.

The obsidian point plunged into the animal. The human and animal screamed. Michael kept a hold of the spear as the monster was lifted off the ground. Its deafening scream was now of fear and pain.

The thrashing thing was above him as blood sprayed down on Michael. He held on to the blood soaked spear knowing either the spear would continue through the bull or the shaft would snap. Either way he would be trampled, crushed, or both.

For an eternity of two seconds the bull buffalo seem to hang above him. Then it continued over. The monster buffalo landed on its hooves, but it legs buckled. The spear stayed lodged in and it was toren out of Michael's hands. The buffalo landed on his side, its legs toward Michael.

Michael watched as the bull gave a few kicks, its eyes on him. Then it went still.

Michael was covered with blood. He got up and walked over to the dead buffalo.

He grabbed a hold of the spear, and tried to pull it out of the dead animal. The shaft was slippery with blood. After the third try it came loose. For some reason Michael thought pulling the thing out would lessen its pain.

Michael walked half-way up the hill and sat down. He looked at the dead bull buffalo — an animal that an hour ago was going about his buffalo life. Then a stupid/crazy kid from Boston decided it would be fun to go on a buffalo hunt. Now it was dead. Michael Dugan wondered what made him think killing would be fun.

He wondered what the procedure was now? What happens next? Does someone pick up the kill? Is it his kill? He didn't really hunt it. It was more or less an accident. A raven came and landed on the carcass. Ah! What did Logan say? "Let's see who the crows get to eat?"

Michael decided to leave his kill for the ravens and the vultures. He had no interest in having any reward for what he had done to this poor bull buffalo.

He stood and started toward the hill before realizing he had one more hill to get over to get to the place where is horse was waiting.

Then he heard something behind him. Voices carried on the wind. He climbed to the top of the hill. Maybe it was the Lakota hunting party.

He got to the top and looked in the direction of the voices. He saw two men on horseback close to the nearby main herd. Even from this distance he could recognize the two.

"The Devilbiss Brothers." Michael Whispered. They were looking in his direction. They both raised their pistols. Michael saw the smoke from the two firing before he heard the shots.

As one, the main herd ran from the sound and right at him. The Devil Brothers had started a stampede. Michael felt the earth shake as the brown wave topped the hill two hills away. He ran down the hill and up the next. He stopped and looked over the next hill where he had left his horse.

The horse with no name was not there.

Michael decided it was not Jarrod and Cain Devilbis's fault. The herd was avenging their brother's death.

Michael decided he would turn and take their punishment with open arms!

CHAPTER IX

Michael Dugan could hear the grunting herd top the hill behind him. He raised his arms and started to turn when a large head rose up before him. He was looking at wide dark eyes, and he felt a burst of warm damp breath from large nostrils pushing against his face.

It was his horse.

He half hugged half grabbed the horse's neck. It dragged Michael as it turned around.

The herd was half way up the hill! Michael grabbed two handfuls of the horse's coarse hair and, in one jump, mounted as the herd topped the hill behind him.

"GO! GO! GO!"

The horse did not run. It was like Michael Dugan was riding the mythical Pegasus! The horse flew down the hill. Michael saw the reins hanging loose. He dared not reach for them. There was no need to control the horse. It knew where it was going. The horse did not go up the next hill. Instead it followed the connecting gullies and soon the hills fell away.

They were heading for camp. Michael heard a loud whistle to his right. It was Thunder Eagle riding like the wind not far away. Michael saw the herd behind them. He knew he and Thunder Eagle could out-run the stampede, but not the slower wagon or carriage.

He saw the wagon and carriage ahead already moving fast. Seward was driving the wagon, and Obadiah was in the back. Miss Kilgore drove the carriage. Ebony was with her.

In the distance about a half mile ahead and to his right Michael saw Braker's wagon, and it was not moving. The Mountain Man was standing in the back and hobbling toward the driver's seat. Michael knew there was no time. He looked at Thunder Eagle and pointed to Braker. The Indian nodded and turned his horse. Braker's only hope was to jump on Thunder Eagle's horse.

It looked like Braker saw the plan. He then started waving the Indian off. As Thunder Eagle closed in on the wagon, Braker brought up his buffalo gun, aiming it at the approaching Indian.

A large buffalo rammed the back of Braker's wagon before he could fire. The Mountain Man's eyes widened as he waved his arms to regain his balance. Another buffalo hit the wagon. Braker's and Michael's eyes met as The Mountain Man fell backwards out of the wagon. The herd swallowed his wagon.

Michael tore his eyes away. Thunder Eagle turned back toward him as they neared the wagon and the carriage. Michael saw a steep hill ahead, but it was a mile off. Michael came next to the wagon as Seward whipped the horses with the reins. Both looked behind. Michael had slowed to pace the wagon and the thundering brown wave was gaining fast. Michael knew if he let his horse run it could make the hill and safety. But not the wagon or carriage. Seward shrugged.

Then came the war whoops from in front.

Michael thought, a Sioux attack during a buffalo stampede? The Great Spirit must be sleeping late.

Six Lakota riders shot right by Michael and the wagon. They expertly turned their steeds and ran along the front of the herd shooting arrows at the lead buffalo. As the animals fell it slowed the herd.

Seward and Michael looked at each other. Seward shrugged, then headed the wagon toward the hill.

Michael kicked his horse in the flank and pulled ahead. Thunder Eagle was even with him. They looked at each other, and Michael looked back at the Indians who were keeping just ahead of the herd still firing. Michael looked back at Thunder Eagle. The Indian shrugged.

Michael didn't notice his horse was slowing until he saw a buffalo coming up on his left not ten feet away. It brought its horns down and angled toward Michael's horse. Michael braced himself.

It appeared out of nowhere. A large black wolf

came running up beside the charging buffalo. The animal's horns were inches from Michael's thigh when the wolf leapt and clamped his massive teeth on the buffalo's ear. The beast gave an outraged bellow as it was dragged off.

The lighter carriage got ahead of the wagon. Michael came up beside the carriage and pointed toward the hill. Miss Kilgore nodded and gave the horse the whip.

A buffalo came up next to the slower wagon and rammed the side.

The animal put on more speed and brought his horns down, aiming at Seward's front wheel.

Seward looked on helplessly as the beast closed.

There was a hiss and a thump. Then another. Seward saw two arrows sticking out of the buffalo as it fell. Seward saw it was Thunder Eagle who felled the beast. He gave a nod of thanks.

Michael and Thunder Eagle rode next to Miss Kilgore as she drove the carriage up the hill. Seward soon followed. He came up next to the carriage, half-way up the hill. The herd charged up but slowed and finally turned back down.

When they all made the top of the hill Obadiah jumped off the wagon, ran over and took Ebony in his arms.

Michael watched as the herd went around the hill — the Indians now riding and shooting among them. Michael could see the herd stretched out in all directions. No hill like this in sight. If the hill had not been there … If the Lakota had not helped …

"What happened to you?" asked Seward jumping from the wagon.

Michael looked down at him from his horse. "Why do you ask?"

"Mr. Dugan, you are covered in blood."

Everyone was looking up at him.

"Any of it bein' yours?" asked Miss Kilgore stepping off the carriage.

Michael dismounted and looked down at himself, and saw he was covered head to toe with the blood of dead bull buffalo.

"I killed a buffalo with the spear," explained Michael matter of factly. "I got some of its blood on me."

"You killed a buffalo?" asked Thunder Eagle.

"Thunder Eagle," said Michael ignoring the remark. "I am sorry. I seem to have lost your spear. Did you get your two buffalo for your tipi?"

The group looked each other then back to Michael.

"The spear was a gift," said Thunder Eagle. "I killed three buffalo, but they were lost in the stampede."

"How far is Westport from here?" Michael asked.

"Why do you----?" Michael held his blood caked hand up to Seward.

Thunder Eagle looked at the group. "Westport is a full days ride from here."

"Could we get there before dark, if we left now?"

Thunder Eagle looked at the sun. "We would have to camp."

"What about the place we camped last night?"

"It is two hours from here."

"Thunder Eagle, you will have to get your two buffalo on your own." Michael turned to the group. "We are going back to where we camped last night," he announced. "Going on this buffalo hunt was a bad decision on my part. One of many I have made recently. First thing in the morning we are heading back to Westport. We are going home."

They all moved toward their means of travel.

"I guess your little buffalo hunt didn't turn out to be as much fun as you thought." Seward said snidely.

Michael whirled and faced Seward, fists clinched.

Seward knew Michael Dugan was deciding whether to throw a punch. Seward was deciding what he was going to do about it.

"Mr. Seward," Michael said curtly. "A man is dead because of me. I would like to get back to Westport before I get anyone else killed."

It was a long two hours, but they finally made it to the top of the plateau. With one wagon lost, the wagon and the carriage faced each other with their spars crossed.

Seward felt it was still too open, but at least they had something at their backs.

Michael took the change of clothes out of the wagon and walked down the hill to the stream. He figured if the Indians left Miss Kilgore alone, he didn't have to worry. He found the pool. He could still hear the bellow of the dying bull buffalo and could still see Braker's wide eyes looking at him as he fell out of his wagon. As Michael undressed he saw Braker's terror filled eyes and heard the sound of the screaming bull. Naked, he dove into the water, hoping the shock of cold water would purge the sight and sound out of his mind. Obadiah had given him a bar of soap. No matter how hard Michael Dugan scrubbed, he could not get the smell of blood off him.

Michael dressed as he saw the image of Braker aiming his gun at Thunder Eagle who was coming to help him. Would the man rather die than have a Sioux save his life?

Was the last thing he wanted to do was kill a member of the tribe he believed responsible for the deaths of his family?

Michael knew if he had not insisted they go on this buffalo hunt, Braker would be on his way to his cabin, and the big bull buffalo would now be proudly walking among the smaller buffalo. And if the Lakota had not shown up, if the hill had not been there, they would all have been trampled into the prairie and no one would have known. Why? Because a spoiled brat from Boston wanted to brag to his friends and family he went on a damn buffalo hunt.

He finished dressing and walked back up the hill to the camp. Obadiah met him and reached for the bloody bundle under Michael's arm. "I will get these things nice and clean when we get back, Mr. Dugan."

Michael kept the clothes away from the slave. "You will never get the smell of blood out of them, Obadiah. Burn them."

"Mr. Dugan!" chided the slave. "Don't you worry about the smell. I gots somethin' that can gets skunk out."

Michael walked past Obadiah and threw the bloody bundle into the fire. Everyone in the group noticed tears in Michael Dugan's blue eyes as they watched the clothes burn.

For the rest of the day Michael lay in his bedding, not getting up until the sun sat and the group gathered to eat.

Michael finally came and sat at the make-shift table.

"I thought we was goin' to be havin buffalo," said Obadiah as he sat the bowls in front of them. "Thunder Eagle was going to show me how the Sioux cook it."

"Your stew is fine," growled Michael.

The group looked at Michael and then Seward as Obadiah served the stew.

"So what happened out there?" asked Seward.

Michael took a roll and tore it open. "It was stupid. I was stupid."

"Crazy or stupid?' Thunder Eagle smiled, sitting across from Michael.

Michael shot a warning look at the Indian. "Stupid. I should do what I should have done in the first place, and just go home. Uncle Mike is dead, and Mr. Hopkins can have the damn house."

None of them heard what Michael had said. Their attention was on a large black wolf standing just in the fire's light looking at them.

Seward reached for the Colt, and Thunder Eagle pulled his knife.

"Nobody move!" said Michael as he calmly stoodup. "That's a friend of mine."

Michael eased himself out from behind the make-shift table and stood up not taking eyes off the wolf.

"Hey!" The wolf's tail swung back and forth as he shifted on his paws and whined.

Michael slowly walked toward it. "You lookin' for me?" He lowered his hands, and turned his palms toward the wolf. "Come 'ere!"

The wolf charged Michael. Seward drew the Colt.

It skidded to a stop and stood in front of Michael. He ran his hands over the wolf's head, ears, and back to make sure it was real.   Michael could not believe the size of the animal. Its nose came up to the middle of his chest, and the back was even with his hip.

Michael turned and started back to the group. The wolf remained where it was. Michael hoped it wouldn't run off again. The animal looked at the group.

"Come on! These are my friends!" He walked toward the group, and the wolf trotted by his side. Michael sat down, and the wolf sat next to him. Michael took a piece of meat from his bowl and offered it to he wolf. The wolf nipped his fingers as he took the morsel.

The group relaxed a bit. Thunder Eagle and Seward kept their chosen weapons at the ready. "Looks like somethin good be comin' out of this, Mr. Dugan," observed Miss Kilgore. "You got yourself a pet."

The wolf turned and looked into the dark before them and gave a deep growl.

The Indians were not there, and then they were there. Six Lakotas quietly climbed into the wagon and carriage — all were aiming arrows at the group. Seward grabbed the handle of the Colt. Every arrow aimed at him was drawn back. It was clear the Indians were quite prepared to kill them all. The wolf growled at the nearest Indian. He aimed his arrow at the wolf. Michael's eyes narrowed at the Indian as he put his arms around the wolf's neck.

"Thunder Eagle, what is going on?" demanded Michael.

"If this was an attack, we would be dead. They want to control us."

"Nobody move." Michael instructed. "Thunder Eagle, ask them what they want."

Thunder Eagle spoke in Lakota to the nearest Indian. Michael heard nothing but anger and contempt in the reply.

"He said I am a traitor to my people and to be quiet."

"Have you ever seen them do this before?" asked Michael.

Thunder Eagle nodded. "Yes, I know these men. I just do not understand what they are doing here."

Someone shouted in Lakota from the darkness.

"What now?" asked Seward.

"Someone is asking permission to join us in our camp," said Thunder Eagle.

Michael realized the Indians were here to protect someone. Whoever it was was asking to come into camp.

"Since when do Sioux ask to come into a camp?" inquired Seward in disbelief.

"Ask who it is," Michael said.

Thunder Eagle rose up on his knees and shouted into the dark. There was a pause.

Then there were responding shouts from the dark.

Thunder Eagle sank back down on his haunches, looking at the ground with fear on his face. "It's my father Fire Oak. He has come with Chases Horses."

"Thunder Eagle, who is Chases Horses?" asked Michael not really sure he wanted to hear the answer.

Thunder Eagle looked up at Michael Dugan. "My … our chief."

Michael thought a moment, took a deep breath, stood and spoke loudly into the dark. "Leader of the Great Lakota people." Michael hoped he was saying it right in Lakota. "We will be honored to have you and Medicine Man Fire Oak to join us in our humble camp."

Michael bent down. "How did that sound?"

"My Chief will be honored that you tried to speak our language. Or."

"Or?"

"Chases Horses will be insulted for your mocking him, and order these men to kill us."

Two figures walked into the light of the fire.

"Everyone look down," instructed Michael. Michael had learned in his studies with his uncle that Lakota only got a feather when they did something special. Chases Horses must of done many special things. His headdress dragged far behind him.

Chief Chases Horses spoke. Michael really wished he had learned more Lakota.

"Chases Horses is honored by your show of respect of your speaking our language. We may look up."

The two walked over to the group. The older Indian spoke as he gestured toward Michael.

"Chases Horses has come to honor the brave hunter, Crazy Boy Who Stands," said Thunder Eagle. Thunder Eagle looked at Michael. "Why is Chief Chases Horses calling you a brave hunter?"

The Chief spoke and gestured to the ground. Thunder Eagle replied and nodded.

"He wants to sit with us. Share food." The Chief spoke and gestured toward Michael.

"And he wants to know if you have shared your story of your great hunt."

Thunder Eagle answered Chief Chases Horses, talking quickly. The Chief smiled and nodded as Thunder Eagle spoke. Michael tried to get the gist of what Thunder Eagle was telling his Chief. However, the only word Michael got was humble said many times. When he gestured to the chief he heard honor. Chases Horses seemed pleased with whatever Thunder Eagle said.

"What did you tell him?" asked Michael as the group sat in a circle around the fire.

"I told him you were too humble to tell the story

of your hunt. I asked Chief Chases Horses to tell us the story. He agreed. This is a great honor for you."

Fire Oak sat next to the chief. Thunder Eagle sat next to Michael across from Chases Horses. The six protective Indians stood scowling looking down at the group.

Obadiah brought Chases Horses a plate of stew, rolls and cup of water. He set it in front of the Indian. Chases Horses smiled up at Obadiah and nodded. Obadiah smiled and nodded back.

Chases Horses began to speak, pausing only to let Thunder Eagle translate.

"If I had not seen it with my own eyes, I would not believe it. Crazy Boy Who Stands' first hunt, and he chooses the biggest buffalo in the group. From his horse he threw his spear. His lack of experience showed. He only hits the buffalo's shoulder. It ran away. Now wounded and twice as dangerous, Crazy Boy Who Stands still followed the animal on his horse. Then on foot, determined to get his kill."

"I just wanted to----" The group, including the scowling Indians, shushed Michael.

"To interrupt very disrespectful," scolded Thunder Eagle.

"He chased the dangerous wounded buffalo on foot for almost a mile. It ran from him."

"As it ran the spear stuck in its shoulder fell on the ground. As the boy picked up the spear the wounded bull buffalo attacked!   The boy cleverly retreated over a hill. Halfway down the hill, Crazy Boy made his stand.   He planted end of the spear in the ground and brought up the spear as the giant bull buffalo came over the hill.   It leapt onto the boy! Crazy Boy Who Stands stood holding the spear and drove it into the buffalo heart.   The buffalo fell dead. And then when the yellow hairs started the stampede, the boy's horse, a loyal Indian Pony, risked its own life to save its master.

"I did not want to see you killed after such bravery. I sent my hunters to save you from the stampede." Chief Chases Horses called into the dark. A rider appeared. He dragged the dead buffalo behind him. "I am honoring your bravery replacing your kill that was lost."

Tears came to Michael's eyes. "Thank you, Chief Chases Horses." Michael said in Lakota

"And the two yellow hairs who started the stampede," said the chief nodding. "I will make sure their deaths are slow and painful."

"No!" said Michael.   "We will deal with the Devilbiss brothers."

Thunder Eagle translated. The chief looked at Michael and shrugged.

"There is one thing the Chief could do for me ... us." Thunder Eagle spoke. The chief looked at Michael.

"If his people could keep watch on the camp

tonight. All of us could use a good night sleep and a safe passage tomorrow to Westport."

Thunder Eagle spoke. The Chief replied, pointing to the wolf standing at Michael's side.

"Chief Chases Horses said the Great Spirit has sent protection in the form of a wolf, you have nothing to fear from us." The six protective Indians left as quietly as they came.

Everyone was looking at Michael Dugan.

"Was all that story true?" asked Seward.

Michael looked at the group. Who was he to call a Lakota Chief a liar?

"Every word," said Michael. "God, I am tired."

CHAPTER X

True to their word, the Lakota protected the camp through the night. Everyone slept soundly. Michael Dugan should have been the warmest. The black wolf slept next to him the whole night. But when Michael woke up he felt a bit of a chill and his body ached. The sky was overcast. Michael assumed it was the lack of sun to blame for the way he felt.

Just after they finished breakfast and packed up, a cold mist blew in from the north.

"You all right?" asked Seward as they mounted their horses. "You lookin' a little pale."

"I'm fine," grumbled Michael. "It's probably all this sleeping on the ground that gave me a chill."

After they stopped for lunch at noon the cold mist turned into a light rain. Michael was not hungry and decided to ride in the wagon. He tied up his horse, climbed in, and laid down. Miss Kilgore gave the reins of the carriage to Ebony and got in to the wagon with Michael.

"You be havin' a bit of a fever, Mr. Dugan," she said feeling his face. "As soon as we be gettin' back be you needin' to go to bed."

Michael pulled his damp coat up around his neck. "First Mr. Seward and I have business in Westport."

Miss Kilgore saw Seward was listening. "What sort of business would you be havin'?"

Anger came to Michael 's eyes. "Deputy Seward and I have business with the Devilbiss brothers."

Michael smiled as he rose and saw the house in the distance. Everyone was home and safe, he thought. Just one more bit of business, and he would crawl into his big, warm, dry bed. Then a couple of days rest and he would pack and catch the next riverboat east!

"Why don't you go get in bed? Let me deal with this," said Seward as he pulled himself into his saddle.

"You are going to arrest the Devilbiss brothers. I am your witness."

The cold rain continued as they came to the Harris House. Three familiar horses were tied up in front.

"Let me handle this," said Seward as they walked into the lobby.

"Can I help you, gentleman?" asked Mr. McCoy, meeting them as they entered.

"Where are the Devilbiss brothers?" demanded Michael Dugan.

"You look ill, Mr. Dugan. Perhaps you should---"

"Where are they?" Michael roared.

McCoy looked at Seward. "I need to talk to them about an incident resulting in a death."

"You will find Mr. Hopkins and his associates in the restaurant."

Michael started ahead. Seward reached out and grabbed the young man's shoulder.

Seward turned him to face him. "What do you think you are doing?"

"We are going in there and arrest those killers!"

"I am going in there and talk to those men." explained Seward curtly. "You are only here to identify them.

"NO! I am also pressing charges!" said Michael, not looking at Seward. "They killed Mr. Braker. They tried to kill me -----you----all of us!"

"Let's go see what they have to say about that."

They walked into the restaurant and saw Jarrod and Cain Devilbiss sitting in a booth with Nick Hopkins eating dinner.

"Good evening Deputy Seward," said Hopkins.

"I need to talk to Jarrod and Cain about an incident yesterday," said Seward calmly. "A man was killed."

Hopkins picked up his napkin and wiped his mouth. "There must be some mistake," he said leaning back. "These two gentlemen have not left Westport in three days."

"That's a lie!" stated Michael. "I saw them start a stampede! They killed Mr. Braker and almost killed us all!"

Nick Hopkins showed only annoyance on his face. "Who saw them do this?"

"I did!" shouted Michael. "And Lakota Chief Chases Horses saw the whole thing! These two are under arrest for murder and attempted murder." The diners around them were now watching.

Mr. McCoy came to the table. "Is there a problem here?" he asked in a quiet voice.

Jarrod and Cain Devilbiss had not looked up from their meal and continued to eat.

"Mr. Dugan is accusing my men here of starting a stampede yesterday in which someone was killed," said Hopkins pretending surprise.

Mr. McCoy turned to Seward. "These two gentlemen have not left town in three days," he informed Seward. "They stayed here at the Harris, and I am sure Mr. Hopkins and several saloon keepers and operators of other establishments----" The three men laughed, "will attest to this."

"THEY ARE ALL LYING!" Michael screamed pointing at the three. "You killed Nathan Braker, and you tried to kill us." Michael grabbed the Colt and drew it

The three men came to their feet, reaching for their pistols. Seward grabbed Michael's wrist and pointed the gun at the ceiling. He then tore the Colt from Michael's fingers. He slapped Michael with the back of his hand, knocking him down into an empty chair.

"My apologies, gentlemen," said Seward. "The boy is out of his head with fever."

Seward grabbed the shoulder of Michael's coat and brought him to his feet. "Excuse the interruption. This boy needs to go home and get to bed."

Nick Hopkins stood and took Michael Dugan by the front of his coat, dragged him across the table, bringing Michael's face close to his. "Boy, NOBODY pulls a gun on me. The next time you pull your fancy gun on me, you are dead! I don't give a damn who your daddy is." Hopkins shoved him hard back across the table. Seward caught him. The two walked out the restaurant and into the hotel lobby.

"There are three shots left!" Michael said angrily in slurred words. "Why the hell didn't you let me use them?" Michael Dugan collapsed. Seward bent down and threw the boy over his shoulder.

"Is there anything I can do?" asked Mr. McCoy.

"Yeah, send Doc Adams out to the Dugan place."

Seward threw the limp form of Michael Dugan across the young man's horse and mounted his. He rode in the stiff rain to the house.

He took Michael off his horse. The doors opened, and Miss Kilgore and Obadiah came out.

""Is he shot?" asked the woman.

"Just damn luck he wasn't," said Seward. "He is burning up with fever."

"We needin' to be gettin' him up to his room," she said following Seward up the stairs. "We be needin' to be gettin' him out of those wet clothes."

"I'll go up and turn down the bed," said Obadiah getting ahead of them.

"I know something that will help with the fever," said Thunder Eagle.

Michael Dugan heard and saw all this through closing darkness. He felt himself being laid on a bed and the odd sensation of his clothes being removed. Then he felt the covers being pulled over him. Then there was nothing but dry warm darkness.

CHAPTER XI

Michael Dugan felt there was someone in the room. He opened his eyes a bit to see the mustached face of Dr. Adams.

The doctor stood and turned to Miss Kilgore. Michael could see that the woman's beautiful face was now tear streaked and showed only sadness and worry.

"Nothing else I can do until the fever breaks," he said to Miss Kilgore. Obadiah stood beside her listening. "Keep him comfortable, give him fluids, and try to get him to eat something."

"That's all we can be doin'?" asked Miss Kilgore with a crack in her voice.

The doctor looked at Michael and ran his finger over his face. "Pray." He closed his black bag and left the room. Obadiah and Miss Kilgore followed him out. The wolf walked up and put his nose on the bed. Michael wanted to raise his hand and rub its massive ears, but his arm seemed to weigh a ton. Just before he fell back to sleep he realized he had not named his wolf or his horse even though both had saved his life.

When he woke again Obadiah was sitting next to the bed smiling at him. He took a wooden bowl off the night stand. He dipped a spoon in the bowl and brought it to Michael's mouth. Michael swallowed the warm, thick liquid.

"That is buffalo soup!" said Obadiah filling the spoon again. "Thunder Eagle helped me make it. It supposed make you strong like an Indian." He brought the spoon to Michael's lips. Michael swallowed again.

"There you go!" Obadiah set the bowl aside. "Mr. Dugan, don't die. Me and Ebony like livin' here and workin' for you. We even liked you takin' us your buffalo hunt up until we almost got trampled to death. We don't blame you for that." The slave's face turned angry. "That was those no count, slave chasin' Devil Brothers doin' ." A smile returned to the old slave's face. "Ebony and me been prayin' every night for you, Mr. Dugan. And don't worry, we is prayin' to your Catholic god." Blackness came again.

Next time he was aware of a familiar voice in the room he lifted his eye lids a bit to see Nick Hopkins standing by his bed looking down at him. Standing on the other side of the bed was Seward.

"How long has he been like this?" asked Hopkins.

"Couple of days. He has been taking water and soup but ..."

"I already had a sealed coffin made to send him home in. I have seen this before," said Hopkins sadly. "It shouldn't be much longer. But, I guess bullet, stampede, or fever, dead is dead."

"You should read the nice letter Miss Kilgore wrote his family about what happened. She had to write the damn thing three times. Her tears kept makin' the ink run."

"His uncle and now his son. His father will probably want to forget all about Westport and this house." Hopkins laughed. "I told Doc Adams I would cover the boy's bill and a little extra if he could do somethin' to hurry things along."

"What did old Doc say?"

"He offered to bet me one hundred dollars even money the boy will pull through."

"You take that bet?"

"I sure as hell did! It'll cover the cost of the casket and sending him home. Plus a little for me for all the trouble he has caused me." Michael felt his right hip, hoping the Colt was there. Darkness came again.

Michael was aware of the smell of smoke and heard chanting in Lakota. He lifted his eye lids as far as he could. At the foot of his bed stood Chief Chases Horses. At one side of the bed stood Medicine Man Fire Oak. On the other side was Thunder Eagle. All were looking up, arms raised, and chanting. Peaceful and passage were the only words Michael recognized. He tried to smile. Getting the last rites from the Lakota. He would have a little explaining to do to St. Peter. Darkness again.

"Mr. Dugan? You still be with us?" He knew that voice. He opened his eyes as wide as he could. He saw those bright green eyes smiling into his. "So you not be passin' into the spirit world yet." Miss Kilgore wore a simple frock, and her long auburn hair hung down. A flickering candle on the nightstand gave Miss Kilgore a magical aura.

"It be Halloween, Mr. Dugan. The world of the living and the dead be very close. It be time you be makin' your trip to the other side."

She reached over his head, bringing her perfect bosoms close to his face. She brought down a clear pointed crystal on a golden string. She put the string over his head and lay the crystal over his heart. She covered the amulet with both her hands, closed her eyes, and mouthed words Michael was sure were ancient Celtic. Miss Kilgore opened her eyes and solemnly picked up a crystal goblet from the night stand. It was filled with clear ruby colored liquid.

"This will help you on your trip."

She brought the crystal goblet to his lips. Michael Dugan understood now. He was dying, and Miss Kilgore was nice enough to give him something to make his passing easier.

The last rites from a Lakota Medicine Man and a Celtic Princess.

He drank all of her potion.

She set the crystal cup aside. She leaned in and kissed him on the forehead. She started to straighten up, thought a moment, and leaned in again. Michael Dugan thought he going to die with the kiss of a Celtic Princess on his lips.

What would St. Peter say?

He was standing in a room. To his left was his father's desk bathed in lamplight.

What was he doing in his father's study? He heard someone laugh to his right. He saw someone was under the masthead of an Angel mounted on the wall. He heard the laughter again. He knew that mischievous laugh.

"Grandpa!" Michael dove onto the floor and slid on his stomach under the massive figure.

The old man held a candle and looked at Michael. "Michael! I am bein' happy to see you." Michael's grandfather had refused to give up his Irish brogue.

"Grandpa! What are you doing here?"

"Why do you think an ol' man such as myself is doin' on the floor? Admirin' art!"

Michael laughed. It was the Dugan's "Nasty" secret. The masthead of the Angel had been a woman with large bare breasts. The Angel was the ship that brought The Dugans to Boston.

His father had bought captain's desk and the masthead. He planned to put them both in his den. His mother would not permit he wooden harlot in her house. Michael's father hired a woodcarver to give the woman hands to hold the Dugan Family Crest to hide the magnificent breasts.

Michael was thirteen when his grandfather secretly introduced him to whiskey and the real

Angel. It was just as Michael remembered it. He and his grandpa smiled up at the forbidden sight of the Angel's breasts. The figure now looked like Miss Jessica Kilgore.

"Grandpa."

"A man have to be appreciatin' a fine set of---"

"Grandpa! Am I dead?"

The old man looked at the boy. "Would you wantin' to be dead?"

"Maybe I deserve to be."

His grandpa set the candle down. "Michael Dugan, Why would you be sayin' a daft thing like that?"

Michael looked down. "I did something stupid, and a man is dead because of it."

"Did you kill him?"

Michael sighed. "I made everyone go on a stupid buffalo hunt. Then someone started a stampede."

The old man's eyes widened in amazement. "Huntin' buffalo, were ya' now? Did you be gettin' one?"

"I killed one with a spear. It was an accident. It was run over in the stampede," but Chases Horses, a Lakota Chief, brought me another buffalo to honor me as a brave hunter."

The old man pulled himself out from under the masthead and stood up. Michael followed him. "This

Indian Chief be sayin' you be brave hunter? He be callin' you stupid?"

"No, my Indian name is now Crazy Boy Who Stands. But in Lakota crazy and stupid are the same word."

His grandfather put his hands on his hips and looked at Michael. "And now you be speakin' Indian and a Chief of the Lakota Tribe gave you an Indian name."

"It was the Lakota Medicine Man, Fire Oak, gave me that name. Fire Oak is the father of my friend Thunder Eagle."

The old man walked over and leaned back against the desk. "You be tryin' to tell me you be friends with the son of a Lakota Medicine man? And you killed a buffalo on a hunt? But you be losin' in a stampede. So an Indian Chief, be rewardin' you as a brave hunter, by givin' you another buffalo."

"And I have a timber wolf as a pet."

The old man stood up, folded his arms and looked down at the boy.

"Michael Dugan, you wouldn't be tellin' your old grandpa tall tales, would ya' now?"

"No, it's all true!" He looked up at this grandfather. "Grandpa, is Uncle Mike here?"

"Mike?" said the old man with annoyance. "What be he havin' to with all this?"

"He tried to cross from St. Louis to the Town of

Kansas in a covered wagon alone and is assumed lost. Is his ghost wandering the plains?"

The man walked over to Michael. "Your Uncle Mike is where he needs to be. You need to be decidin' where you need to be."

"Grandpa, what should I do?" pleaded Michael.

"What did you name your wolf?"

"I haven't named him yet."

"Everyone be knowin' the first thing you should be doin' when you be findin' a pet is name it."

"He found me."

The old man looked at Michael, thinking. "Damien. You should name your wolf Damien."

"That's Uncle Mike's middle name. Thunder Eagle said the wolf is … "

"Damien is a good name for a wolf." The old man turned and walked toward the darkness. "You wanted me to tell you what you should do. I did. You should name your wolf Damien. "

"Tell me what I am supposed to do!"

"Die, don't die. Grow up or be runnin' back home to your mother and father. It is all up to you now."

Darkness swallowed the old man.

"Grandpa, wait!" He reached out and tried to take a step to follow. Something had a hold of his legs.

He fell forward and landed on the floor and his legs were tangled in the sheet on the bed.

Then hands were pressing down on his shoulders.

No. They were paws! A big cold nose sniffed his face. Then came the monster wet tongue. As Michael laughed the tongue went in his mouth. "Damien! Stop it!" The licking stopped. "Now, get off." The wolf obeyed. Michael kicked himself free of the bedding. He planted his hands on the bed and pushed himself up to his feet. Michael had never felt so weak. Leaning on the bed, he made his way close to the door.

He flung himself at the doorknob. He caught it, barely standing. He opened the door, and the wolf went out. He got on his knees and crawled to the banister. He pulled himself up.

He steadied himself. He heard voices coming from the dining room. He also smelled food. Michael realized he was weak from hunger. He unsteadily made his way down the stairs using the bannister. The wolf went ahead of him.

"Whose turn is it to feed this animal?" Michael heard Seward ask.

"I am tired of cleaning up after that thing," complained Obadiah. "After Master Dugan is dead I gonna' shoot the wolf myself."

"He be probably leavin' when Mr. Dugan passes," said Miss Kilgore in resignation.

"My wolf's name is Damien, and nobody is

going to shoot him." said Michael leaning against the doorjam focusing only on the table of food. "And for now Damien and I are not going anywhere." Michael dropped into a chair, grabbed a roll, and bit into it.

There was stunned silence, but also cheers of joy.

"Mr. Dugan, you look like death warmed over," said Seward.

Obadiah placed a platter in front of him stacked with dripping slabs of buffalo steaks.

Michael took the top one in both hands and bit into it.   After he swallowed he did it again. He finished the steak then sat back. Ebony brought him a glass of milk. He drained it.

"Happy Halloween, Mr. Dugan," said Miss Kilgore.

"What are your plans now?" asked Seward

"First, I have decided not to die," announced Michael. He looked at the group, knowing what they wanted to know. The wolf put his nose in Michael's lap.

Michael petted Damien and scratched his ears. "I plan to eat and then go back to bed."

"What bein' your plans after that?" asked Miss Kilgore. "I seemed to be rememberin' you be sayin' something about goin' home."

The wolf looked up at Michael with sad blue eyes and whined. Michael smiled down at his wolf. "Miss Kilgore, for now, I am home."

CHAPTER XII

Michael Dugan pictured wintering in Westport would be cold and boring. He realized that if he was staying in the house alone it may have been just that. But he was not alone.

His constant companion was Damien his wolf. Much to everyone's relief, Michael had gotten Damien house trained. Whenever the wolf wanted out he would take Michael's arm firmly in his mouth and bring him to the front door. This was annoying when Michael was trying to work. But in the middle of the night? Fortunately, this did not happen that often.

He named his horse Dollar, because that is what he paid for it. During the winter his repair business was slow but steady, as was Miss Kilgore's. Seward agreed to pay half his deputy pay for renting the room. Obadiah made agreements with various farmers to supply all the meats they required. When anyone went into town they never went alone.

The residents of Westport quietly disapproved of the living arrangements at the house.

Obadiah and Ebony lived in the servants'

quarters. Thunder Eagle had rebuilt his tipi. Michael would visit him. A few times on very cold nights Michael would sleep in the tipi, so Thunder Eagle could show him how warm it was. And when he escorted Miss Kilgore to town they seemed invisible. But the people were friendly enough when it came to Miss Kilgore's services.

The obvious thing was not happening. Nick Hopkins and the Devilbiss brothers continued to keep their distance. Michael assumed it was because they had a deputy as escort and boarder.

It was a mild fall. For Thanksgiving they set up a table outside. All the people who attended the Sunday meeting were invited. Indians, slaves, and their children came. Michael, Miss Kilgore, and Seward were the only white people to attend.

The Sunday meetings went on. The group preferred the Old Testament. Everyone liked the battles, vengeful God, and the miracles. There was too much talking in the New Testament. There were a couple of times issues came up in which Michael struggled for answers.

There was an awkward question regarding Jesus and Satan in the desert.

"Why didn't Jesus kill the evil one right there?" asked Thunder Eagle.

"What?" asked Michael.

"It was only the two of them out in the dessert." stated the Indian. "Jesus had the power of his father.

Why not kill him? No one would know, and there would be no more evil."

They all nodded and looked to Michael for an answer.

Michael recalled the incident with Mr. Hopkins and the Devilbiss Brothers. Why did the amoral hired gun stop him from killing those evil men?

"Because," Seward spoke up, "Satan was not threatening Jesus," he said looking at Michael. "Killing Satan would be murder." Michael turned away not wanting to meet Seward's accusing look. "And Jesus is not a murderer."

The question of conversion came up more than once. One time the standard answer did not seem to apply:

"My father, Fire Oak, would like to know." said Thunder Eagle. "What if the Lakota learn about your Jesus and, like the Lakota belief in the Great Spirit better?

Michael saw Miss Kilgore standing off to one side. She crossed her arms, raised an eyebrow, and waited for an answer.

"The priest will be able to explain better than me. You will all want to convert."

"Like the Celts be wantin' to convert in Ireland?" inquired Miss Kilgore.

"Exactly! It will be just like St. Patrick. He came and told the Pagans ..."

"Celts!" corrected Miss Kilgore.

"Celts about Jesus and they all converted," said Michael wanting to change the subject. "It was known as the Bloodless Conversion."

"Then you be knowin' the legend of your St. Paddy, do ya' Mr. Dugan?" asked Miss Kilgore.

"The story is not in the Bible. But St. Patrick did drive the snakes out of Ireland."

"Mr. Dugan, surely you not be teachin' these people that fairy tale!" said Miss Kilgore. "There never be any snakes in Ireland," stated Miss Kilgore. "They be talkin' about your people drivin' the Celts out of Ireland!"

Michael had heard that somewhere before. Would the Lakota be like the Celts, Michael wondered? But that was fifteen hundred years ago during the Dark Ages. Michael was sure such a thing would never happen to the Lakota or any of the other Indians.

"Here is what I believe," said Michael. "This is a very big country. Much bigger than Ireland." he said looking at Miss Kilgore. "We have Freedom of Religion in our Constitution. I am sure if any of the Indians wish to keep their beliefs, they will be able to."

"You promise, Crazy Boy Who Stands?" asked Thunder Eagle.

"Yes," said Michael in Lakota "I believe I can promise that."

Miss Kilgore turned and walked back to her parlor in a huff.

Like Boston, after Thanksgiving the weather turned colder. When it snowed Damien would bring Michael out to play in the snow.

It took two weeks, but Michael finally found the perfect Christmas tree. They cut it down and hauled it back in the wagon. It was put up in the corner of the living room. The Sunday group made ornaments by hand. Candles lit every branch. There were mixtures of Lakota, Christian, and Celt decorations throughout the house.

As Christmas neared Michael began to feel like he was a child at home. Everyone seemed to be sneaking around. Talking in hushed tones, and stopping when he came in the room.

Whatever it was, Thunder Eagle and Seward swore they knew nothing about it.

Seward escorted Michael to town to do his Christmas shopping. He bought practical gifts for everyone. He had held back a clock for Miss Kilgore. It played Mozart, her favorite composer, at the top of the hour.

Christmas Eve they had a special meeting of the Sunday group. They ate dinner and afterwards exchanged presents. They gave Michael some wool long johns. Damien the wolf got a big buffalo bone. The group listened as Michael read the Nativity from Luke as Thunder Eagle translated. Then they sang Christmas Carols.

Finally everyone left, and Michael walked up the stairs and went to his room. He undressed, put on his nightshirt, and got into bed. As usual Damien jumped in beside him and laid his nose on Michael's stomach. He scratched the wolf's massive ears. He then turned over and felt Damien put his large paw on his shoulder. He slept.

Before Michael could open his eyes he felt Damien squirm his body around and looked at the door. Michael knew someone was coming up the stairs. There was a knock at the door.

Michael raised himself up on his elbows. "Come in."

Obadiah opened the door. "Merry Christmas, Mr. Dugan," the slave said with a grin.

"Merry Christmas, Obadiah."

"Better get dressed." Obadiah was positively beaming. "Breakfast is ready, and Santa Claus done come and brought you somethin'."

Michael dressed and came downstairs. The tree glowed in candle light and presents were under the tree. At home Michael's father would insist they open presents between breakfast and morning mass. Michael decided that last night's meeting would pass for midnight mass, and he was too excited eat.

Chairs were taken from the dining room and placed facing the tree. Then presents were handed out. Miss Kilgore loved her clock. Everyone oohed and ahhed over Michael's unimaginative gifts. After all the presents had been opened, Michael Dugan had not received a single one.

"Now bein' your turn, Mr. Dugan," said Miss Kilgore nodding to Obadiah.

Ebony went into Miss Kilgore's parlor and brought out a large beautiful box. On it was a pretty envelope with a snowflake painted on it. "To Mr. Dugan," was written in fine script on the envelope. Ebony smiled. "Mr. Dugan, I did the snowflake," she whispered to Michael as she gave him the box.

"Thank you, Ebony," Michael said smiling at the girl. "It is very pretty," he said setting the box on his lap.

"Be readin' the card," urged Miss Kilgore with excitement.

Michael opened the ornate envelope and pulled out the card. "To a great boss and landlord," he read aloud. "But a really bad buffalo hunter." The group ahhed as Michael laughed and tried to blink back his tears.

"Open the damn thing." Seward said in frustration.

Michael lifted the lid. In the box was a dark brown coat made of, what he thought, was cowhide. He lifted it out of the box. It had tassels running down the side of each arm. He turned it around and saw the tassels along the shoulders. On the back was a figure of a man standing. Before him stood a buffalo on its hind legs. The beast was three times the size the man.

The man was impaling the buffalo with a spear.

"That was made from the buffalo Chief Chases Horses gave you." Thunder Eagle said with reverence. Michael could tell that others besides Thunder Eagle had a hand in making the magnificent coat.

Michael pursed his lips as the tears flowed. "Thank you all." He looked at Thunder Eagle who was smiling. "Tell Chief Chases Horses I said thank you." Michael said in Lakota.

"Be stoppin' showin' off your Indian talk and be tryin' the coat on!" Miss Kilgore insisted. Michael got to his feet and pulled on the coat. "We be havin' to use your coat for the size. I be hopin' it fits."

It fit perfectly.

"That ain't all," said Obadiah as he reached into the box. The slave pulled out something long also made of buffalo skin. It had intricate beaded patterns sewn to it. Seward reached behind the tree and brought out a large and familiar rifle. He offered it to Michael.

Michael's blue eyes widened. "That is Mr. Braker's buffalo gun," he said taking it from Seward.

"Thunder Eagle and Obadiah went out on their own and found the damn thing," said Seward.

Obadiah handed him the strange long object. "This goes over it."

Michael found the open end of the sheath and slid the barrel in.

"There you go," said Seward. "You have your buffalo skin coat and buffalo gun.

You will look like the proper frontiersman when you go home to Boston."

When I go home, thought Michael. The whole scene turned into a watery blur as tears again overflowed his eyes and ran down his face. "Dammit!" he said as he tried to wipe the tears away with his hands. Michael sat the gun against the wall and took off the coat and hung it carefully on a chair. "Merry Christmas, and may the Great Spirit bless us, everyone! Let's eat!"

A week later Seward went out and rang in 1846. Michael stayed in. In bed Michael Dugan lay listening to the louder than normal parties going on in Westport. Michael did not feel homesick. Actually, he wished his family and friends from Boston would have come to this place for a holiday party and dinner.

He and Miss Kilgore would be host and hostess. He would introduce his new friends.

Oh! If only Fire Oak and Chief Chases Horses could come. Yes! A real Lakota Chief and a Medicine Man! Why yes, that is a real wolf. His name is Damien. Why yes it is my late uncle's middle name, and no my grandfather said I should name it that. Will, you have to meet Miss Jessica Kilgore. Miss Kilgore, you see, is a Celtic Princess. She gave me a potion. I don't know what was in it, but I found myself in the Spirit World talking to my dead grandfather. Michael would bring them out in the cold to demonstrate his new found skill of riding a horse bareback! Oh, in the frontier you don't pick your pets, the pets pick you! Have you met Deputy Seward? Yes, I hired him as my protector. Saved my life more times than I can count. Then they would sit down for dinner, and Michael would regale the group with tales of Indians, gun fights, and buffalo hunts.

Of course, after dinner, his father would quietly take him into the study. First, his father would not approve of what Michael had done to the study. He would ask how dare Michael lie about Uncle Mike. He would tell Michael he should have gotten whatever he could for the house and come home. Instead he wasted half a year in godforsaken Westport.

Well, he did stay. He stayed and did all those things. He was happy, and he was proud.

Yes! Proud of what he had done here. And he would tell his father just that when he returned home in the spring. Yes! There were many things he had to discuss with his father.

Then what? He would go to business college. Then he would become head of Dugan Manufacturing.

He would have to hide his buffalo gun in the back of a closet. He would hang his buffalo hunting coat there too. In the back closet in the house he and Jane would move into after they were married. At the formal company and family parties he would tell of his trip to the frontier. People would to listen politely.

He would leave out the scary parts. He would have children then grandchildren. All wanting to hear how much fun it had been to live on the frontier. Did you kill any bad men? Did you fight Indians?

But all that started when he went back to Boston. He had months before he had to concern himself with that. Three months. It was about midnight January first. Exactly three months from the next morning he would be boarding the Riverboat Chariot and heading east. Back to his father's house. But he assured himself, as he scratched his wolf's ears, that was all a long time off. He turned on his side. Damien put his paw on his shoulder and gave a deep sigh. Three months is a very long time.

No, it wasn't. Before Michael knew it the snow was coming less. Then it was gone.

Then it was March. Then it was the last day of March. Everyone would be moving out after he left the next day. Michael was finishing up some work. Mr. Ewing assured him he would bring the repair shop back to his store after Michael was gone. Obadiah said he would get the study like he was never here. All would be as it was. Miss Kilgore arranged to have her things brought to the Chariot. Before that she would drive Michael in the carriage, making sure he was safely on board. He was leaving the house to Hopkins. His father would take issue with giving the house away. Michael had more important issues to take up with his father when he got home. Michael and Miss Kilgore would have a long farewell on their way back to St. Louis where they would part ways. He knew it was very unlikely he would see Miss Jessica Kilgore again. Obadiah and Ebony would move back to the barn. Seward was the only one not moving out.

Everyone decided to stay in the house on the last night. They had their last dinner together. It was a quiet meal.

That night Michael came knocking on Seward's door. "Mr. Dugan," he said opening the door. "Is there a problem?

"No, but there is one thing I have yet to do, Mr. Seward," said Michael with a wry smile. "I would like to take you out for a drink."

Seward leaned against the door jam. "Well, Mr. Dugan, I don't go out for a drink I have drinks and get drunk," explained Seward. "And most of the time I end up in a fight or with a woman."

"Sometimes more than one woman if I remember correctly," said Michael. "If we go out, no guns, no women."

"I can't bring the Colt for old time sake?"

Michael went into Seward's room and found the Colt still in the holster. He picked it up and stood in front of Seward holding up the gun and holster. "I am going to be wearing this damn thing when I get home. I will be handing it to my father and tell him It was exactly as I said. I had no use for it!" Michael opened the door to his room, and threw the gun onto his bed.

"What about when he notices those used three shoots?"

"I will honestly say I did not use the gun," stated Michael. "My last night in Westport I want to get drunk in one of your frontier saloons. We are celebrating me leaving without me or anyone else getting killed.

"You buyin', Mr. Dugan?"

"I am buyin', Mr. Seward."

"Ya know, Crazy/Stupid Boy Who Stands," Seward said closing his door. "This is either the best or worst idea you have had since I have known you. I know just the place!"

They walked past several establishments Michael felt were suitable. Seward explained they were too expensive, bad booze, in one a woman swore she would shoot him if he ever came back.

Finally, Seward stopped in front of a pair of swinging doors. He smiled and nodded at Michael. "Mr. Dugan," he pointed into the loud, smoke filled place. "This is the place."

They pushed open the door and were greeted by howls of welcome.

A scantily clad barmaid met them as they came in the door. "Deputy Mike Seward. Where the helL have you been?" She gave Michael Dugan the once over. "And who is this fine lookin' young man?"

"Delila, honey, it is Mr. Seward tonight. This is my soon to be former boss, Mr. Michael Dugan. We are here to celebrate."

"What is the occasion?" she said moving up the bar toward Michael.

"Mr. Dugan is leaving tomorrow, and he is not dead," said Seward. "We will be needing a table for two."

She narrowed her eyes accusingly at Seward. "You got any money?"

"I do," said Michael. "And I am buying."

Delila looked at a brute not far away. "Payin' party of two!" she yelled at him.

The large man walked over to a nearby table. The two men seated at the table looked up at the hulk. The giant folded his arms. The men's eyes grew big, and the two stood up and backed away.

"Gentleman, we just had a table open up."

They sat down. "What will you have?" asked Delila, leaning over the table, giving Michael a view of her bosoms.

"Irish whiskey, please," Michael said.

Delila cocked her head at him. "We got whiskey. I am not sure what country it is from."

"A bottle of your best and two glasses," said Seward.

The woman smiled over at Seward. "You gentleman want some company tonight?" asked the woman. "The Sapphire triplets are available."

Seward raised his eyebrows and smiled over at Michael. Michael shook his head.

Seward gave a disappointed sigh. "We won't be needing company tonight."

She looked at Michael and licked her lips. "Maybe you and me could ... "

"No! Thank you Miss Delila," said Michael.

"Maybe after you get some whiskey in ya' you will change your mind," she said giving him one last look.

Delila returned with a bottle and two glasses. Michael put a twenty-dollar gold piece on the table. "Let me know when that runs out." Delila gave Michael a positively ravenous smile as she picked up the coin.

Seward uncorked the bottle and filled the glasses. They picked up the glasses.

"What do we drink to?" asked Seward.

"To my future boring life." They touched their glasses, and gulped their drinks down.

Seward filled the glasses again. They drank. And again.

"I thought you said you didn't drink," said Seward over the noise.

"I said I did not drink. I didn't say I had not drank before."

"I have been reading your Shakespeare," said Seward filling the glasses

"To Shakespeare!" Michael said raising his glass. They toasted and drank.

"He was my uncle's favorite." Michael filled their glasses.

"You remind me a little of Hamlet." Seward drained his glass. "But you ain't him."

"I don't get your meaning." Michael gulped.

"You know. That to be or not to be stuff."

"To be or not to be," recited Michael filling their glasses. "Whether to suffer the slings and arrows of outrageous fortune." They drank.

"Yeah!" said Seward snatching the bottle away from Michael. "Outrageous Fortune!" He filled the glasses. "After a little of that outrageous fortune on your buffalo hunt." He swigged his drink down. "You were ready to go running home to Mommy and Daddy."

Michael glared across the table as he emptied his glass. "I got a man killed and almost all of us with him."

"You didn't start that stampede. You were just using that as an excuse to hide out all winter and wait for spring to run home."

"We are supposed to be celebrating."

"People celebrate when they do something. You have not done anything."

Michael leaned in toward Seward. "That's not true."

Seward leaned in, bringing his face to Michael's. "One month from now no one will know you were even here. Nick Hopkins will be living in that house you are giving him. Obadiah goes back to sleeping in the barn where slaves belong. Hopkins will probably sell Ebony. And as for your Miss Jessica Kilgore, she will be back in St. Louis preparing for her annual spring trip on the Riverboat Sultana down to New Orleans. What will she say about Mr. Michael Dugan? He was the perfect gentleman, but boring." Seward leaned back in his chair and laughed.

"I killed a buffalo!" Michael said loudly.

"You yourself said that was an accident. And what about daddy's gun? Someone else had to shoot that for you." Seward's tone turned angry. "Because you were too afraid."

"If I knew what was goin on—"

"If you saw Nick Hopkins and his men drawing down on you." Seward laughed and shook his head a he filled his glass. "The only different thing you would have done was mess your pants, and I would still have to do the shootin'. You were a scared little boy then, and you are a scared little boy now. A little outrageous fortune and you are ready to run home to mommy and daddy."

Michael jumped up, knocking his chair over as he did. He walked around the table to stand over Seward. He looked down at the man, his eyes narrowed. "Mr. Seward, shut up."

Seward finished what was left in the bottle then came to his feet. "Or what . . .Boy?"

Seward was barely aware of Michael's lightning fast upper cut. The force knocked him back onto a table behind him.

Someone grabbed Michael's shoulder and turned him around. He saw a fist flying toward his face. He blocked the punch with his left, and slammed his fist into his attacker's face, knocking him out.

Michael is put in a bear hug from behind. Two men came at him fists raised. Michael raised his feet and planted them in the pair's chests, pushing them backwards onto a table. The table tilted backwards and fell. Michael broke the hold on him. He turned and punched the man in the stomach and then an upper cut sent him falling into the crowd. Everyone was suddenly fighting. Michael put his back to the bar. Someone lunged at him. He side-stepped him, and the man fell across the bar. Michael grabbed his belt and shirt and threw him the rest of the way over. The man's boots smashed into the glass shelf holding some bottles, bringing it all down with a loud crash.

Michael saw Seward with assailants coming from all directions. Michael put up his dukes and made his way over to Seward. By the time he got there Seward had already dealt with his attackers and was taking on more.

Michael and Seward stood shoulder to shoulder. "I don't recall a saloon fight on your agenda for this evening." Seward blocked a punch and threw another.

Michael hit an attacker with a right cross, and he

dropped to the floor. "You seem very good at this sort of thing, Mr. Seward." Michael said giving three fast jabs to a man's face.

"You are not so bad yourself, Mr. Dugan."

"Boxing Champion, St. Mary's High School." He said bringing his foot up between an attacker's leg, then punching him in he face. "Three years in a row."

Seward looked across the room. Delila was glaring at them. Behind her was the brute that got them their table. She pointed at them. The large man started toward them, throwing people out of his way.

"I think our maître d' would like to discuss our bill," observed Michael.

"So I see, let's get out of here!" Seward said nodding toward the exit behind them.

The large brute was reaching for them as they reached the exit. They ran.

Half-way to the house they stopped.

"Why are we running?" asked Michael. "You're the deputy."

"You wouldn't let me bring the Colt."

They walked home. Michael was feeling good. Whatever they were drinking must have been watered down. He was not as drunk as he wanted to be. Damien followed him up to his room. He saw a light under Miss Kilgore's door. He went into his room, got undressed and put on his night shirt. He sat on the bed, and Damien jumped up and sat next to him. He stood and walked to his door and opened it a crack. The light still shone under Miss Kilgore's door. He opened his door, went out, and closed it to keep the wolf inside.

He walked up to Miss Kilgore's door. He willed himself to knock on the door. His hand remained at his side. He sighed and started to turn away when the door opened.

"Good evening, Mr. Dugan." Miss Kilgore stood in a very sheer nightgown. The many candles lighting her room showed she wore nothing under the gown.

"Miss Kilgore, there is something I have been meaning to ask you to do for me since we met."

"And what bein' that, Mr. Dugan?" she asked looking coy.

"I would like you to tell my fortune."

A genuine look of surprise came over Miss Kilgore's face. "No! I am sorry. It is late. You are dressed for bed, as I am.

"Mr. Seward and I went out. We were drinking and …"

Miss Kilgore took his hand. "Mr. Dugan, I be thinkin' you would never be askin' ."

She led him into the room and shut the door. She motioned to the overstuffed chair. Michael sat. In front of him was a square antique table. Miss Kilgore took her seat across from Michael. He noticed the two top ties on her night gown were undone. He seriously considered pointing it out to her.

She reached up to a shelf and brought down a wooden box and set it on the table. The box was very old and carved with intricate symbols. She opened the box and took out a deck of cards and set them on the table. The cards looked very old. She set the box aside, and picked up the cards. She smiled as she went through them. Then she looked at Michael, and took a card from the deck, and set it in the center of the table.

"The Knight of Wands," she said.

"I know nothing about these cards." explained Michael. "What does that mean?"

"That, Mr. Dugan, be you. It is a skilled young man of strong mind and body who be goin' on a trip or is on one."

"That fits me, I guess." She placed the cards in front of him. "What do I do?"

"Shuffle the cards, please."

Michael cut the deck into two stacks. When he tried to merge the two stacks of cards they flew all over the table. Michael gave a nervous laugh. "I don't play cards." He started to pick up the cards.

"Mr. Dugan," Miss Kilgore reached across the table and covered the young man's hands with hers. "If doin' this be makin' you uncomfortable we can be stoppin'."

He looked into those green eyes shimmering in the candle light. "No," he assured her.

"It is just … I have never done anything like this before." She smiled and leaned back in her chair as he put the cards back in together.

He tried to shuffle again, and this time the cards went together smoothly.

"When do I stop?"

"When the cards feel right."

One more shuffle and he set the deck on the table. His heart was racing as his breath deepened. Michael could not remember when he was so excited. Miss Kilgore's elegant hands picked up the cards. Taking the card from the top, she placed it face down on the Knight of Wands. The next card she lay side ways face up across the two cards.

"The Page Of Cups," she said. "See how the fish is coming out of the cup?"

"Yes."

"The boy here be raisin' that fish in that cup but now the fish be ready to be getting' out of that little cup."

"I see water behind him," observed Michael.

"That be the sea. But he be not wantin' to lose his fish to the unknown dangers of the big dark sea. This be an uncertain time for the boy and his beloved fish."

Michael nodded as she put down four more cards — one at the bottom of the three cards, one to the left, one above, and one to the right, forming a cross. All were laid face down.

"When do I get to see the cards?" Michael said with childlike excitement.

A knowing smile came to Miss Kilgore's lips. "Patience, Mr. Dugan," she said laying a card close to her right. She laid another above it and made a line of four cards up the side of the cross. All these cards she laid were also face down.

She picked up the Page of Cups and set it at the top left corner of the table.

"The child needin' to make a decision."

Michael watched as she turned the card over that lay on the card she said represented him.

"The Ten of Cups."

Michael saw ten glowing cups in the arch of a rainbow and under the arch there was man and woman with children nearby. All seemed very happy.

"This be the happily ever after card." She turned the card just below it. "The Seven of Cups."

Michael saw a figure looking at cups on a shelf. Each cup contained different things. Some things were beautiful, others not.

"This card be meanin' be makin' the choices that best for you. You be havin' to be decidin' what will be makin' you happy, Mr. Dugan."

She turned the card to her left. "The card of the past. The King of Wands upside down."

"What do they mean when they are upside down?"

"It mean they be against you and be havin' none of your best interest."

Michael remembered the letter from his father to Uncle Mike. "I know who that is."

She turned the card at the top of the cross. "The King of Pentacles, upside down.

This bein' a man whose only interest be money and power."

"That's my father too. The company always comes first. To hell with what anyone else wants to do."

She turned the last card of the cross. "The future."

"The King of Swords, and it's upside down too," observed Michael.

"He be an evil powerful man; he be takin' whatever he wants."

"That is Nick Hopkins. Why is he in my future? I am leaving him the house. He doesn't have to take it."

She turned the bottom card of the four in the line on her right. "The Knight of Pentacles."

"At least he is right side up."

Miss Kilgore gave a sigh of relief. "This be a very smart young man. He be doin' what he is supposed to be doin'."

"Boring." Michael smiled and pointed to the card. "That is me from now on!"

She turned the card above the Knight of Pentacles. "The Fool upside down."

"It's a man walking off a cliff." Michael said looking at the card. "But it's upside down. That means he is not going to walk off that cliff, right?"

"No, Mr. Dugan. That be meanin' he be doin' somethin' very stupid."

"But you said the Knight of Pentacles always does what he is supposed to do. Why would he do something stupid? It doesn't make sense."

She turned the second card to last. She gasped. "The Tower."

Michael didn't have to be told what the card meant. It showed lightening striking a tower with two figures on fire falling from it.

"This be a very public defeat," she said quietly without looking up.

They both looked at the last card as she reached for it. Michael covered her hand.

She looked up at him. Michael saw worry and sadness in those green eyes. "What does this card mean?"

"It be the final outcome."

He slowly removed his hand.

Miss Kilgore turned over the last card.

"Death."

Michael stood. "I am going to face an evil man

in public and do something very stupid and people are going to die."

"Sometimes the Death card not be meanin' a physical death. It may just mean a transition. Your whole time in Westport has been …"

"A mistake. Stupid/Crazy Boy Who Stands is not going to do anything crazy or stupid ever again. I plan to get up very early tomorrow morning and make sure I am on board the Chariot before Nick Hopkins and his men know I am gone. I am going to be that smart boring knight and do what I should have done in the first place. I am going home."

Miss Kilgore stood and walked over and sat on her bed. She motioned Michael to join her.

Michael looked at the door and then looked back at Miss Kilgore sitting on her bed in a nightgown looking at him. He knew what he should do. The boring knight would go back to his room. He thought about doing that for all of two seconds. He sat with Miss Kilgore.

She took his hand. "Mr. Dugan, I would be likin' to be askin' you a very personal question, and I be wantin' the truth."

"Of course Miss Kilgore. Anything."

She slid closer to him. "What bein' the real reason you be decidin' you may be wantin' to become a priest?"

Michael looked down. "I will tell you, but you cannot tell anyone."

She made a cross with her dainty finger over her heart. "I be promisn'."

Michael took a deep breath. "Jane is my more or less fiancé. We have known each other since we were children-----very young. We decided that we should try … making love."

Miss Kilgore bent her head down, trying not to laugh. It had been so long since she had seen a man blush. "I see," she said.

"Jane liked reading those novels of romance, and she said they made it sound so wonderful."

"I be familiar with those sort of … books," she said.

"I also had read books. The sort of books my parents would not approve of."

Miss Kilgore turned away again, wishing Michael Dugan would stop blushing!

"I have heard of such … books."

"Believe me, Miss Kilgore, the only reason I read all those books is for research. To get the basic idea to know what one should and should not do."

Miss Kilgore cleared her throat. "Of course, Mr. Dugan, there is no other reason you would be reading all those … books but for research," she said trying to keep a straight face.

"Exactly! But in all those books everything seemed to come so natural." explained Michael. "Even for people who have never done it before."

"So you and … Jane attempted … "

"To make love."

"And it was not … successful?'

"Oh, Miss Kilgore, it was horrible," stated Michael. "We tried for an hour."

"If nothing else, Mr. Dugan, you were … persistent."

"I knew priests don't have to ... you know. Uncle Mike seemed to be perfectly happy and he is not doing it."

She moved closer the Michael. "Mr. Dugan, I be findin', as in many pursuits, that books can be takin' you so far. Sometimes be takin' an experienced instructor to take you the rest of the way." She looked into Michael Dugan's wide blue eyes. "I am not be sayin' I have that much experience, but perhaps I can be showin' you what you be doin' wrong, so when you return home you can—"

"Miss Kilgore anything you----" She pressed her lips to his as she undid the ties of his nightshirt. Their kiss deepened as he pulled his night shirt down to his waist.

She then got off the bed and stood before Michael, the candles created an aura around her perfect form. She undid the ties to her nightgown, and it fell open. Michael reached up and pulled lightly on the nightgown. Miss Kilgore let it fall. She reached down and pulled the nightshirt down over his legs and threw it on the floor. She brought her lips to his. Their kiss deepened. She brought him down on top of her.

Miss Kilgore was a fine teacher. It helped that the young man proved to be an enthusiastic and naturally gifted student. If there was one word to describe Michael Dugan that night it would be proficient.

CHAPTER XIII

Michael Dugan lay naked on his back in Miss Jessica Kilgore's bed. He looked across the room at the door Miss Kilgore had left an eternity of a few minutes ago. He also saw his traveling clothes laying over the back of the chair he had sat in to have has fortune told the night before. Of all last night, Michael remembered the least his fortune being told.

The door opened, and Miss Kilgore entered wearing only a robe.   She carried a large tray with breakfast on it. She set it on the table she had read his cards on last night.

Miss Kilgore stood at the foot of the bed. She untied her robe, opened it, and eased her form onto Michael Dugan.   Her actions had the effect she wanted. He took her in his arms, and their lips met as she eased Michael Dugan into her.

He smiled looking up at her. "Our breakfast will get cold," he said kissing her shoulder.

"Let it." she said huskily as she started moving up and down.

Miss Kilgore wanted just one more mutual

eruption inside her with the young man. She wanted the climax of pleasure to make her forget, if only for an instant, what the cards had said. The naïve knight, the evil man, and then … "He was moving with her now. "God Yes!" she screamed as she arched her back hoping the fire of passion that was now consuming her body would burn away her memory of what the cards foretold for this man she loved. For one more glorious moment it was only her and him. No past. No future. Just pure white, hot love. She lay back down on Michael Dugan, fulfilled. She opened her eyes wanting to look into his bright blue eyes.

She only saw the empty black eyes of the skull of the Death Card.

"I be havin' Obadiah pack your bags," she whispered in his ear. "I told him to be hitchin' up the carriage. I will be makin' sure you be on board the Chariot before Nick Hopkins be knowin' you left."

Michael laughed, and got a playful hungry smile on his face. He flipped Miss Kilgore on to her back. grabbing her wrists and pinning her. She felt him probing her. She welcomed him. Yes! Again, she thought, before the evil man kills you.

"We'll have time for this on our way to St. Louis." He said rolling off the bed. He saw something in her eyes, "What is it?"

"I just bein' hungry." She got out of bed and took a seat at the table. Michael looked at his nightshirt still on the floor where Miss Kilgore had thrown it.

He sat in the chair naked. He looked across the table at the woman, her robe open.

Michael suddenly realized he was starving. He dove into his eggs and bacon.

"How do you be feelin, Mr. Dugan?" asked Miss Kilgore biting into her toast.

Michael thought for a moment. "It is like someone took my body and brain apart and put it back together. Now I have to see if they work."

"And do they?"

He looked at her with a wry smile. "You tell me."

They finished breakfast and got dressed. Miss Kilgore put on the green dress she had wore when they met.

They went into the hall. Michael went into the master bedroom. His bags were packed and lay on the bed. His buffalo coat lay on top. He strapped on the Colt then put the coat on and then his wide brimmed hat. He then picked up the buffalo gun in its beaded sheath. "You be lookin' like a man returnin' from the frontier," observed Miss Kilgore.

Michael turned back into the room, remembering something. He opened the top drawer of the dresser. He pulled out Uncle Mike's crucifix and put it on.

"It's the only thing I have to remind me of him," he said. Michael did not see that Miss Kilgore turned away when she saw it. "Have you seen Damien?" he asked.

"The door to your room be open when I be getting' your clothes," she said.

Michael closed the door and looked at Seward's door.

"You be thinkin' we be needin' Mr. Seward?" she asked.

Michael didn't see why he would need an escort to the Chariot. "No, let him sleep."

Obadiah came running up the stairs.

"Good morning, Obadiah," said Michael. "Have you seen Damien?"

"He took off just now when I was goin' out to hitch up carriage."

Michael was not sure what he was going to do about Damien. Maybe the wolf had made that decision for both of them.

"Obadiah, grab my bags and take them to the carriage." Michael said as he and Miss Kilgore started down the steps.

"I couldn't hitch up the carriage, Mr. Dugan," said the slave with dread in his voice.

"Why in blazes not, Obadiah?" inquired Miss Kilgore. "Mr. Dugan needs to be to goin.'"

"Someone else wants to take Mr. Dugan down to the Chariot they self." Obadiah looked at the Colt on Michael's hip. "Master Hopkins and the Devil brothers are out front. They is armed."

Michael's eyes narrowed. "Obadiah, bring my bags."

He and Miss Kilgore pushed open the double doors and came out onto the porch. There a smiling Nick Hopkins waited. To his left and right were Cane and Jarrod Devilbiss. The three men did not really concern Michael Dugan. His main concern was the Colt revolvers all three had in their chest holsters.

"Good mornin' Mr. Dugan. Miss Kilgore." Hopkins said with a big smile. "Boy, you look like a real frontiersman." Michael suspected Hopkins had been already celebrating his victory.

Obadiah came out. Ebony followed. The slave quietly set down the bag on Michael's right. Michael also felt the slave take the buffalo gun from him, freeing up the young man's right hand. Michael felt the Colt at his fingertips. Michael realized the three men standing below were in pointblank range. At this distance Michael could not miss his targets. But now the targets were experienced hired guns.

"What can I do for you, Mr. Hopkins?" asked Michael curtly.

"Oh, it is what I can do for you, Mr. Dugan. I … We are here to make sure you safely get on board the Chariot to start your trip home." He gestured to the old wagon waiting not far away.

"Mr. Dugan will not be driven out of town in one of your dirty slave wagons, Nick Hopkins," declared Miss Kilgore.

"Mr. Hopkins," Michael said trying to remain calm. "You are trespassing."

"I beg your pardon, Boy. This is April first. This is my house now."

"This is Dugan property," said Michael Dugan trying to keep his anger out of his voice. "I consider you armed intruders, and you are being ordered off this property."

Nick Hopkins put his hands on his hips. "Or what, boy? Your hired gun ain't gonna be doin' your shootin' for you this time. And you only have three shots left in that gun."

Michael's eyes narrowed at Nick Hopkins. "You should have brought more men."

"You've three shots to our eighteen? Unless you are crazy or stupid, I suggest you get yourself in that wagon."

Miss Kilgore moved behind Michael and took his gun hand in hers. "Mr. Dugan," she said in a lilting voice in Michael's ear. "I be decidin' that I be needin' some more ..." She squeezed his hand, digging her nails into his skin. "Breakfast. The Chariot not be leavin' til noon. That is hours away."

Michael smiled over his shoulder. He looked back at Hopkins. "When we come back out, you and your men, a better be gone." Michael turned to go back into the house.

"She didn't tell you, did she?" said Hopkins.

"There be no need to be tellin' anybody anything, Nick Hopkins," said Miss Kilgore angrily.

Michael turned back, taking his hand out of hers. "Tell me about what?"

"The truth about your beloved Uncle Mike. Also known as the honorable Father Mike Dugan."

"All right, that bein' enough Nick Hopkins. He'll be ridin' in your slave wagon, and you can be takin' the damn house. Just be keepin' your mouth shut."

"What about my uncle?"

"About me meetin' your uncle in St. Louis. It was at the Bon Voyage party bein' held by none other than the river witch/whore herself, Miss Jessica Kilgore and your uncle Mike.   They were headin' down to New Orleans on the Riverboat Sultana," explained Hopkins. "I offered your Uncle Mike one thousand dollars if he changed that contract to have this house built in Westport."

"He didn't think twice." continued Hopkins. "With my money and the money he was supposed to use to build his church, your uncle and Miss Kilgore sailed down the Mississippi on the Sultana and wintered in New Orleans. Together."

"Father Mike Dugan left alone from St. Louis on the first of March." stated Michael. "He said in a letter he hoped to reach the Town of Kansas the first of April. He is assumed lost."

"He crossed to the Town of Kansas." Hopkins laughed "But it was on the Chariot with the river witch/whore, Miss Jessica Kilgore. He arrived safe and sound one year ago today."

"Why you be tellin' him this, Nick Hopkins?"

"I want this boy to go home and tell his family the truth about Father Michael Dugan." He looked back to Michael.   "So he and Miss Kilgore arrived April first. They stay at this newly completed house for a week or so. Obadiah, here, took care of them. Anyway, I paid him three thousand dollars for the house. He caught the first wagon train west. Just before he left he traded that cross you got on to your Indian friend for one of his Sioux trinkets."

"Miss Jessica Kilgore got back on the Chariot and went back to bein' the river witch/whore. All I had to do was wait six months, and the house would be declared abandoned. All nice and legal. I even sent for Mike Seward to come to Westport to hire him to kill your uncle should he show back up. One week before the deadline you show up." Hopkins laughed. "You hired Mike Seward and let him stay right where your uncle would have shown up. Mike Seward has been working for me since he got here. And I offered him a nice bonus if he made sure you got killed so that it did not look like murder. Now here we are. I am not the villain here, Father Mike Dugan is."

"Mr. Hopkins." Michael's fingers curled around the Colt. "You are a liar."

Obadiah took Miss Kilgore's hand and brought her and Ebony behind him.

"Boy! You have been more damn trouble than you are worth, and the only reason you are still alive is because you come from a rich family. But, nobody calls me a liar.

"As of right now your little frontier adventure is over. You get yourself in that wagon before I lose my temper. Because one way or another, I am taking this house. Today!"

"No."

"Boy! You … "

"Shut up." Michael Dugan's eyes narrowed as he jooked at Nick Hopkins. "How dare you. How dare you insult the honor of this woman I love. How dare you stand there and say those things about Father Mike Dugan. As far as I am concerned Mr. Hopkins, you shot my uncle in the back as you tried to do me and then you buried him in an unmarked grave in your quarry. Mr. Hopkins, you are a known murderer and a liar. I am Michael Dugan, and this is Dugan property. You will get this house over my dead body, you son of a bitch!"

Obadiah saw Nick Hopkins reach for his gun and pushed Ebony and Miss Kilgore down and covered them with his body.

To Michael Dugan the Colt seemed to jump out of his holster. Nick Hopkins' gun had not yet cleared his holster when he saw Dugan's narrowed blue eyes looking at him down the sights of a Colt revolver. Michael lowered the barrel, aiming as he had been instructed, at the heart. Michael Dugan pulled the trigger. He knew this was a crazy and stupid act. His Colt had not been fired in six months, and he had not fired it since his first and only lesson almost a year ago.

Would the Colt fire?

Would he hit anything if it did?

It did.

He did.

He barely noticed the gun's report, concentrating on keeping control of the gun, hoping to get one more shot before the hired guns shot him.

"Boy! Just what the hell are you just doin' ?" he heard Cane Devilbiss say as Michael turned to his left. Michael saw Cane point his Colt at him as Michael brought his gun down.

Cane fired, and a rock exploded three feet to Michael's right. Cane was aiming again as Michael aimed at Cane's chest and fired. His shot hit Cane squarely causing him to hit a foot above and to the right of Michael's head. How can someone miss at this range? He thought surely they became familiar with the Colt revolver. Why? They expected to face a scared boy with only three shots in his gun. Not a man with a very wise father who forced his son to become proficient with the Colt revolver!

Michael accepted that he was lucky with the first two shots. Hopefully he would get the third man before Death claimed him.

He heard a shot from his right, and dust erupted a foot to his left. Michael was bringing the Colt down when there was another shot. Michael felt rock dust spray the side of his face. As he was aiming he saw Jarrod doing the same.

Before either could properly aim, they fired.

Michael shoved the empty Colt in its holster. "Let's see who the crows get to eat."

Nick Hopkins and the Devilbiss brothers were still standing. For a moment Michael thought he had missed. Nick Hopkins pointed at Michael then fell backwards. Dead.

The Devilbiss brothers looked at their boss, then at each other looking very confused.

Blood ran down from the hole between Jarrod Devilbiss' eyes. The brothers looked at Michael Dugan in what seemed to be annoyance. Then they also fell. Dead.

Michael knew it was now his turn. He knew Jarrod could have not missed him. His mind simply would not allow him to feel the pain of the bullet. He waited for his legs to buckle.

"Be getting off of me!" he heard Miss Kilgore say. She ran over to him. Yes, he would die in her arms. He was killed defending the honor of the woman he loved and the Dugan Family name. That is what Miss Kilgore would say in her tear stained letter to his family. Michael hoped the undertaker still had the sealed coffin Mr. Hopkins had made for him.

"You damn fool! The man I love standin' up here lettin' yourself be shot at.

If ya' be wantin' to know what the Fool upside down be meanin'? That be it!"

Michael had the odd sensation of Miss Kilgore's dainty fingers running over his body.

"Where are you hit?" she asked

It occurred to Michael that he had yet to fall dead.

He felt fingers pinching his upper left shoulder.

"Ow!"

"You been shot!"

Michael opened his coat, expecting to see his chest covered in blood. "Where?"

"In the shoulder. It just bein' a graze." Miss Kilgore bent down and ripped a strip off her petticoat. She wrapped the cloth around his arm and pulled it tight.

"Miss Kilgore! That hurts!"

"It be servin' you right. That Indian be havin' you pegged. You be crazy and stupid."

It was then Michael Dugan realized he had just killed three men!

Three armed men!

Three armed men with Colt revolvers!

Three men with Colt Revolvers who were shooting at him!

Michael Dugan didn't know whether to faint or cry.

Then a man rode up. It was Sheriff Winkleman. "What the hell happened here?" he said getting off his horse.

Michael folded his arms in front of him. "Nick Hopkins and the Devilbiss brothers tried to take my house by force." Michael said simply. "I was forced to defend Dugan property. Sheriff, please remove these bodies from my property."

Sheriff Winkleman saw a Colt revolver lying next to Nick Hopkins. He knew the boy only had three shots in his gun, and he had used them. He walked over and bent down. He would pick up the gun and kill the Michael Dugan. He just touched the Colt when two large black paws planted themselves on either side of the Colt. The Sheriff looked up at a maul of snarling teeth and angry blue eyes. The sheriff thought if he moved fast enough he could probably kill the wolf and the boy.

Then he heard a horse walk up on him. He saw an Indian on horseback. His face looked like someone had held it to a fire. The Indian held a multi-colored spear with a black point on it, and he was holding the spear as if ready to throw it at him. Three? Could he get three shots before … ?

There was movement from the tipi on his right. A young angry looking Indian was holding a knife ready to throw. At him.

Then he heard a click from the house. Standing on the porch was a young angry looking negro girl with what looked like a the barrel of a small cannon on her shoulder. Behind her was Obadiah with his finger on the trigger of the large gun aimed right at him.

There was a small click. He saw Michael Dugan still looking at him with his arms folded. To his left was Miss Jessica Kilgore with a derringer also pointed at him.

"Sheriff Winkleman," said Michael Dugan. "Attempting to use a Colt revolver without the proper training can result in injury or death."

Sherriff Winkleman stood and raised his hands.

"As I requested before, please remove the bodies of these armed intruders. Leave the Colt revolvers where they are. Me and Deputy Seward will bring them down when we make our report."

"Obadiah, get down here and help me," ordered the sheriff.

The two slaves put down the gun and started down the steps.

"Obadiah," said Michael looking at the sheriff. T

The two went back and picked up the gun and pointed it at the sheriff.

Everyone watched as the fat sheriff struggled to get the three bodies into the wagon.

"Boy, this ain't over," said Sheriff Winkleman finally hauling himself into the driver's seat of the wagon. "Not by a long shot."

Michael smiled and waved as the wagon rolled away

Michael walked down the steps and walked over to the nearest Colt. He reached down and then fell to his knees. He saw his father's itinerary poking out of his buffalo coat. He took it out and looked at it.

Damien walked over, looked at Michael, took the paper in his teeth, pulling the page out of Michael's hand. The wolf laid down, put the paper between his paws, and started chewing up Michael Dugan's father's itinerary.

Michael sighed. What did he do now? What did he want to do now? He turned and saw Miss Kilgore smiling at him from the porch. She shook her head and shrugged. Breakfast, he thought. He would think about all this after … breakfast.

He stood and walked toward the house. A horse walked up and blocked his path.

Michael knew who it was.

"Crazy Man Who Stands," said Fire Oak in English.

"Great Medicine Man, Fire Oak," Michael said in Lakota keeping his eyes down.

Fire Oak brought the spear up and aimed it down toward Michael Dugan. He threw it down as hard as he could.   It stuck into the ground between Michael's feet.   Michael looked up.   Fire Oak was smiling (Michael guessed) down at Michael and raised his right hand. Michael Dugan smiled and raised his right hand.

Fire Oak turned his horse and brought it over to the stunned Thunder Eagle. He looked down at the young Indian and said something. Thunder Eagle smiled and nodded. The Indian went over and jumped on his horse. He smiled at Michael and raised his right hand. Then he and his father galloped off.

Michael left the spear where it was deciding it was either a gift or the Lakota were coming back to kill him and burn his house down. When he came to the bottom of the steps there was Seward, dressed in his suit complete with pistols. He and Michael looked at each other for a bit. Finally, Michael walked up the steps to the hired gun.

"What did I miss? Did I hear shooting?"

Miss Kilgore came at Seward.   "And where be the great protector when Mr. Dugan was nearly bein' killed!" she demanded.

Michael calmly held up his hand to her and turned back to Seward.

"It was very exciting," said Michael folding his arms in front of him, looking at Seward.

"I had a disagreement with Mr. Hopkins over ownership of this house. I knew I had the law on my side. He had the guns on his. He and his men drew their Colt revolvers."

"And."

Michael's eyes narrowed. "That is when Deputy Mike Seward, knowing there were only three shots left in my Colt, drew it and under fire killed Nick Hopkins and the Devil brothers. "

"That did not happen," said Seward.

"That is what the report will say when we go down to talk to Sheriff Winkleman. Or you can leave Westport right now, and I will swear out a warrant for your arrest for conspiracy to commit the murder of one Michael Dugan."

Seward shrugged, "I am wanted for worse."

"Why does that not surprise me?" said Michael "But I think Dugan Manufacturing will put up a substantial reward. Dead or alive."

"So it is Heroic Deputy Mike Seward."

"The man who be riddin' Westport of the evil Nick Hopkins," put in Miss Kilgore.

"Or Mike Seward a wanted man with a substantial price on my head."

"Wanted dead or alive." said Michael Dugan.

Seward looked out at Westport. "Westport without Nick Hopkins. Just me here to run things."

"I'll be here to keep an eye on you." He put his

arm around Miss Kilgore. "Me and Miss Kilgore are engaged."

"Yes, I heard you engaging all last night." Seward looked a Michael. "Do I get the Colt back?"

"Get your own, Deputy Seward. This was a gift from father."

Michael turned to Miss Kilgore. "Did you say something about wanting more breakfast, Miss Kilgore?"

Miss Kilgore put her arm around Michael Dugan. "Welcome to Westport, Mr. Dugan."

They walked into the house, planning on a happily ever after.

T H E

N

D

R. E. Mahoney is a "semi" retired custodian who still lives in a two bedroom basement apartment in Westport, Mo. He now has a better computer that no longer turns off for no reason. He also insists he is NOT mad. That being said, Mr. Mahoney says if one more person asks him about a sequel he wil kill them and feed them to his three cats!

OUTRAGEOUS FORTUNE
ACT II

FAMILY SECRETS

a frontier ghost story

by
Robert E. Mahoney

This is dedicated to

All the people of Westport(and beyond) who suffered through that barely readable first edition of "Outrageous Fortune" And to all of you who asked for "more".

Be careful what you ask for.

I would like to acknowledge Saphira Rain had ABSOLUTELY NOTHING to do with this work and I am not REAL sure why she wanted that made clear.

Everybody's so different
I haven't changed
Life's been good to me so far

~ Joe Walsh

PROLOGUE

It was Michael Dugan's birthday, and the first
anniversary of his arrival in Westport. He was not
supposed to be aware of a surprise party for him. He
was told to act surprised.   He and Miss Kilgore (he
still called her that) were taking the day off. Michael
had given Obadiah orders not to wake them.

His arm lay across her waist, and he rested his
hand on the swell of her stomach. He felt the baby
kick. Miss Kilgore swore the child was conceived
in the wee hours of April Fools day which, Michael
now knew, was the Celt (not Pagan) New Years.
Miss Kilgore was sure it was going to be a girl, and
she would be named April. Michael was hoping for
a boy, and he would name it Michael — Mike for
short. They both joked that as soon as a Catholic
priest or a Druid came into Westport they would get
married. For now Michael Dugan was happy to just
lay listening to the breath of the woman he loved and
waiting for the baby to kick again.

Damien lifted his head from where he slept
across the room.   The wolf looked toward the
windows and gave a half bark, half growl. Michael

could hear loud voices outside. He turned over and raised up on his elbow. It was Obadiah.

2 "You need to go, now!" he heard Obadiah say.

"Boy, you need to go get your master, now!" said an oddly familiar voice.

Michael got up and went to the window. The eastern sky had a slight glow. A lone figure stood half-way up from the road. Michael assumed it was another panhandler looking for a handout. They always came there because it was the biggest house.

Michael hoped Obadiah was waking Deputy Seward.

There was a tap on the door. Obadiah opened it.

Michael rushed to the door. "What is it, Obadiah?" he whispered not wanting to wake Miss Kilgore.

"There's someone out front."

"What does he want?"

"He wants to talk to Master Hopkins."

Michael sighed. Maybe it was someone who had not heard that Mr. Hopkins was dead, Michael thought. He pulled on some pants and a shirt and started out the door.

"He is armed." Obadiah warned

Michael went to the closet and reached in the back. He moved his buffalo coat and took down the holster hanging behind it.

"Why didn't you wake, Deputy Seward?" Michael asked strapping on the Colt.

3"Mr. Dugan this is somethin' you need to take care of personally."

Miss Kilgore lifted her head. "What is it, Michael?"

"It is just another panhandler." Michael whispered. " I will deal with it. Go back to sleep."

Michael remembered he'd forgotten his boots when he walked across the rocks of the drive. The figure was just a silhouette against the glow in the east.

"Can I help you?" asked Michael.

"I told the slave, Obadiah, I needed to talk to his owner, Nick Hopkins. That stupid nigger didn't seem to understand."

"Obadiah works for me. Are you a friend of Mr. Hopkins?"

"I sold him this house."

Michael thought the voice sounded familiar. "You are Father Mike Dugan?"

"Nobody has called me Father in a long time." Michael saw a glint on the figure's chest.

He recognized one of Thunder Eagle's trinkets hanging around his neck. Michael also saw the pistol in his chest holster.

"Where have you been?"

"Everywhere. I took the money they gave me

to build the church and sailed down to New Orleans with a witch/whore named Miss Jessica Kilgore. We wintered down there." He laughed. "Everyone thought I was wintering in St. Louis."

"I heard you said in a letter to your family you were attempting a solo trip by wagon to the Town of Kansas."

"Yeah, I sent that letter the same time I sent my letter of resignation to Rome."

Tears welled up in Michael's eyes. "You were assumed lost."

"It is better that way. I knew a long time ago I was never meant to be a priest. I decided when they assigned me to The Town of Kansas it was my chance to start a new life. I sold this house to Nick Hopkins for three thousand dollars and headed west."

Tears ran down Michael's face. "Why did you come back?" he said with a steady voice.

"I made it to California, but I ran out of money. I had to work my way back on three different wagon trains. Took me all summer."

"I can give you money to get back to your family in Boston. They'll probably be happy you are least alive."

"And be thrown in jail for fraud and embezzlement? No thank you."

Michael suppressed a sob. "You should at least let your family know you are alive. You don't have to tell them what you did."

The man continued as if he had not heard. "No sir, I came here to see if Nick Hopkins will let me work in his quarry or something. Just to get a stake to go back west. You need somebody here?" The man started toward Michael. "I don't believe I caught your name."

"It's me. Michael," he said.

The man stopped. "Michael? What are you doing here?"

Michael swallowed and took a deep breath. "I came here a year ago to surprise you. You remember, don't you Uncle Mike? I was thinking about becoming a priest. I came to spend the winter with you." Tears soaked Michael's face. "To help you build your church."

"What? Where is Nick Hopkins?"

"Nick Hopkins is dead. I killed him. Men are dead because of you! And I killed three of them!" Michael sobbed.

"Let's go in the house and talk. You can sell the house. Me and you can go out to California and ..."

"I have a business here. I have a wife and a child due in four months. I will give you money only if you go back to Boston and tell the family what you did." Tears dripped from Michael's face.

"Michael, you are going to give me that money."

Michael took a breath. "I have a Deputy Sheriff living here. Leave now, Uncle Mike, and if I ever see you again I will have you arrested and held for the Federal Marshal. He will be able arrange to have you returned to Boston to face charges. One way or the other I will be writing our family and telling them everything."

"I can't let you do that Michael. Everyone thinks I am dead."

Michael's eyes narrowed. "Then you should never have come back."

"I'm sorry, Michael but..." He reached for his pistol.

Michael pulled his Colt and aimed. He pulled the trigger and flagged the gun's hammer with his palm. The man was jolted as he was hit with the rapid fire rounds. Even after six shots Michael kept pulling the trigger and flagging the hammer until he fell.

Obadiah came running up behind him. "Mr. Dugan, I ... we all knew but ... "

"Obadiah." Michael said keeping his voice down.

"Its just we didn't see what good it would do. And now that you and Miss Kilgore are ... "

"OBADIAH! WILL YOU PLEASE SHUT UP!"

Seward came running out in his long johns carrying his Colt. He looked over Michael's shoulder. "What the hell happened?"

Michael continued to look down at the figure. "It was an armed intruder. He was trying to rob the house."

Seward sighed. "Another poor bastard for one of those dollar graves in your quarry, Mr. Dugan."

Michael turned and saw that Miss Kilgore had come out on the porch. Michael turned to Obadiah. "Help Mr. Seward take the body down to quarry. Miss Kilgore is to know nothing of this," he instructed the men quietly .

"What is there to tell?" asked Seward.

Michael turned and walked back to the house, trying to wipe his tears away.

Obadiah ran up to Michael. "Mr. Dugan that was … "

Michael turned and brought his face close to the slave's. "That was only an armed intruder," said Michael Dugan in a loud harsh whisper. "Father Mike Dugan was lost while attempting a solo wagon trip from St. Louis to the Town of Kansas. If I hear anything about this, Obadiah, the first thing I will do is shoot you and feed you to my wolf! Do I make myself clear?"

"Yes, Master Dugan."

Michael turned and walked to the house. He smiled as he walked up the steps and took Miss Kilgore in his arms.

"Trouble?" she asked with a sleepy smile.

"Nothing I couldn't handle," he said looking into her green eyes as the first light of day hit them.

"Michael, you be cryin'?"

"What was that tarot card? The one about the evil man?"

"You be meaning from when I be tellin' your fortune the night we first … ?"

"Yes," he said holding her. "What card was the evil man?"

"The King of Swords upside down. Why?"

"And the one who will have all the cups?"

"That be Seven of Cups. Making the right choice."

"You said I had to make a choice."

"Yes," she said putting her arms around him.

"And my favorite card. The one with the all cups in a rainbow and people dancing under it."

"The Ten of Cups."

He brought her closer. "You called it the happily ever after card. You said it was up to me to choose what would make me happy. Miss Kilgore, I am very happy with my choice, and my choice has made me very happy."

He got a stern look on his face. "I thought I told you to go back to sleep."

Miss Kilgore put her arm around Michael Dugan, "Welcome to Westport, Mr. Dugan.is neck. "I be wantin to be the first to be wishin' you a Happy Birthday, Mr. Dugan."

Chapter I

Four month old April Kilgore Dugan's wide blue eyes looked up at Miss Jessica Kilgore as she suckled her mother's breast.

"Good morning, April," said Michael Dugan as he entered the dining room. He bent down and kissed his daughter's forehead as he pulled the child's blanket up to cover the woman's breast. "Happy Conception Day." He then kissed the woman. "Happy Pagan New Year, Miss Kilgore."

Since their daughter's birth was on the Winter Solstice, Michael and Miss Kilgore had agreed it was too close to Christmas. They decided the day of their daughter's conception would be a celebration instead.

Michael took a seat next to Miss Kilgore who, as always, sat at the head of the table. "How is April today?"

"She be happy and hungry as always," she said with a smile as she ran her lovely hand over the child's already thickening red hair. She looked back at Michael. "You be lookin' dapper in your suit."

"As we agreed.   No work today. My only duties today will be playing host to your hostess at our cookout and the dinner party tonight."

"Good, at least one day you won't be goin' down into that pit of yours." Miss Kilgore said tersely.

"It is not a pit. Actually, legally it is a mine. I could not buy it outright. I had to file a claim on the property."

"It be a horrid place to work and a worse place to be livin'," she said looking at her daughter.

"It was like that when I took it over."

"Those negroes be workin' and livin' in those terrible conditions while your white day workers be collectin' their pay and be goin' to their nice rooms in town."

"Our slaves have it better than others I have seen."

"Michael Dugan, they be livin' in caves."

"And now that spring is here I am having them build a big stone lodge. I pay those slaves the same way as I do Obadiah, " he said stealing a piece of bacon from Miss Kilgore's plate. "I put the money aside. If they wish to leave I give it to them."

"And where are they to be goin', Michael? The Kansas Territory? Those damn slave catchers be goin' after them. They be stealin' the money you be givin' them and be bringing them negroes back to be sold."

"If they are found roaming, they can be caught and sold. Just like a wild horse."

"We be nearly halfway through the nineteenth

century, and a man can still own another human being.   I be knowin' certain people who be helpin' negroes escape north."

Michael looked around. "Miss Kilgore," he said lowering his voice. "You remember the Baker place that burnt down over the winter?"

"They be sayin' that was Indians."

"No, Miss Kilgore. The Bakers were involved with doing exactly what you suggest. Helping escaped slaves."

"The Bakers and their two little girls were killed," she said with sadness in her voice looking at the baby at her breast.

A young negro girl came in from the kitchen with two full plates of breakfast and set them in front of Michael. She then poured his coffee.

"Good morning, Ebony. You are serving breakfast today?" asked Michael as he watched the girl pour cream into his coffee.

"Good morning, Mr. Dugan. Yes, father is out back cookin' that buffalo over that big fire. He been out there since before sunup," reported the negro girl, her dark brown eyes wide with excitement. "He and Mr. Thunder Eagle done made up this sauce. They had to make TWO buckets of it for the whole buffalo. They said they had to. . ." Ebony struggled with the word. "Morinate."

"Marinate." put in Miss Kilgore.

"Yessum! That is what Father is out there doin' to that buffalo."

"Ebony, will you be takin' April upstairs. I laid ' out some clothes for her to be wearin' at the cook out. Be gettin' her dressed."

"Yessum! Miss Kilgore." Ebony took the baby out of the woman's arms. Miss Kilgore waited until the girl was out of ear shot.

"There is somethin' I need to be tellin' you Michael. I be wantin' to be the one to tell you first before you be hearin' it from someone else."

"Tell me what?" asked Michael cutting into a stack of hotcakes before him.

"I'd not be botherin' ya with it but there be so many people be tellin' me." Michael could see fear in the woman's eyes.

"What is this all about, Miss Kilgore?"

She looked at Michael. "People been sayin' they be seein' a priest around town."

Michael set his fork down. "A priest? Where?"

"Here in Westport and the Town of Kansas."

"How do they know he is a priest?"

"He be wearin' the collar for one thing. He be dressed all in black."

Michael Dugan gave a dismissing laugh. "Miss Kilgore, we---I am the only Catholic that I know of between here and St. Louis. If he is a priest, why would he not come see me?"

Miss Kilgore hesitated. "They be sayin' he has black hair and bright blue eyes."

Michael stared at the woman for a moment. "Like Uncle Mike," he finally said.

"I be knowin'."

Michael looked down at his plate. "It can't be Uncle Mike."

"And why not?"

"Because, Miss Kilgore, Uncle Mike is dead. I---" Michael stopped himself.

"You not be knowin' that. Not for sure."

"I am the one person that knows that for sure!" Michael wanted to say. Instead he finished cutting a piece of flap jacks and popped it in his mouth. "Uncle Mike was lost in a solo wagon trip from St. Louis. Everyone knows that."

Miss Kilgore looked down to avoid the man's eyes. "What if he be dead. What if it be-"

"His ghost, Miss Kilgore?" Michael laughed. "And I would be likin' you to be tellin' me why not."

Michael looked into the woman's bright green eyes. "Miss Kilgore, we Catholics can go to Heaven, Hell, or Purgatory, but we do NOT come back as ghosts."

"Why would you be sayin' your uncle be goin' to Hell?"

The sight of the his bullets hitting the figure

flashed before Michaels eyes. "I only meant Catholics do not come back as ghosts."

"Good mornin' all," said Mike Seward as he entered the dining room.

"Good morning, Deputy Seward." Said Michael "Have YOU heard about the ghost?"

Seward stopped and looked at Michael Dugan. "How would you know about The Ghost?"

"Miss Kilgore was just telling me about him," said Michael popping a piece of bacon into his mouth.

Seward eased himself into the chair next to Miss Kilgore. "Miss Kilgore, how the hell would YOU know about The Ghost?"

"He has been reported seen," said Michael taking a sip of coffee.

"Seen? Where and when?" Seward nearly demanded.

"It seems the ghost of my dead Uncle Mike has been recently seen haunting Westport and the Town of Kansas."

Seward was visibly relieved. "No! I have not been seein' any ghost priests in my travels."

"What ghost did you think we be talking about?" asked Miss Kilgore.

"Neither of you need to be worried about it," said Seward getting out of the chair. "I want to be there when the Chariot docks."

"Just to pick up the mail?" asked Michael

"Yeah," said Seward. "I know you are expectin' that letter from your father."

"And don't be forgettin' to pick up our order at the general store," said Miss Kilgore. "We be needin' those things for the dinner party tonight."

"Already had Obadiah hitch up the wagon. I'll pick up the Westport mail personally. See you two at the cookout. I WILL keep an eye out for that ghost priest." Seward quickly left.

"You still not be gettin' an answer from you last letter?" asked Miss Kilgore took a sip of milk.

"No, Miss Kilgore, you have no idea how Father infuriates me. DEMANDING I sell the house and return to Boston at once."

"You be homesick, Michael?"

"I DO miss my family and old friends. But this is my home now. You and April are my family, and this is my life now. Father simply will have to accept that. Last time I wrote him I sent that letter in which he ADMITS he bribed those people to make sure I failed everything I tried."

"I be likin' the story we be tellin' em about me and April."

"How you were left in Westport with child on the way while your husband went west, promising to send for you."

Miss Kilgore laughed. "And how I be takin' in laundry to pay me rent."

"My Mother scolded me for making you pay rent."

"But she did be sendin' some nice clothes when April was born."

"Something I didn't tell you. In one of my letters, I MAY have SUGGESTED to my parents you were. . . Catholic."

She playfully slapped Michael on the shoulder. "Michael Dugan! Why would you be tellin' such a lie. Why don't you just be tellin' them the truth?"

Michael laughed. "The truth? You want me to write my Catholic parents that I am living with a Celtic Princess, and we have have had a child together?"

"What would they be sayin?"

Again Michael had to laugh. "Saying? Before you know it they would be here to rescue me from the clutches of a witch that had a spell on their baby boy. I think my mother would like you. But Father? I don't even want to think about it."

Seward brought the wagon to a stop at top of the hill overlooking the Town of Kansas and the river beyond. Michael Dugan had given him a bit of a start talking about The Ghost.

Seward remembered the conversation with John Smith they day before. Seward suspected John Smith was not the man's real name. People came out west for many reasons. Smith owned two of the biggest saloons/brothels. One in Westport and the other in the Town of Kansas. Seward made extra money working for Smith as security. Smith was also one of Seward's best informants. For a price.

Smith sent word he wanted to talk to Seward. When Seward arrived Smith met him with a beer in hand. He motioned Seward over to a back table.

As they sat down, Smith set the beer in front of Seward. "I hear in a week or so your problem with Mr. Dugan may be taken care of."

"Problem? What Problem?"" asked Seward sipping the foam off his mug.

Smith looked around the crowded saloon, making sure no one was listening. "With that boy gone, some people are sayin', you could take over Westport."

Seward set down his beer and leaned back in his chair. "And where will Mr. Dugan be goin'?"

"Where ever a Catholic like him goes when they die, I guess."

Seward looked at Smith and picked up is beer . "So, someone plannin' on killin' Mr. Dugan, are they?" He said sipping his beer.

"You ever heard of the The Ghost?"

Seward straightened up in his chair and set his beer on the table. "The Ghost? I heard he was strictly east coast." He picked up his beer and took a swallow.

"Then you HAVE heard of him," said Smith, nodding. "He is a killer for hire like you used to be."

"The Ghost is nothing like I was" said Seward dismissively "I was a hired gun. The Ghost is more like an assassin."

"Exactly. Gets hired, come into town, and a week later the target is dead. I heard he never uses a gun."

"Yeah I heard about him," said Seward looking off in thought. "Mostly makes it look like an accident. They call him The Ghost, because he makes himself invisible."

"Yeah, he blends in. Like that lizard I heard about."

"Yeah, the chameleon." Seward shook his head. "The Ghost is too high priced. Nobody in Westport has that kind of money."

Smith leaned in closer. "You are right there. They pooled their money and wrote offering his fee. He wrote back sayin' it wasn't worth the trip."

"But he is still comin'?" Seward took a big drink of his beer.

"Someone offered double his price."

Seward nearly choked on his beer. "Double?"

Smith smiled and nodded. "I hear they sent him his regular fee. The rest to be paid here when the job is done."

Seward took a big drink from his beer. "Somebody in WESTPORT will be paying him? Nick Hopkins could not put together that much money. Alright," said Seward draining his beer. "When is this Ghost supposed to be comin' into town?"

"THAT will cost you," said Smith with a smile. Seward put a twenty dollar gold piece on the table in front of Smith. Smith shook his head. Seward put another coin of equal value on top of the first. "He is comin' in the same way your boy did. On the Chariot. Tomorrow. Story will be she is staying in the Town of Kansas for repairs for a week. The Ghost is payin' Captain Foster to keep her here. They say when the Chariot leaves, the Dugan problem will be solved."

Seward was torn from his reflections with a blast from a ship's whistle. He saw a wisp of black smoke rise above a bluff. He reached into his vest pocket and pulled out a piece of paper. He knew he had seen it in Sherriff Winkleman's office.

He had to dig through all the wanted posters. The frontier ones were on top. The ones unlikely to be found on frontier were toward the bottom. There it was. The Ghost. Just the drawing with a wispy shape. Ten Thousand dollar reward. Dead or alive. Seward folded the paper up and put it back in his vest pocket as the Chariot came into view. He slapped the reins on the back of the horse and started down toward the Town of Kansas and the pier.

The man known and Mr. Smith had little to do with the other passengers on the Chariot. All anyone knew for sure was he was coming west on business. He was a taller stocky man, with trimmed red hair which was showing yellow at the temples. He had blue eyes that always seemed to have anger in them. Since he boarded in St. Louis, Mr. Smith mostly stayed in his cabin and ate alone in the dining room. He was also seen walking the upper decks, always looking forward, as if annoyed The Chariot could not go faster.

Mr. Smith constantly seemed to be in a state of annoyance and impatience. Bob was one of his prime annoyances.

Bob was a short, stout tow-headed man who boarded the Chariot in St. Louis the same time as Mr. Smith. Mr. Smith made the mistake of paying Bob to carry his bags on to the steamboat. Since then Bob was the first person Mr. Smith saw when he left his cabin.

Bob told Mr. Smith (and anyone else who would listen) that he was working for passage on the Chariot to the Town of Kansas after which he intended to get some work to get money to go west. Bob claimed to be working to pay his passage, but Mr. Smith had not actually seen the man do any real work with the exception of doing things for the odd coin. Bob DID seem to be interested in everyone.

The Chariot came around the bend and to his left Mr. Smith saw the pier lined with other boats.

He had paid Bob to bring his bags to the gangway which was to be set-up mid-ships. "Did you say you were goin' to Westport?" asked Bob as the vessel turned toward the pier.

"Yes, I am staying at the Harris House. I asked

them to have a carriage waiting for me when the Chariot arrived."

"Hotel, huh?" said Bob sadly. "I'm not really sure WHERE I will be stayin' tonight. Westport. That's where all those wagon trains leave to go west, right?"

Mr. Smith watched the bow of the Chariot as it neared the dock. "I am not really familiar with Westport. I don't plan to be there long. The Chariot is leaving in a week. I should have my business taken care of by then."

"What business is that, Mr. . . . Smith?"

Mr. Smith looked down at the man. "My own."

"Hey! Can I get a ride with you to Westport in that carriage you have waitin'?"

"If there is room."

Seward drove the wagon down the road toward the pier. Suddenly there was a man dressed in black standing on the side of the road. To Seward the man was nearly in the road.

Seward pulled back on this reins and slammed his foot on the wagon's brake. The horse screamed in protest as it came up on his hind legs then dropped back down bringing the wagon to a stop. Seward looked to his left expecting to see the man. He saw no one. He climbed down off the wagon and looked underneath, thinking he may have run the man over. Nothing. He looked around. No one was near the wagon. Seward got back up on to the wagon and slapped the reins on the back of the horse. As the wagon started Seward realized the man was wearing a priests' collar.

Soon Seward brought the wagon to a stop as the Chariot maneuvered close to the pier. He climbed down and walked over to the dock. Men were in line waiting in their positions for the lines to be tossed to them. As the boat drew closer, members of the crew dropped large bumpers over the side. Smaller weighted ropes were then thrown to the men on the dock. The men snatched them out of the air and started pulling them hand over fist. Tied to the other end were the mooring lines with loops at their ends. The men fought to keep the heavier lines out of the water. They dragged the large loops and dropped them over the massive cleats on the dock. Captain Foster was standing mid-ships looking forward and aft. He saw Seward and waved. Three slaves appeared carrying the long gangplank and waited for instructions. Under the captain's directions, they eased the gangplank over the side and set the end down on the pier with a bang.

Captain Foster stepped on the gangplank to make sure it was setting secure. He then walked backwards toward the pier, watching the crew members figure eight the lines on cleats on the boat. "Make sure those lines are tight!" the captain shouted angrily.

"Good morning, Captain." called Seward over the din.

Captain Foster glanced over his shoulder. "Good Morning, Deputy."

"How long you plannin' on stayin'? Couple of days as usual?"

"Get those lines tight, dammit!!" instructed the captain. "Or we will be having her drifting into one of these other boats." He looked at Seward. "I am here for a week this time."

"A week? Why so long?"

The captain watched the men. "Repairs." he said simply.

"I didn't know the Town of Kansas was a place to have a boat repaired."

Captain Foster walked down to the end of the gangplank where Seward stood. "If a man can repair a wagon, he can repair a boat." He walked by Seward as he watched the men wrap the lines on the boats' massive cleats. "Why the interest?"

"Anyone say they were sure to be leaving with you in a week?"

"Hey! Dammit! All of you! Unwind those lines and get the slack out of them!" ordered the captain. "Most people just returning. The rest are going west." The captain stopped and thought a moment. "There is one passenger. As he tells it, he did not want to come west. He has made it very clear the sooner he heads back east the better."

"Who would that be?"

"A Mr. Smith." The captain stepped on to the gangplank and looked forward and aft as the men rewound the lines.

"Really? Smith?"

"Says he has business in Westport," said the captain walking up the gangplank as he checked the lines. "He is staying at the Harris House."

Seward looked around the pier and spotted a carriage from the Harris House waiting nearby. He walked over to the young driver. "Waiting for a Mr. Smith?" inquired Seward.

"Yes, sir."

"He won't be needing you. I'll make sure he gets to the hotel."

"Are you sure, Deputy?" asked the driver. "My instructions were quite clear."

Seward saw people lining up to disembark the Chariot. "I will take responsibility."

The driver shrugged, gave the horse the whip, and was gone.

Seward walked back to the gangplank of the Chariot as the passengers started walking down. Some he recognized, some not. He smiled and nodded as they passed. Then a young lady stepped upon to the gangplank. Her nice figure caught Seward's eye. She wore a simple blue dress and her brown hair was done up in a bun.

She looked at Seward. "Are you here to escort a

nice Christian lady as myself, deputy?" she asked with a nice smile as she walked down the gangplank.

"I admit, Miss, a woman like that is very rare in these parts."

She came to the end of the gangplank. Seward offered his hand. She took it and stepped down. She was about a head shorter than Seward. "I am Scarlett Herrington."

Seward lightly kept hold of her hand. "Deputy Mike Seward at your service." he said. "What brings a nice blue eyed young lady such as yourself to the Town of Kansas, Miss Herrington?"

She moved closer "Please, call me Scarlett. Do I call you Deputy Seward or Mike?"

Seward noticed she made no effort to remove her hand from his. "Mike will do."

"And my eyes are blue hazel. The blue in them has a brown halo," she said leaning closer to Seward.

Seward looked into those beautiful eyes. "I can honestly say I have never met a woman with a halo."

"To answer your question. I am a just out of school. I am a certified school teacher."

"I am afraid the Town of Kansas already has a school and schoolmarm."

"I am just visiting towns. Seeing which one I find . . ." looking at Seward, "interesting."

"How long you gonna' be in town?"

"I bought a round trip ticket to as far west as I could go. Unfortunately, the Chariot will be here a week. But Captain Foster says I can stay on the boat."

"That sounds a like a boring first day, Scarlett. I am on my way to an old fashioned frontier cook out if you are interested."

Her round face exploded with a smile looking up at Seward. "I would love to!"

Seward saw a tall stocky man standing at the top of the gangplank, scowling as he scanned the pier.

"Miss Scarlett, I have some deputy business to tend to. My wagon is right over there," he said pointing to the wagon. "I will be right with you."

Seward watched Scarlett Herrington's form as she walked toward the wagon. He looked back to see the man saying something to Captain Foster. The captain looked up and down the pier, then turned to the man and shrugged.

The man had curly red hair, and there was anger in his blue eyes as he walked down the gangplank. He was followed by a short, dumpy man carrying two large, matching suitcases. The taller man stepped off the gangplank and looked up and down the pier.

"Is there a problem?" asked Seward as he walked up to the man.

"The Harris House was supposed to have a carriage waiting for me," said the man in annoyance."

"I am heading to Westport. My wagon is right over there," offered Seward.

The man looked at Seward. "You are armed and wearing a badge. I assume you are the sheriff."

Seward pointed to the lettering on his star. "Deputy. Of Westport."

"Mike Seward" asked the man.

"That is me."

The short man looked at Seward.

"You have heard of me, Mr. Smith?"

"Let 's just say we have a mutual acquaintance." The man's red brows furrowed. "How do you know my name, Deputy?"

"The captain may have mentioned it. As soon as I get the Westport mail, I can give you and your man a ride to the Harris House."

"I am NOT his man," said the short man dropping the suitcases. "I am Bob," he said offering his hand to Seward.

"You got a last name, Bob?" asked Seward taking the man's hand.

"Just Bob for now. I am goin' west. I plan to pick a name when I get out there. I just worked passage on the Chariot from St. Louie. I plan on gettin' some work to put money together to catch a wagon train west."

Seward smiled to himself. When he shook hands with Bob, his hands were soft. Seward seriously wondered if Bob had ever done any real work.

"There is plenty of work here in town." said Seward.

A slave with a canvas bag came running down the gangplank. "Deputy! Cap'um says to give this here to ya." He handed the bag to Seward. "It be the Westport mail."

"Mr. Smith, our chariot awaits." Bob picked up the bags and Seward led them to the wagon.

"Mr. Smith, this is Miss Scarlett Herrington. She is fresh out of teaching school.

"Are you the new schoolmarm?" asked Bob

Seward took the bags from Bob and threw them into the wagon on top of the supplies. Seward got a look at the matching leather suitcases. They were very nice and looked handmade. They were even monogrammed P S D

"Mr. Smith said I could get a ride to Westport," said Bob. "Westport is where all the wagon trains leave from. I was thinkin I could get work there and catch a wagon train when I am ready."

Seward watched Mr. Smith climb up into the wagon and take a seat next to Scarlett Herrington. "Sure, Bob, but you'll have to ride in the back."

As Bob climbed in the back, Seward got into the front seat next to Scarlett.

"You live at the Dugan Place," said Mr. Smith as the wagon made its' way up the hill and out of the Town of Kansas.

"Yes, do you know that?"

Mr. Smith looked straight ahead, ignoring the question. "I have business at the Dugan Place. Perhaps when you drop off the mail, you can wait for me to get checked in and drop off my bags. And I can get a ride with you."

"What sort of business do you have with the Dugans, Mr. Smith?"

"Dugans? There is only one Dugan living there."

"What kind of business do you have there?" inquired Seward again.

"A personal matter I need to take care of, is all."

For a while, they rode quietly uphill.

"I have never heard of Westport," mentioned Scarlett.

"Not surprised," said Seward as he handled the reins. "It is the starting point for people going west. It is about four miles south."

"Does Westport have a school there?" she asked excitedly.

"Not that I know of," said Seward. "It's a pretty rough town."

"Sounds exciting!"

Seward smiled and shook his head as the wagon turned onto the road toward the Harris House. "How long you plan on stayin' in Westport, Mr. Smith?"

"I plan to leave on the Chariot when it leaves in

a week." The man said as they came to a stop in front of the Harris House. "Frankly, Deputy Seward, I have no use for your god-forsaken frontier. The sooner I am heading back east the better."

"What a beautiful hotel," said Scarlett. "I think I am going to like the Westport!"

Mr. Smith sighed and shook his head as he climbed down off the wagon.

Seward handed the reins to Scarlett. "Stay with the wagon. We won't be long."

"What if the horse starts to move?" asked the woman looking at the horse.

"Pull on the reins real hard and yell 'whoa,' " instructed Seward.

She looked at him with surprise in her blue-hazel eyes. "They actually say 'whoa' out here?"

"Yes!" Seward said climbing off the wagon. Bob threw the bags off the wagon and jumped down, then picked up the bags and the three walked into the hotel.

"Good morning, gentleman," greeted the front desk clerk as the three walked up to the counter. "How may I help you?"

Seward put the canvas bag on the counter. "Have someone go through this and see if there is any mail for the Dugans." The clerk handed the bag to a bellman, who disappeared into the back.

The clerk turned to Mr. Smith. "And how can I help you, sir?"

"I am Mr. Smith. I have a reservation."

The clerk pulled open a small drawer and went through some cards. "Yes! Mr. Smith." said the clerk looking at the card. "You will be with us for one week." He set the card, a pen, and an inkwell in front of Mr. Smith.

"Yes and I was SUPPOSE to have had a carriage waiting for me when the Chariot arrived," growled the man as he filled out the card.

"Yes sir, I understand the driver was told it would not be needed."

Mr. Smith looked up at the clerk. "Who told the driver that?"

The clerk nodded toward Seward. Mr. Smith turned to look at Seward.

"Let's just say you are in my custody for the time being."

He turned toward Seward. "Custody? What have I done?"

"Possible conspiracy to commit murder," said Seward.

Smith shook his head and turned back to filling out the card as the stunned clerk looked on.

"Deputy! Who is he conspirin' to kill?" asked Bob excitedly.

"Michael Dugan."

The man turned suddenly in frustration to face

Seward. The deputy realized the man was a good half foot taller and had fifty pounds on him. He gripped his Colt.

"Michael Dugan?" Mr. Smith said angrily. "And WHY would I want to kill my—Michael Dugan?"

"If someone is paying you to do it."

"He is a hired killer?" exclaimed Bob.

"What fool made you a deputy?" demanded Mr. Smith.

"Sheriff Winkleman. It was supposed to be temporary. But Mr. Dugan blackmailed me into keeping the job. It is a long story."

Mr. Smith shook his head as he turned back to the counter and signed the card. "Please have my bags taken to my room. I will pick up my key when I return. Providing I am not in jail."

The bellman who had taken the mail bag reappeared. "No mail for the Dugans," he reported.

"Dammit."

"Bad news?" inquired Mr. Smith.

"NO, no news. Mr. Dugan and his father have been having an argument by mail. He has not gotten an answer to his last letter. That father of his." Seward shook his head. "You would not believe what that son-of-a-bitch has done to that kid. From how Mr. Dugan talks about him, I am glad that bastard's back in Boston."

Mr. Smith dug into his pocket as he watched the

bellman take the bags from Bob. He pulled out a coin and offered it to Bob. "Thank you, Bob, for your help. Good luck with your trip west."

"Thank you, Mr. Smith," he said as he took the coin. "I was wondering if there may be work for me at the Dugan Place," he said looking at Seward.

"Mr. Dugan IS always looking for a good day worker as long as you don't mind working along with slaves." Seward said as they walked out of the hotel.

"Never worked with slaves. I don't think that will be a problem."

They came to the wagon. "Ok, Bob, you climb in the back. Scarlett, slide over. Mr. Smith you are next to me."

"Yes, I know. I am Deputy Seward's prisoner."

"What do you mean you're his prisoner?" asked Scarlett

"Yes, it seems I am a hired killer, Miss Herrington. I am surprised I am not in irons."

"Forgot to bring 'em," said Seward slapping the reins on the back of the horse.

"Hired killer? Prisoner? Mike, what is this all about"

"Just another day in your exciting Westport, Scarlett. You are in luck Mr. Smith. There is a big cook out at the Dugan place. It is Conception Day AND the Pagan New Year. There is also a fancy dinner party tonight."

Mr. Smith looked at Seward. "Who was conceived? And why would my—Michael Dugan be celebrating the Pagan New Year?"

Michael Dugan surveyed the scene from his back porch. Between the house and the barn were three picnic tables. The guests had begun arriving. To his left, Obadiah turned the buffalo over the fire. The slave would stop turning to let someone cut off a piece for a taste. The negro smiled when the people showed their approval. Michael walked over to a group of men.

"Good morning everyone," greeted Michael

"Good morning, Mr. Dugan. Fine day for a cookout," said the owner of the general store. "But there is trouble a-brewin."

Michael looked at the men. "This problem wouldn't have to do with Indians, would it?" They all nodded.

"You ARE friends with that Medicine Boy, his father, and that chief."

"What is it now?"

"Same problem. Attacks on wagons." Said the man who owned the livery.

"Tell them to pay the tribute. Like all Indians, you show them respect they will leave you alone."

"Respect? For godless savages?"

Michael sighed. "That kind of thinking will just get more people killed. Miss Kilgore and I are taking April out to the Lakota camp tomorrow. I will talk to Thunder Eagle. But you all just have to remember. They were here first. Now, if you excuse me, I need to have a word with the cook." Michael walked over to Obadiah. "About ready to start serving, Obadiah?"

"Yessum, Mr. Dugan." The slave lowered his voice. "Those two got away last night."

"That's good to hear."

"I hear there are a couple in the Town of Kansas ready to go."

"No, Obadiah. We agreed. They have to come from at least fifty miles away. The quarry is the perfect place for hiding escaped slaves. If someone finds a local slave in my quarry, I could be arrested or worse."

"I knows what kind of danger you puttin', you, Miss Kilgore, and now that baby in just helpin' the few that you have, Mr. Dugan."

"Michael!" called Miss Kilgore standing at the back door holding April. "Deputy Seward is bringing the wagon around."

"Good! He is bringing the supplies for the dinner."

"He be havin' strangers with him. Was he supposed to be pickin' someone up?"

"Not that I know of, but everyone is welcome." He turned to the slave. "Deputy Seward is back. Time to eat, Obadiah."

The crowd moved to surround the buffalo and men cut off pieces of meat and put them on offered plates. Miss Kilgore came to stand next to Michael at the head of the middle table.

The baby reached for her father and Michael took her. Michael did not notice the people on the wagon as Seward pulled up. He was too busy watching everyone admiring his daughter. April smiled at the attention. It wasn't until he saw Miss Kilgore looking off with a furrowed brow. Damien his wolf came up next to him and gave a growl. Seward stood at the other end of the table with the people he had brought. Michael was not surprised that Seward was with a woman. Nor did he take note of the shorter man. No, he was looking at the tall stocky red haired man with anger-widened blue eyes. He watched as the man turned and suddenly slammed his large fist into the Deputy Seward's face, knocking him to the ground.

Miss Kilgore looked to Michael Dugan, "Michael!"

Michael Dugan smiled. "That, Miss Kilgore, is Father."

. . .